Runaway Romance

Runaway Romance

Book One

BY MIRALEE FERRELL

Runaway Romance
Published by Mountain Brook Ink
White Salmon, WA U.S.A.

The website addresses shown in this book are not intended in any way to be or imply an endorsement on the part of Mountain Brook Ink, nor do we vouch for their content.

This story is a work of fiction. All characters and events are the product of the author's imagination. Any resemblance to any person, living or dead, is coincidental.

Scripture quotations are taken from the King James Version of the Bible. Public domain.

ISBN 978-1-943959-41-9

The Team: Miralee Ferrell, Nikki Wright, Cindy Jackson, Judy Vandiver
Cover Design: Indie Cover Design, Lynnette Bonner Designer and UP TV

Mountain Brook Ink is an inspirational publisher offering fiction you can believe in.

Printed in the United States of America

Dedication

To God, who brought this about, and to Chevonne O'Shaughnessy who inspired the story and helped it come to life

Acknowledgments

Where do I even start? This has been an amazing journey—my first movie—and I had very, very little to do with it happening. I'm going to thank several people on this page, but for the full story of how this all came to be, please read the Author Note at the end of the book. You'll get the behind-the-scenes scoop on my adventure from book to movie.

First and foremost, my gratitude goes to the Lord Jesus Christ, my friend and savior who made all of this possible. Again, you'll see the amazing sequence of events that only HE could have brought about, when you visit the Author Note.

Second, I owe so much to Chevonne O'Shaughnessy who brought this to reality. She brought the initial idea to me of a reality star running away from her life, wanting something more, and landing in Amish country. From that point, I came up with a lot of the storyline, but her help and brainstorming kept it flowing and moving ahead. She is not only a professional and an expert at what she does, she's an amazing woman and someone I've come to call a friend. I'm so blessed God brought her into my life. And of course, a huge thank you goes to the entire ACI team who brought this movie to the screen, as well as the actors and actresses who brought their talent to the production. Thank you all for making my dream come true!

I so appreciate my family who encourages and blesses me each step of the way, especially my husband who hung in there through two years of ups and downs, waiting for a final thumbs-up on this project. And of course, I'm blessed by each and every person who reads my work and shares their excitement and enthusiasm with their friends. If it wasn't for you, there would be no movies or books. Please keep sharing—it's such a blessing when you do!

Chapter One

ANN STANWAY SAT IN HER TELEVISION producer's office trying to still the butterflies doing battle in her belly. No, not butterflies, more like buzzards. At least, that's what the atmosphere felt like, even if Doyle had a smile on his face. She'd always liked Doyle—he reminded her of a kind older uncle, but when it came to the decision-making part of this industry, he could turn into the wicked stepfather—if there was such a thing—when pressed by the woman who held the purse strings, Veronica Adson.

Tanya and Jan, both twenty-somethings, hovered nearby. Jan worked in publicity and marketing, and Tanya seemed to be Doyle's shadow much of the time, implementing his orders, oftentimes before they escaped his lips.

Doyle perched on the corner of his ostentatious, over-sized desk. "Did they offer you water? Or would you rather have coffee?"

Ann waved a perfectly manicured hand, and with the other, she pushed a brunette curl from her eyes. "I'm fine. Now, what's up? Is something wrong? We didn't have a meeting scheduled today." She was proud of how steady she'd managed to keep her voice. At least her acting skills had paid off that much. No one would guess her nerves were screaming. This meeting could only mean one thing. Trouble.

Jan and Tanya both spoke at the same time. "No, everything's fine. Great!" Tanya glanced at Jan with a fixed smile. "Like, seriously good. No worries."

Doyle nodded. "Actually, we have exciting news about tweaks we're making to the show. You'll love it."

Ann sat up straighter, her gaze fixed on Doyle. “Tweaks?” Maybe this wouldn’t be so bad. As long as Doyle made the decisions and it had nothing to do with Veronica.

“Yes. For three seasons now, reality fans have loved seeing you and Scott develop a deeper relationship on *Life with the Adsons.*”

Tanya bounced on her toes. “You guys are the cutest couple, ever. I want a relationship like yours.”

Jan’s face took on a dreamy look. “Me too. It’s like a fairytale. Naive Pennsylvania girl moves to Hollywood to become an actress, meets the hottest reality star in the country while catering his party, becomes his girlfriend and an overnight reality celeb with endorsement deals!”

Ann raised her brows. “Yes, Scott has made me feel like I’m living in a fairytale, but what’s that got to do with anything right now? I’m not sure what you’re getting at.”

Jan settled into the seat next to Ann and touched her shoulder. “Our research department has given us a few new findings.”

“And?” Ann shifted her position. It wasn’t that she didn’t like Jan most of the time, but something felt off. Very off. Everyone was almost too cheerful, but Ann read a different message in Doyle’s eyes. He could cover his feelings with his words, but his eyes never lied.

Tanya stepped closer. “Our viewers are bored.”

Jan nodded. “Cute is out. Something else has to be done.”

Doyle looked at the door as it opened then snapped closed behind the stylish, fifty-something woman who walked in, stopping to survey the room. Doyle shot upright, then took two steps toward her. “Veronica. Uh, Ms. Adson. I didn’t realize you were attending our meeting today.”

She raised perfectly plucked brows. "Why wouldn't I be here? This meeting has to do with my son and our family's highly-rated television show, does it not?"

He wiped the back of his sleeve across his forehead. "Yes, ma'am. Of course you should be here. I simply didn't expect—"

"Well, I'm here now." The words came out clipped and cold, then she motioned toward Jan and pointed at the chair. Jan jumped out of her chair as though it had suddenly been wired with electricity.

Doyle walked to his desk. "Your relationship with Scott has hit a plateau, Ann." He sank into the plush leather chair and leaned back.

Ann shook her head, the sense of dread even deeper now that Veronica Adson was in the room. The woman's usually fake 'happy' façade wasn't in place today. She'd only intimidated Ann a couple of times, but now . . . This didn't make a bit of sense. "You mean because we get along and love each other?"

"No one wants to watch true love, darling." Veronica spoke in her trademark drawl that viewers seemed to love. "Each week, you and my son make goo-goo eyes at each other. The whole cook-turned-owner-of-her-own-catering-business, country-girl-meets hot-reality-star angle has grown cold."

"Exactly." Doyle's brows rose toward his thinning hairline.

Tanya gave a fake yawn and followed it with a catty smile. "Where's the fun and drama in that?"

Ann swung her gaze from one to another, her stomach tightening as the tension in the room seemed to suck the air from her lungs. "You mean because Scott and I actually *are* in love? What's wrong with that? What ever happened to having a happily-ever-after reality show. That *is* our reality."

Veronica crossed her ankles and sighed, a bored expression covering her perfectly made-up face. "No, it's not, Ann. It's *your* reality. It's always only been your reality. And our ratings are dropping. We must turn things around to keep public interest strong."

Doyle drummed his fingers on his mahogany desk. "We're going to increase the drama by having Scott date Jess Oliver this year."

Shock nearly threw Ann out of her chair, but she gripped the armrests and stayed put. "What? That doesn't make a bit of sense! Jess is the girl who dated Scott's brother before he left the show two seasons ago, then she left to get counseling. Why would you bring her back?"

Tanya nodded. "You nailed it. She's the one—the one and only Jess who was here the first season and generated so much chatter on social media for the high drama she brought to the show."

"She got the help she needed, and she's agreed to return to the show to boost our ratings. We're convinced she'll be a success." Jan's eyes sparkled.

Doyle tipped back in his chair, his mouth stretched in a grin. "Market research shows our fans love watching Jess. She brings a whole different dynamic to the show. Her new relationship with Scott will spice things up."

Ann crossed her arms. "Scott will never agree. No way. He and I have a deep relationship that goes beyond a reality show." Rage battled with confusion in her heart, but she tried to hold both back. She must get to the bottom of this before it got completely out of control.

Veronica's smile looked more like a barracuda pursuing its prey. "I'm sorry, dear, but he's already agreed."

"Let me get this straight." Ann pushed to her feet. "My boyfriend is dumping me. Through you."

"He wanted to be here," Veronica said. "But you know how crazy his schedule is. It's not like he doesn't care, darling. He's a busy man. Surely you can understand that."

"There isn't a single thing I understand about any of this. So you're saying I'm off the show?"

Doyle shook his head. "Not at all. Scott told us it's important you understand that this isn't about you. It's about the ratings."

Ann didn't know whether to laugh or scream. She and Scott had been dating for three years. Three years of her life given to this show and this man, and her relationship with Scott was real. After all, it *was* a reality show. Didn't that mean that what happened *was* real? Weren't the cameras simply following their lives and filming what happened? Sure, when they started the show, she knew part of it was staged but surely not all. She and Scott had fallen in love. How could someone choose to do this? Bring in another woman and announce she and Scott were breaking up? *That* was not reality.

Jan's voice broke into her thoughts. "We know you've always been a team player, Ann. You've always wanted what's best for the show."

"Right," Doyle said. "And you'll still play an important part."

Ann gave a harsh laugh. "As Scott's ex-girlfriend."

"Exactly." Doyle's smile returned. "Pathetic. Lost. A recurring role of you trying to win Scott back. Our viewers will eat it up."

Tanya tapped her iPad. "The whole Ann-Scott-Jessie triangle is testing through the roof. Our viewers are eating it up. You'll see, your social media numbers will go crazy."

Ann felt like she'd been tackled by a three-hundred-pound linebacker and flattened with no warning.

Jan stood and walked to Ann, placing her arm around her shoulders. "Come on. It'll be fun. Just think—this will be a whole new part for you to play. Something that will stretch your acting talent."

Tanya laughed. "Yeah. Research has shown that you're much more popular when you're unhappy."

Ann shook off Jan's arm and stepped away. "Well, isn't that reassuring." Right now, all she wanted to do was get away from these people and think. She'd trusted these people for three years. Surely Veronica and Scott couldn't agree. They were like family. They would never betray her. No way could her life change this fast.

Doyle pushed to his feet. "Come on, Ann. Reality TV is acting, exactly like any other job. It's not personal, so don't take it that way. Give it a little time. You'll get used to the idea."

Someone tapped at the office door a second later, and Ann's heart jolted when Scott entered the room, closing the door with a soft click. He strode across the space between them, the top button of his white shirt unbuttoned as was his habit, his well-cut jacket showing his square shoulders, and his dark-blond hair, as usual, in need of a cut. He reached out to Ann, his handsome face wearing a rueful smile. "Sorry I'm late. An accident on the freeway. Is everything settled and understood? We okay here?"

Veronica gave a short nod. "Perfectly understood."

Ann pulled away from his outstretched arm. "You both knew about this? You approved it without so much as discussing it with me first? What about our engagement?"

He sucked in a sharp breath. "You know that's very unofficial. It's not like we've announced it on the show or anything. After three years, I thought you'd know how this thing goes. We have to keep the ratings up. We need to do what's best for the show."

She took a step toward the door and away from him. "You're saying you'll be dating Jess now, and we won't see each other?" She crossed her arms. "If our engagement is unofficial, then maybe I need to officially get out of your life. Is that what you want?"

"No, of course not. Jess is all for show. You and I can see each other on the side. But we can't let anyone know. The cameras can't follow us anymore."

Ann drew in a deep breath and looked from one expectant face to the next. "Right. I get it. We'll sneak around. Keep it a secret. What I *thought* was you being in love with me was all about the ratings. Nice." Fury built and pushed the confusion aside.

Scott reached for her again but dropped his arm to his side when she didn't respond. "I'm sorry. . . really. Try to understand, okay?"

"Oh, I understand—I understand that I was naïve enough to think I could have a happy, healthy relationship that would end in marriage, when in 'reality'," she gave a half-laugh, "nothing about this was real. The only time the audience will be happy is when the 'characters' are unhappy. It's apparent I need to make a decision."

"You need to think long and hard, young lady." Veronica's ice-blue eyes bore into Ann's as she stepped close. "You're still under contract."

Ann nearly choked. "My contract is up for renewal next month, and we don't start shooting the new season for three months. I'm going to take a vacation and think about whether or not I even want to sign that contract."

As soon as the words were out of her mouth, a deep sense of relief filled her.

Scott jolted beside her. "That's not smart."

Ann smiled. "You know what's not smart? Getting caught up in this reality lifestyle and believing for even one minute that it's real." She leaned over and grabbed her Coach purse where it hung over her chair, more determined than ever to get out of this room and leave these people behind. "You guys set this all up—set me up to fail—and I never saw it coming. Talk about naïve." She shook her head. "No more." She pivoted and walked from the room, slamming the door behind her.

Scott stood rooted to the spot, unable to believe the woman he loved had walked out on the show—worse yet—walked out on him. Had they all made a mistake?

Tanya's face reflected shock. "What now? I can't believe she's thinking of quitting and stormed out. She's usually extremely easy to deal with."

Scott reached for the doorknob. "I didn't expect her to be so upset. I had no idea she'd react like this. I need to go after her."

Veronica put her manicured hand on his arm and squeezed lightly. "No, darling. Let her go. She needs time to realize what she's walking away from."

"But Mom, this isn't like Ann. I've never seen her so . . . so determined. What if she follows through and refuses to sign a new contract?"

Veronica pulled him into a brief hug then stepped away. "Never fear, dear boy. She's not going to throw away the best job she's ever had and return to catering parties for rich people. She should count her blessings that we noticed her three years ago at the Nelson's party and offered her a role on the show."

"You do remember don't you, that shortly after she came on the show, our ratings went up significantly? Besides, I do care about her. I mean, this is Ann. We've been discussing getting married."

She patted his arm. "And you've played your part beautifully, darling. Now it's time to move on for the sake of the show. Like you said, you can still date Ann on the side occasionally, if you'd like. But I'm guessing you'll be head-over-heels with Jessie before long. Give it a chance to work out, all right?"

He shook his head, refusing to be bullied this time. "I don't agree. I must talk to Ann. She needs to understand I still care."

Veronica looked from one expectant face to the other. "That might be wise. We'll give Ann a few hours to come to her senses, then you can contact her again, Scott."

Relief flooded him, and he closed his eyes for a brief second. "Thanks, Mom. I hate hurting her like this. But I agree, I think she'll come around."

Veronica shifted her attention to Jan. "What's the name of that assistant Ann gets along with? Gretel? Gertrude?"

Tanya winced. "Gretchen."

"Right. Put her on alert. She doesn't need to do anything yet, but I want her to be able to drop everything at a moment's notice if we decide we need to send her to Ann's house."

Jan punched in a number. "I'm on it."

Ann pulled up at a red light in her new Mercedes SUV—something she wouldn't have dreamed of owning three years ago when she'd turned twenty-one. She'd come to this town with barely enough money to start her catering business and figured it would take years before she could buy a modest car and home.

She glanced at her phone lying face up on the seat next to her, then pressed the button to wake it up. Scott's contact info showing his smiling face looked at her as if expecting her to call. She glanced at the street light again. Still red. Her thumb hovered over the button—one touch and Scott could be on the line, making this all go away—making her life right again.

Was that what she wanted? She'd allowed Scott, his family, her producer, so many people, to step in and figure out what was best for her these past three years. Did she want to do that again?

She glanced up. The light turned green, and she put both hands on the wheel, willing herself to ignore the phone. Slow tears trickled down her cheeks as she drove the rest of the way home.

Pulling up in front of her house, she switched off the ignition and sat, staring at her townhouse. How many women in their mid-twenties owned something like this, in California, no less? When she'd purchased it, she'd wanted nothing more than a home of her own, but looking at it now, she realized the house had never attained that goal. There had been something missing the entire time. She'd thought it was Scott—that when they married, and she had her own family, everything would change. Now that seemed a distant dream.

As she walked into her house, she glanced at the pictures sitting on the entry tables. Scott and her at the beach. Scott, his mom, his sister, and herself at his mom's house. They all looked so perfect, as though they'd walked off the set. Now she wondered. Was it all staged, exactly like *Life with the Adsons*? Had it all been a hoax—something created for the viewers, or did Scott's family love her and want her as part of their family, as they'd declared for the better part of two years?

The phone jingled Scott's special ringtone. She reached for it, then paused. There was no reason to pick it up right now. Maybe it wouldn't hurt to make him wait.

It hit the fifth ring and went silent. Good. She needed more time before dealing with whatever he had to say.

Chapter Two

VERONICA WAITED UNTIL THE DOOR TO Doyle's office closed behind her son before she swung toward Doyle, her face contorted in anger. How dare that little snippet of a girl stand up to her, Veronica Adson, and flaunt what she'd decreed would happen, in front of her producer and his staff.

Doyle stood and waited for her to sit. When she continued to stare at him, he drew in a deep breath. "We might need to rethink this. Scott was upset. Ann's a nice girl, and she's been like a part of the family the past few years. Maybe we shouldn't bring Jess in."

Veronica pressed her lips together to keep from exploding. After all, image was everything in this business. She kept her next words slow, measured. "This show is called *Life with the Adsons*, not *Life with a Little Caterer* who my son happens to have a childish crush on."

"I think it's more than a childish crush."

She couldn't help rolling her eyes this time. "Oh, please. How many women has Scott dated on the side since this show started? A couple of episodes with Jess Oliver, drama queen, and the ratings will soar—and Scott and the audience will forget all about Ann Stanway and her childish tantrums."

Doyle's brows rose. "That's news to me. You're saying you don't want to give Ann another role on the show at all?"

"Not if she continues like this." She sighed and sank into the plush chair near his desk. "She's too sweet. It was over-the-top to even offer her a recurring role as the dumped girlfriend. Her ungrateful attitude shows she doesn't deserve even that much consideration."

Doyle took his own chair. "Yeah, but Ann's *always* been a nice girl."

Veronica huffed. "*Nice* doesn't increase ratings or create buzz. We'll need to be sure things don't tip the other direction."

Doyle frowned. "I don't follow. You think she might reach out to our competition or speak to the press? I don't believe she'd do that."

She drummed her fingers on the arm of the plush leather chair. "We're not taking that chance. We need to consider damage control. What was the name of that personal assistant again?"

"Gretchen? You see her every day. She's worked for us several years now."

"Right." She narrowed her eyes, not caring for the tone he took with her. She was the star, not him. If she didn't choose to put any effort into remembering every assistant's name, who was he to complain? "It's time to send Gretchen over to Ann's house to talk. Tell her to be there within the hour and report to you or me. We need to get a handle on this. If Ann is truly considering quitting, we'd better get ahead of it and control the story. We'll find a way to use it, whichever way it goes."

An hour later, Scott pounded his fist on the arm of the same leather chair his mother had used in Doyle's office. He looked up into the worried faces of Doyle and Tanya and shook his head. "She's still not picking up. I've tried twice now."

Doyle didn't stop pacing. "Call her again. You know

she can't hold out against you for long. She'll answer. She always has her phone with her. It's part of her contract requirement."

Scott hit redial and waited, his foot tapping against the polished hardwood floor. He ran a hand over his dark blond hair that he wore fashionably long, annoyed yet again that he'd been called away from his stylist. "She'd better answer this—Ann? Is that you? Where have you been? I've been so worried when you didn't answer. I thought something might have happened." His voice dropped to the loving tone he knew Ann expected. This wasn't the time to upset her when she appeared so close to bolting. "I got a call from Doyle, and he's worried too."

"Oh really?" Ann's voice carried into the room. "You told your producer to dump me so you can date Jess. How do you think I should act?"

He shot a quick glance at Doyle who scowled. "It's not like that, hon—we went over this when you were here. The whole thing with Jess is for the viewers, that's all. It's nothing to get upset about."

"I can't believe you and your mom agreed to this."

"I didn't know until a couple of days ago. It was my mom's idea. It's not a big deal. You need to chill and see it as part of the show, that's all. You're making too big a deal of it."

"Chill." Her voice almost froze him through the phone. "You're saying the people who I've come to consider my second family think it's a good idea we break up. Nice. I need to go."

He held up a hand as though he could stop her. "Wait. Don't hang up. Please. Hear me out. My family stars in the most popular reality show in America. That means we have to do things differently in public than in private, but it doesn't change how I feel about you. I love you. You know that."

She gave a sad laugh. "Do I? I'm not so sure anymore."

"What do you mean?" He stood and began to pace, waving Doyle to his seat behind the desk. "We're all you have, Ann."

Ann wanted to hurl the phone across the room. She didn't know why she was talking to Scott again—not after what had happened in Doyle's office. But they'd had a past together—yesterday she'd have said a life together—so maybe she owed him another minute or two. Was he right? Was his family and this show all she had? Possibly, although she hated to admit it. With her father dead and her mom not seeming to care what she did or where she lived since her father's death, Scott's family had become like her own.

Then her eyes landed on another picture. An old one, this time from her childhood. A lovely, quaint home in the country with two people standing out front, their arms wrapped around her shoulders. How she missed her grandparents. They were the last real family she'd had until they passed away four years ago, not long before she'd landed this dream job in Hollywood. What would they say to this mess?

"Ann? Are you still there?" Scott's voice jarred her back to the present. "You need to calm down and come to the office. You and I can go for coffee and talk. You'll feel better after you get things in perspective."

She shook her head, not caring he couldn't see her. "I think we need space. Time to think things through. I don't want to return to the office."

"Okay, so tomorrow morning. Breakfast. I'll take you to our favorite little place. Will that work?"

She gave it two whole seconds before she responded. "I told you I'm taking a short vacation. I was considering a bit longer than a day or two. I need distance from everything. Time to think."

"What are you talking about?" His voice rose, and she pulled the phone away from her ear. "You can't walk away from this life. You're famous. Where would you go? You'll be recognized pretty much anywhere in this country. Anonymity isn't an option."

She peeked out the window as she heard a car door slam. "I always have options, Scott. Hey, I need to go. Someone is here. 'Bye." She clicked off the phone and slipped it into her pocket then hurried to the door as the chimes rang.

Ann swung open the door. "Hi, Gretchen." She stared at her PA, a personal assistant who worked for *Life with the Adsons*. A red-head with freckles and a turned-up nose, she never quite seemed happy, somehow. No doubt Veronica had screamed at her again. Hopefully the poor girl hadn't been fired as a result of the 'talk' in the office with Doyle and crew earlier. She drew her inside. "You look beyond tired. They have you running non-stop today?"

"Pretty much since dawn. You know how it goes. I'm a lowly personal assistant." She laughed, then put her hand over her mouth. "Sorry. I shouldn't have said that. I'm very thankful for my job. Please don't tell Scott or his mom?"

Ann gave her a brief hug. "Hey, no worries. I think you're the only person who's ever been completely real with me since I signed onto this gig. Come in and have an iced tea or a mineral water."

They walked into the kitchen. "Iced tea sounds

great, thanks. And to answer your question, yeah. They sent me over. They said they're worried about you. Veronica, Scott, and Doyle."

Ann waved Gretchen toward a chair and emitted a brittle laugh. "You look like you're about to fall over. Sit. Worried about me, huh? Right. They're worried about the show. That's all any of this has ever been about. I'll admit, some of it has been fun—exciting even. The last thing I expected after being in LA for three months and starting my catering business was to be asked out by Scott Adson. I agreed to go on the show to be close to him. It's not like I came to this town to act. Why did they send you, anyway? I mean, did they tell you what happened in the office today?"

Gretchen shrugged. "They wanted to make sure you're okay. I honestly don't have a clue. They didn't tell me what's going on—but I got the feeling it's more like I'm supposed to keep an eye on you. They said I was to call them immediately and let them know if you're . . . acting weird or anything." She took the tall glass Ann offered. "Thanks. Guess I probably shouldn't have told you all of that."

Ann smiled and sank into the opposite chair, cradling her own icy glass. "Don't worry, I won't repeat it. I'm sure Veronica's worried I'll run—or worse yet, that I'll be vindictive and try to get even." She settled in and gave Gretchen a quick recap of what had happened at the office.

Gretchen's eyes widened, and she almost choked on her tea. "I'm so sorry. I honestly had no idea things were so bad."

Ann reached across the table and quickly squeezed Gretchen's hand. "It's okay. Veronica wants to control the Adson storyline, including my part in it, and I'm not interested in letting that happen. I don't want you to get in trouble, but I need your help. I have to get out of here for a while. Like, out of town. Think you could give me a bit of a head start before they figure out I'm gone?"

"Sure." Gretchen grinned. "You're the only one from the entire cast who ever calls me by name or is kind. I'd be happy to help."

"Thanks. But I don't want you to lose your job." Ann bit her lip, worry tugging at her heart. If Gretchen called Scott, he'd be hot on her trail before she could get two miles down the road.

Gretchen waved an airy hand. "It doesn't matter. I think I might quit, anyway, if they put too much pressure on me. I've started a travel blog, and this might be a good time to get my courage together and pursue it full time."

"Seriously?"

"Yeah. I've been working it on the side for over a year. I've gotten a lot of interest from places that want to advertise on my site." She finished the last drink of her tea. "Where do you plan to go if you leave here?"

"I'm not sure. My grandparents lived in Pennsylvania but they died years ago, so there's no pull there. At this point, I'm going to drive and see where I end up."

"Aren't you worried about being recognized?"

"That would be a problem." A slow smile widened Ann's lips. "Unless I can get you to help me."

Gretchen sat up straight, her smile matching Ann's. "You've got it. What's the plan?"

Scott jumped to his feet when his mother walked into

Doyle's office like she owned it. Well, she pretty much did, since a lot of their family money had gone into starting this show in the first place. "Mom. You're here." As usual, his mother was dressed to perfection. With the cosmetic work she'd had done and the professional make-up, even the most discerning eye wouldn't know she'd passed her fiftieth birthday.

She gave a short nod and lowered herself into the chair Scott had vacated, ever the lady with her designer dress, Coach bag, and Jimmy Choo sandals. Veronica Adson did everything exquisitely, and she expected others to treat her as though she were royalty. "Of course I'm here." She waved at Jan and Tanya hovering near the door. "Out. Both of you."

She waited until they'd closed the door behind them, then turned to Doyle, who appeared ready to fall over himself to please her. "So, what's this I hear about Ann? She's still pouting at home? Poor baby girl." Her perfect lips pulled into a smirk. "Too bad she was never this dramatic on the show, but we couldn't seem to get through to her that people want to see a bad girl, not a nice one."

Scott blew a breath out between pursed lips. "I tried talking sense into her. I even asked her to breakfast tomorrow, but she blew me off. I think her feelings are seriously hurt. She said she needs time—distance—from me and the show. I'm worried she's going to run."

Doyle stopped pacing in front of Veronica's chair. "Do we need to take some kind of action? Should we be worried?"

Veronica waved her expensive manicure under his nose. "No, darling, I don't think so. After all, no one else is going to hire a girl who's been demoted from a starring role to a groveling ex-girlfriend desperate to get her claws into her fiancé again." She trilled a laugh.

"You wait and see. After she realizes what she's lost, she'll come crawling to us in a matter of days."

Scott ran his fingers through his hair. He hated it when his mother dominated the room and the conversation. It was as though he didn't exist, and *he* was supposedly the star. If Mom made Ann feel the same way on top of demoting her, maybe he could understand why she ran.

No. He shook off that thought. She'd come to them with nothing and been handed everything. Ann had no right to complain. "What if she doesn't return? I've never seen her like this before. What if she decides she's done and sticks to her decision?"

Doyle grunted. "Then we play up your new relationship with Jessie in social media, that's what. We'll use Ann's departure to make Jess look even better. Viewers will love it."

Veronica gave a slow nod. "There's nothing like a little jealousy to stir things up."

Scott moved uneasily from one foot to the other. Jess was fine, but there was something about Ann that had always drawn him. Surely, she'd come to her senses soon. "Maybe we could write Ann into the script as my girlfriend again after a suitable time?"

A slight smile tugged at Veronica's lips, and she hunched one shoulder. "We'll see how the ratings go, darling."

He hated when she called him that. Ann was a breath of fresh air after being around his mother for five minutes. "How about I drive to her place and talk to her? Maybe I can get her to come around." Even more than how his mother spoke to him, he hated the pleading tone in his voice. Why couldn't he stand up to Mom and insist Ann not be cut? It wasn't like their ratings had tanked. He'd almost added 'please' but bit back the word.

She drummed her fingers on the leather chair arm. "All right. Maybe I'm being too harsh. She's a rather sensitive girl, and she's done a decent job for us in the past. A little in-person chat might be helpful. Go ahead and try it your way, Scotty. It can't hurt." She pushed to her feet and leveled a hard stare in his direction. "But make it snappy and call me as soon as you finish. I want a report."

He winced. Scotty. His name from childhood that he'd detested for years. Why couldn't she see that he was twenty-eight years old, and let him make a few decisions for himself? He wanted to jump for the door and run from the production office, but he forced himself to stroll, not wanting his mother to get any more amusement out of him today. Maybe he'd grab a burger before going to Ann's and let his mother stew, wondering what was taking him so long. He smiled. Small victories, but he'd take what he could get.

Chapter Three

ANN LOOKED THROUGH THE PEEPHOLE THEN swung open her front door. "You made quick time. I'm so glad. I've been worried someone from the office might show up. Did you get it all?"

Gretchen nodded. "Yes, I went to the drugstore, and they had everything on your list." She handed a plastic bag to Ann and waited.

"Excellent." Ann gave Gretchen an impulsive hug, then ushered her in and shut the door, turning the deadbolt. "Come on, I'll need your help. Let's go to my bathroom. I've already got a bag packed, so I'm ready to go once we finish."

She stepped into the room that was more like a spa than a bathroom and looked around one last time. What a far cry from where she'd grown up. She'd never dreamed she'd have something so nice when she was little. But as the past few hours had shown her, money and fame weren't necessarily enough. How had she gotten so far from her roots? She hadn't been to church in over two years, and she wasn't sure she could go back. Somehow, doing so would feel almost hypocritical—ignoring God when things were going well, then running to Him when it all fell apart. Wasn't that what people called a fair-weather Christian? She shrugged off the thought. No time right now to dig that deep.

Ann pulled a box out of the sack and held it up. "Medium blonde. Perfect. I've been brunette for so long, it's going to be strange to have my natural color again. Of course, one nice thing, I won't have to worry about it growing and having to dye it again." She grimaced. "I never agreed with Veronica about changing my hair color, but she insisted fans would like brunette better as it makes me look more warm and approachable. I really don't get her. First, she wants me warm and approachable, then she tells me people don't like nice girls." She shrugged. "So I caved. Like I did about almost everything." Squaring her shoulders, she smiled. "What did you think of my car?"

Gretchen's brows rose. "Uh, you know, it's a great ride. I mean, what's not to like? Of course, it can't hold a candle to my ride. I've got the best 2001 Ford sedan ever made, know what I mean?" She laughed. "Kidding. Seriously, your Mercedes is my dream car. Why do you ask?"

Ann smiled. "You'll see."

An hour later, Ann's long hair gleamed a rich honey-blonde, as she sat in front of the make-up mirror. "Just do it, Gretchen."

Gretchen's face had paled two shades, and her hands were shaking. "I can't cut off your gorgeous hair. No way!"

"We don't have much time. Hurry up. Blunt cut it right below my shoulders. I want to look ordinary and blend in. Besides, it'll grow if I want it long again. You said you used to cut your grandmother's and sister's hair all the time, so this can't be too different."

"Whatever." Gretchen sucked in a deep breath and got to work, moving faster after the first two long strands of hair hit the floor. "We probably should have cut it first then colored it." She giggled. "It would have only taken one box instead of two."

Ann surveyed herself after her friend finished. "Not bad. You even gave me layers."

Gretchen stepped back. "How about make-up?"

Ann shook her head. "I only want the bare

minimum. They always had me so heavily made up I barely recognized myself. Without makeup, with this hair color and cut, *I* don't know myself." She laughed. "It kind of feels like playing dress up when I was a kid in my grandmother's attic." Her smile faded. "Only this is for real."

She pushed to her feet. "You are the best friend ever. I couldn't have done this without you. You're sure you're going to be okay?"

"Absolutely." Gretchen wiped a tear from her cheek. "Now you've gone and made me cry. Come on, we'd better get you to your car."

Ann smiled and shook her head. "That's where you're wrong. Come on. You're going to help me one last time."

Scott parked across the street from Ann's house, taking a moment to rehearse yet again what he planned to say. He'd swear his undying love, assure her he understood how upset she was, and make her believe it would all turn out right in the end. Then bring her to the studio so they could get her to sign her contract for next year. At that point, they could all take a deep breath and relax. Maybe he'd even take Ann to a nice restaurant for dinner to celebrate their new beginning, since the public didn't yet know they were breaking up and that he'd be dating Jess. One last fling with Ann would be perfect before he started his new relationship.

He stepped out of his BMW and smiled. Ann would be putty in his fingers. She always was when he told her how beautiful she was and poured on the compliments. He reached in and grabbed his sunglasses then slipped them on. A soft rumbling swung him around. Ann's garage door was lifting. Good. He'd stay here and flag her down. Pasting on a large smile, he waited as the garage door closed, and the SUV with its heavily tinted windows moved into the street.

Scott took two steps toward it, lifting his hand. "Ann. Wait up. We need to talk." He pulled off his sunglasses, but he still couldn't see a thing through her windows. All that showed was the silhouette of a woman through the passenger side. "Ann!"

Her car almost jumped forward and accelerated down the street. Away from him. What in the world was she thinking? "Ann! Stop." He jogged a few feet up the road then realized he'd never catch her. Turning, he hit the button on his key fob and slid behind the wheel, activating his Bluetooth while he inserted his key in the ignition.

"Yes, Scott. Done with your little errand?" Mom's lazy voice drifted over the speaker built into his dash. "Did you and Ann kiss and make up, so you can break up with her on camera?"

Scott pulled out on the road, but he'd totally lost sight of Ann's car. "She drove off. I got here right as her car was pulling out of her garage."

"Then what are you doing talking to me? Follow her and get her back here! This is ridiculous, and it's gone on long enough. Wasn't a PA sent over there to watch her?"

"I have no idea where the PA is, Mother. And I *am* following her. At least, I'm trying. I wasn't in my car when she left, but I think I know where she turned."

"Get her on the phone. Hang up and call her *right now*." The perfectly modulated voice she used with anyone she wanted to impress had disappeared. This was the mother he knew most of the time.

"What if she doesn't answer or refuses to come with me?"

"Good grief. Do I need to tell you everything? Then we do it my way. You get on the phone with the PR team and let them know what's happening. We'll do everything in our power to make her look like a mess. It won't take long for the press to get hold of the story and make her life a nightmare. She won't be able to go anywhere else to work, and she'll come crawling back. Now call her."

Scott nodded then heaved a sigh as he saw the brilliant blue metallic SUV turn a block ahead. "I don't feel good about treating Ann this way, but I guess I have to do it for her sake as much as mine. I see her." He hit the end button, then spoke Ann's name into his phone. He waited. Two rings. Three. Four. Voicemail. "Come on, Ann. I see you a block ahead. I'm catching up with you. Pick up the phone and let's talk. I know you're upset, but we can talk this through. Give me a chance, okay?"

He increased his speed, barely making it through a yellow light. Great. He didn't need a ticket. Although that could be good press, if he couldn't get Ann to return. Distraught fiancé runs a red light trying to chase Ann after she has a nervous breakdown and runs away. He shook his head. Better not try that without Mother's permission. She'd have his head if he messed up the show. Wasn't he supposed to be dumping Ann for Jess? Yeah. He'd better be careful and not get the paparazzi on his tail without a good excuse.

He followed Ann's vehicle at a discrete distance. Relief flooded him when three miles up the road it pulled into a gas station. He parked behind her and jumped from his car, then strode to her window and tapped.

It slowly rolled down, and a young woman with red hair and raised brows stared at him. "Yes?"

He took a step back. "Who are you?"

She gave a slow smile. "I'm Gretchen Sanderson. I'm Ann's PA, and I've worked on your show for three years. But don't worry. If you don't want me to work for you anymore, I can certainly give notice now that Ann's gone."

Chapter Four

ANN REACHED THE CALIFORNIA/NEVADA BORDER driving Gretchen's old sedan and breathed a deep sigh. The car was running great, and she'd left California behind. Freedom—or despair. She hadn't quite figured out which yet, but she hoped she was driving toward freedom. What would Dad or Grandma have thought of her crazy scheme? She glanced in the mirror and smiled. They'd like that her hair was the color it used to be, even though they'd be sad she'd cut it. Dad had always loved her long hair, but no matter what she decided to do, if he were alive, he'd be proud of her. He'd say she was being a good soldier—to do the right thing and not look back.

She bit her lower lip hard, determined she wouldn't cry. Losing him in Afghanistan had about killed her, and it had driven her mother over the edge. She'd lost both of her parents that day, and she'd only been a young teen. If it hadn't been for Poppy and Nana, she wouldn't have survived.

This time she couldn't control the tears that welled. She didn't try to. Her grandparents wouldn't mind her crying for her parents, as long as she didn't do it too long or let it interfere with her new purpose. Nana would tell her to lift her chin, smile, pray, and take whatever step the Lord showed her to take. But did God even care? How could He possibly, after she'd ditched Him for fame and the spotlight?

The miles sped by, but she barely noticed them. Ten hours later, she crawled into a hotel bed in a mediocre but clean room. From now on, nothing fancy that cost big bucks for her. There was simply no reason to waste money, and she didn't want to stay any place where she might be recognized.

She slipped behind the wheel the next morning. No way would anyone recognize her with her new look and the plain, almost drab clothes she'd purchased at a store in the last town. She grinned. It was time to return to her roots. Nana and Poppy always called her their Annie, so Annie it would be, wherever she chose to stop. She'd use cash and her grandparents' last name, Farley. She'd be Annie Farley from now on.

This might even be fun, once she got over Scott's betrayal. Something about Veronica had always put her off, even though the woman had treated her with the utmost courtesy. There was an edge to her voice whenever she spoke to her household staff, and more than once Ann had heard her snap at someone when they hadn't met her expectations. Ann had always attributed it to the older woman being stressed with so much to deal with—the show, her family foundation, her wealth, and position.

Ann had wanted to believe Veronica saw her as part of the family, but now—well, now she wasn't so sure any more. Hadn't Scott said it was his mom's idea to have Jess take her place? That certainly didn't sound like a woman who loved her son's fiancé and wanted what was best for her. More like a callous woman who was out to make her show hit the top of the charts, whatever way she could.

Scott paced Doyle's office, not caring that his hair wasn't in place and his clothes looked like he'd slept in them. He hadn't slept since this entire fiasco with Ann, and he wanted this resolved. He swung and faced his mother, who sat with her normal smug look in the chair facing Doyle's window, a few feet from his desk. "Ann isn't returning my calls. Gretchen claims she hasn't heard from her at all. It's ridiculous that Ann would give her a car like that, but I can't have her arrested or fire her for it, since Ann apparently signed over the title." He thumped his fist into his open palm. "Who does that?"

His mother gave him a smile that didn't reach her eyes. "Someone who's ungrateful. We're finally seeing her true colors. You need to move on, darling."

He stopped pacing and faced her. "I keep telling you. She's not like that."

"You told Ann it's over, right, Doyle? You left her a voicemail that if she didn't return before her contract is up, we'll make sure she's finished in the industry?"

Doyle nodded but seemed to realize he needed to let this remain between Scott and his mother.

She gave another half-smile. "We tried to treat Ann like an adult, but she chose to run away instead, all because she won't be a regular on the show. She's behaving like a spoiled child."

Scott bit his lip, not sure what to think anymore. The lack of sleep and Jessie's recent phone calls wondering when they were going to get together weren't helping, either. "You really think so?"

His mother slowly rose from her chair and took a step toward him. She placed her hands on his shoulders and looked up into his eyes with her best motherly look. "I know you're disappointed, honey. But it's in times like these that we must pull together and protect the family. Family always comes first. Ann didn't understand that, but I know you do, right? I can count on you to be strong for the family and make good choices, can't I, Scott?"

He took a deep breath then looked at Doyle who nodded. "All right. Sure. So, what do you want me to do?"

She lowered her hands but only enough to stroke his cheek with her knuckles. "We have a big surprise for you. There's a limo waiting downstairs. First, they'll take you home so you can get a bit more . . ." She surveyed him from head to foot. ". . . presentable. Then you'll pick up Jessie Oliver in time to make your reservation at Lombardi's."

Scott felt a little jolt at her words. "Lombardi's—with Jess? That's kind of quick, isn't it?"

"No, darling, not at all. Doyle and I thought it would be nice if you two could spend time together before our first new episode where we let people know she's your new love interest."

He sucked in a deep breath and blew it out through his nostrils. "Right. I suppose dinner couldn't hurt. Thanks, Mom. I'll get going."

As the door was shutting behind him he could hear his mother's voice, normally carefully modulated, but a bit higher in pitch this time. "Barry? It's Veronica. He just left. Be sure you get a few good shots of them at the restaurant. We want our viewers to forget all about Ann before the evening is over."

Scott nearly turned around and stormed into the room again, but he stopped as his fingers touched the knob. What good would it do? Mom would ram anything she wanted down everyone's throats whether they agreed or not. He could refuse to go to dinner, but there would be another time—and other than quit the show and disappear from LA, there wasn't a thing he could do about it but play along. Exactly like he'd been programmed to do since childhood.

By the time Ann had driven past Oklahoma City, then St. Louis and Indianapolis, there'd been at least fifteen voice mails from Scott. She'd ignored them all. She had no interest in talking to him now. Maybe it wasn't fair to ignore her ex—she wasn't entirely sure—but at this point she didn't care to examine her emotions at a deeper level.

Late at night, after long hours on the road, she second guessed herself. More than once she reached for her phone, only to withdraw her hand, remembering what Doyle had said. Scott knew. He approved. The order had come through him, from his mother. He'd always been a mama's boy. Apparently, the family money talked louder than his supposed love for his girlfriend.

All she could say was good luck to Jess if the girl believed this new 'relationship' was real or would last. They'd use her up and spit her out as soon as the fans tired of her or the ratings dropped. Why it took being cut from her part to open her eyes she couldn't imagine. But it had, so no use crying about it now. Time to move on.

Ann's phone chirped as she sat in line at a gas station. She picked it up. Another tweet. *#AnnStanway disappears. She was a loser anyway. Glad she's off the show.*

As soon as Ann deleted that one, another one came in. *You seriously don't need #AnnStanway, Scott. #AnnStanway was boring. You can do better.*

Ann bit her lip. She had worked hard the last two days to ignore them, but they flooded her inbox, each one seeming to be more disparaging than the last. Had no one liked her? Were fans so fickle that they could swoon over her while she was on the show and hate her as soon as she was gone?

She crossed the Kentucky line a couple of hours later, still not sure where she wanted to stay. Each hotel had been like the last. She wanted—no, she needed—a sense of home. But where could she possibly find that? Nana and Poppy had lived on a farm most of her life. She'd loved that. A small one, only about ten acres, but it had an old-fashioned farm house, chickens, a milk cow—all things she'd loved as a child. What she'd give if she could go back there now.

She flipped on the radio. Music would be good. She let it skip through stations until suddenly she jerked up short and hit the hold button. A man's voice filled the car. "And in entertainment news, rumor has it Scott Adson has moved on after his reported breakup with Ann Stanway. He's been seen with Jessie Oliver at Lombardi's. Jess is rumored to become a new series regular on *Life with the Adsons*. Meanwhile, still no sign of Ann. She hasn't posted on any of her social media accounts in four days, leaving many to wonder if her fifteen minutes of fame are truly over."

Ann's hand shook. She knew this would happen. She'd thought she'd been prepared. She had to get off the road. Spotting what looked like a gravel, two-lane road leading nowhere, she turned onto it and punched the accelerator.

The voice on the radio continued. "And to add a shocking twist to the subject, it appears that Ann, who everyone thought was our little Dorothy, turned into the Wicked Witch of the East. Rumor has it that Scott proposed, and she turned him down flat, then demanded a larger role on the show. When the producer told her that couldn't happen, she stormed off in a huff and refused to return. Maybe Scott's better off with Jessie. What do you all think?"

Ann tried to blink the tears away so she could see the road, then she pounded the steering wheel. "I didn't break it off or demand a bigger role." It didn't matter where she ended up, but she had to get away from the images that wouldn't stop pursuing her. Scott—the first time he'd kissed her. Sure, the cameras were rolling, but it had felt so real. Later he'd said it was magical—not staged at all—it simply happened, and he couldn't stop it—hadn't wanted to stop it. And she'd believed him.

Her phone chirped. A text. Maybe it was Gretchen. She slowed and glanced at the screen. Scott. Again. The past four days had been full of texts and voice mails. She'd deleted them all, some without even listening or reading them. This time, she did. *Ann, you're making a mistake. You're going to be sorry if you keep this up. You need to come home—you know you love me. Please think about this and give me another chance?*

Ann lifted her chin, exactly like Nana taught her. She was finished. Done. She was sick of Scott's texts, his phone calls, the tweets, and everything else. She grabbed the phone and tossed it out the window, then glanced in her mirror. It bounced across the gravel, and she saw it break into pieces. A sense of loss mixed with triumph filled her. She'd done it. She was free. No more crying over the past or worrying what Scott or her 'fans' thought anymore. It didn't matter. She looked up and gasped, as a deep ditch loomed ahead. Hitting the brakes, Ann gritted her teeth and willed the car to stop in time.

Chapter Five

ANN OPENED HER EYES and stared out the window. Green fields surrounded her. A fly buzzed past her nose, making her jerk her head back. The engine had quit running, but the ignition was on. What had happened? She unsnapped her seatbelt and peered to the side.

Great. Gretchen's poor car had gone into a deep, dusty ditch and rammed the far side of the bank where a tree grew. Hard. The air bag hadn't deployed, but thankfully, she always wore her seatbelt. Now to find her phone and call a tow company, if there was one in this rural area.

Searching the seat for her phone, she came up empty. Where . . . Oh no. She'd tossed it out right before she'd crashed. Had it really broken into pieces? Maybe the back popped off and the battery came out. She pushed against her door, but it wouldn't open. Panic started to swell, but she refused to entertain it. From now on she had to think of herself as Annie Farley, Nana's granddaughter, the girl who'd been taught to keep her chin up and move forward, not Ann Stanway, the girl who hadn't made the best choices in life.

Grabbing her purse, she scooted over the center console and tried the passenger door. *Whew.* It opened easily. She slipped out and pushed to her feet, taking a moment to survey the damage. The nose of the car was buried in dirt as were the front tires—all the way to the top of the wheel wells, and the right fender was shoved hard against the tree trunk. She moved to the rear of the car and peered underneath. *Great.* It looked like the poor old car had managed to land smack on top of the only boulder within sight. No way could she push the car over that behemoth unless she turned into Superwoman.

Annie trudged along the gravel road, scanning side-to-side for her phone. A glint of metal showed on the edge of the road, and she hurried to it. Stopping, she leaned over and groaned. The face was smashed, the back was off, and there was a long crack through the inside cavity where the battery had been. And the battery was nowhere in sight.

So much for her phone—it was beyond help. She kicked it into the ditch, disgusted she'd lost her temper and tossed it. Now what?

Scanning the countryside, she noted rolling hills in the distance, pasture land surrounded by fences, and shade trees dotting the landscape, but not a house in sight. Where were all the people? This wasn't the seventeen-hundreds, for goodness sake. She returned to her car and waited, hoping someone would travel this apparently little-used road, sooner rather than later.

Five minutes turned to a half-hour and still no movement other than a cow that meandered into view. Should she start walking? But the nearest town behind her had been at least twenty miles, and the sun was already starting to set. Surely someone would come along before dark. Another thirty minutes passed, and a smidgen of panic licked at her mind. She raised her eyes to the sky. "Father, please send help or show me what to do. I'm kinda stuck here. I promise I'll try to do better. And I'm not saying that so You'll help me. I know I've messed up my life, and I truly want to turn things around."

A movement and the sound of a motor made her look up the road. A large green van slowed to a stop next to her car and the doors opened. Annie's eyes widened as a lovely Amish young woman, who appeared to be near her own age, stepped out. Not that she'd ever met an Amish person in real life, but she'd seen documentaries about their faith and lives. Her light brown hair was pulled into a neat bun, and a white bonnet covered her head. She wore a soft gray dress that came to within inches of her ankles, loose sleeves covered her arms to right below her elbows, and the front of the dress was covered by a white apron. "*Ach*! Are you all right?"

Annie nodded. "I'm fine, but I don't think my car is. It appears it's sitting on a boulder."

The young man who'd been driving the van walked to her car and peered underneath then straightened and looked at her. His sandy brown hair fell over his forehead, and he had freckles across the bridge of his nose. He appeared to be a few years younger than her, maybe only a couple of years or so out of high school.

His glance turned into something like an intense stare, and one brow rose. "I don't think it's totaled, but you'll definitely need a tow. I know a mechanic who can fix this car up in a few days, as long as it doesn't need anything too fancy in the way of parts."

Ann pulled her sunglasses off her head and put them on, wondering if he stared at all women like that, or if she hadn't done a good enough job with her disguise. Whatever it was, she'd better be careful. "Great. That's what I was afraid of." She swung toward the woman. "Hey, my phone is broken, so I can't call anyone. Can I borrow one of yours, then maybe I can call a tow truck and Uber can take me to the mechanic's shop."

The young woman's forehead scrunched. "I'm afraid I don't own a phone, and I have no idea what an Uber is."

Ann chuckled. Of course, she didn't have a phone—she probably wouldn't have a TV either, which would be a good thing—there was no way an Amish woman would have ever watched *Life with the Adsons*. "Thank you both for stopping to help."

The young woman bobbed her head. "This is my driver, Jimmy Snyder. He has a car service, so I'm sure he can take you wherever you need to go."

Jimmy nodded. "Or Jim, or Jim-bo. Back in the day, the guys called me Jimmy the Playmaker on the football field." He flexed his muscles and grinned.

The young woman laughed. "Did they really call you that? I've never heard it."

His eyes widened. "Yep, sure did. I earned that nickname like I earned the most improved player award on our eight-man team my senior year at Allentown High."

The woman turned sparkling eyes to Annie for a quick second before smiling at the young man again. "I apologize for not knowing that, Jimmy. I think we have a celebrity in our midst and I didn't even know it."

Ann started, then relaxed as she realized that last comment was aimed at the young man. She raised her brow and gave Jimmy the slightest of smiles. It appeared this guy was fun-loving and maybe a bit of a flirt, but she didn't want to encourage him if he was trying to flirt. She was off men, with no desire to pursue another relationship anytime soon.

He sobered quickly. "Seriously, there's no need for a phone. I have one, but there's no reception here. I can take you straight to the mechanic's garage."

Ann remembered the text she'd gotten right before she'd gone into the ditch. That must be why Scott hadn't left yet another voice mail. "Thanks for the offer.

I'll probably take you up on that. Is there a hotel in town? Maybe you could drop me off there."

"*Nein.* There's no need for that," the young woman said. "I run an Amish inn on the edge of Cave City. I'd be proud to have you stay there while your car gets taken care of."

Jimmy laughed. "If you don't mind living simple, as the Amish say. You won't find anything fancy at Sarah's Wildwood Inn—no internet, TV, or phone service there, and Sarah only has a generator for the most basic electric needs. She has a modern propane fridge and stove, and you will have a light in your bedroom. Think you can handle that?"

"It sounds heavenly. I could use peace and quiet right now. I'd be honored to stay, if you're sure you have room? I'm sorry. Where are my manners? I'm . . . I'm Annie Farley. It's good to meet you." She bit her lip. She'd better start thinking of herself as Annie, too, or she'd mess up and tell someone else she was Ann.

"*Ya.* Plenty of room. I'm never full. And I'm Sarah Stoltzfus. Please call me Sarah." She bobbed her head in an almost shy manner. "Come on, we'll get you home and settled in no time. Do you want Jimmy to bring your luggage from your car and load it into the van?"

"Please. That would be wonderful." She unlocked her trunk and waited for him to move her three cases, then shut it again. Home. The word evoked a ton of memories in Annie's heart, both good and not so good, but somehow, she knew the young woman's idea of home was exactly what she needed right now. She settled into the middle seat next to Sarah and stared out the window for a moment, taking in the peaceful countryside. "You've lived here all your life?"

"*Mamm* and *Daed* have a farm not far from my inn. I'm the oldest of seven children."

"You're not married?" As soon as the personal question left Annie's lips, she wished she could take it back. "I'm sorry. I shouldn't ask something like that. It's only . . . you seem about my age, and . . ."

Sarah gave her a sweet smile. "And most Amish women are married and have at least a couple of *Bopplies* by now, *ya*?" She shrugged.

Annie scrunched her forehead. "What's a *Bopplie*?"

"I'm sorry. I forget you don't know our language. A baby. I was married, but my Ezra died a little over a year ago. We ran the inn together, and he made furniture in his workshop on the other side of my property. When he died, I kept the inn open, and another Amish man is using the workshop for his business. He pays me a little, so I get by."

Annie bit her lip, unsure what to say. I'm sorry sounded so trivial in the face of such a tremendous loss.

Sarah patted Annie's hand. "Please don't worry. *Gott*—God, is healing my heart, and I am better. Now, tell me, are you from this area and returning home, Annie?"

Annie gave a small jolt. Even though she'd decided to use her grandparents last name for herself, it sounded strange on someone else's lips. "No, I'm not returning home, but my grandparents lived on a farm outside of Philadelphia years ago. So being this close kind of feels like coming home."

Jimmy looked at her through his mirror. "Are they still living? Was that where you were headed when you hit the ditch? What brought you to our neck of the woods, anyway?"

"No. They passed away a few years ago. I was just driving . . . nowhere in particular." She swiveled toward Sarah, hoping to keep Jimmy from asking more personal questions.

Jimmy's eyes kept darting between the road and the mirror, peering at her. "Where do you live now?"

Sarah tsked. "Jimmy, so many questions. She wrecked her car. We need to let her rest."

He shrugged. "I'm curious, that's all. We don't often get gorgeous single women wrecking their cars out here."

"Right." Annie straightened. "I live in LA. Have you lived here all your life?"

He appeared to miss the question or maybe he simply ignored it. "What did you do out there? You look kinda familiar."

She slipped her sunglasses on again, her heart pounding. "I was a . . . a caterer. I had my own business. But I don't anymore."

Sarah brightened. "Oh, so you know how to cook? That's *wunderbar* . . ." She smiled. "I mean, that is wonderful. I think you will find our little town quite different from what you're used to."

Annie gave her a grateful smile. "That's fine with me. I was raised in a small town...on a farm, actually. So how does this work? You can't drive or own a car, but you can ride in one?"

"*Ya.* We hire drivers from among the *Englischers* like Jimmy, when a buggy isn't suitable for our needs. But we walk or use our buggies whenever possible."

"Uh—*Englischer*? I don't follow."

Sarah laughed. "I'm sorry. That is someone who is not Amish."

Annie raised her brows. "Oh. I guess I have a lot to learn."

"*Nein.* I would be lost in your world too. Do not worry. I will help you. Ah, we're here." She waved her hand out the window.

Annie turned and stared. "It's lovely. It almost looks like a gingerbread house, or a Victorian mansion. Two stories and it appears to have a garret above. You must love it here."

"*Ya.* Very much, although it's a big house for one person when I don't have many guests. I'm glad you've come." She gave Annie another sweet smile then stepped out of the van when Jimmy slid the door open.

He reached in to take Annie's hand, but she turned to grab her purse, pretending not to have seen him. She swung around. His face fell as her steady gaze met his. "I'll get your luggage and take it to your room. Hey, Annie, I wondered . . ." He twisted his lips to the side then shook his head. "Never mind. Sarah, which room would you like her in?"

Sarah gathered two wicker baskets and slid the handles over each arm then started for the door with Annie following. "The only one occupied at the moment is the one at the top of the stairs. You can put her in the one beyond that if you'd like."

Jimmy slipped through the open door juggling all three cases and headed up the stairs.

Sarah turned to Annie. "I think he may be a bit smitten with you."

Annie bit back a laugh. "I hope not. I think he's a bit young for me, and I'm not looking for a relationship."

"He's twenty-one, if I remember correctly. He's a sweet boy and means well." Sarah squeezed Annie's hand. "I don't think he'll bother you if you don't encourage him."

Jimmy bounded down the stairs a moment later, his wide smile directed toward Annie. "All set. I'll head out now and stop to see the mechanic. Oh, you want to give me your keys so I can get it towed tonight? You said your phone is broken, so I could pick you up tomorrow to see what they have to say, then we could get coffee if you'd like." He stopped and swung around. "You have a nice room. It's next to the bathroom."

Annie's eyes widened. "Next to the bathroom?" She glanced at Sarah. "I don't have a private bath?"

"I'm so sorry, but each floor has one bathroom, which is shared. Will that be a problem, do you think?" Sarah tipped her head to the side, her lips pressed together in worry.

"Oh. Sure. Not a problem. I haven't shared a bathroom since I was a kid living with my grandparents, but I guess it's fine." She dug the keys out of her purse and handed them to Jimmy. "I'm glad to have a place to stay, so anything is fine. And I appreciate the help. Maybe you could swing by and let me know if the mechanic needs to talk to me, then I'll decide what to do."

Sarah shifted the grocery baskets in her arms, and Annie reached to take one. "I'm sorry I didn't offer sooner. Those look heavy."

Sarah motioned toward what looked like the entrance to the kitchen. "We can put them in here. And Jimmy, I have a phone in the shed outside, and you have the number. If you need to leave a message for Annie, you can do that, if you don't want to drive all the way out here again."

A wide grin lit his face. "It's no bother at all. I'll see you tomorrow, Annie. Unless you decide to stay in our one local hotel."

"Why would I want to do that?"

He gestured at the bag over her shoulder. "'Cause that's a $500 bag you're carrying, and Sarah doesn't have Internet. I'm guessing you won't last long."

Her eyes widened. "I'm sure I'll be fine. Thank you,

Jimmy."

He waved. "We'll see. I'll talk to you later when I find out about your car. 'Bye, Sarah."

She waved then headed for the kitchen as he let himself out the front door.

Annie helped Sarah unload the groceries, pulling a jug of orange juice out of the bottom of the bag. "Where do I put this?"

Sarah turned and plucked two juice glasses off a shelf. "How about you fill these first, then you can put it in the fridge, right around that corner. I hope you will be comfortable here, but I understand if you decide it will not suit you. We rarely have *Englischers* stay, as we mostly cater to the Amish community."

"Not at all. I appreciate your hospitality to a stranger."

Annie filled the two glasses then took a drink from one. "Mmm. Good. I didn't realize I was thirsty. Thanks." She picked up the juice bottle, still holding her drink and took a step forward.

Hunter Lewis followed the sound of voices around the corner from the sitting room into the dining nook off the kitchen. Jolting backwards at a sudden impact, he barely noticed the thud of something heavy landing on his toe. He simply stared at the woman pressed up against his shirt—against his very *wet* shirt. Orange juice trickled over his skin and dripped onto the floor.

"Oh my! I'm so sorry!" The melodic voice trapped him as he stared into a pair of amazing brown eyes. The woman gripped his shirt in one hand and an empty glass in the other. Then suddenly, she jumped, set the empty glass down, and reached for a dishtowel. She started scrubbing the orange stain as though it were her final mission in life.

Hunter couldn't contain the chuckle that vibrated through his chest. He gripped her hands, stopping her frantic motion. "It's fine. Really. No harm done. This is my paint shirt. It's supposed to have stains." He held her hands a second longer than necessary and heard her suck in a quick breath.

Finally, he mustered the will power to take a half-step away and glanced at Sarah, then at the young woman again. Blonde hair that accentuated her eyes. Pale skin that had very little color at the moment, and lips that would probably be quite attractive if they weren't pressed together as though she were holding back the urge to cry—or could it be laughter? A glint of something shone in her eyes that he couldn't quite interpret. "I wasn't aware you had another guest, Sarah." Then he turned his attention to the woman who'd bent to pluck a full jug of juice off the floor. "And I apologize for making you spill your drink."

"Oh, it wasn't your fault. I was in a car accident an hour or so ago, and I think I'm still a bit jumpy." She quit worrying her bottom lip and smiled.

"Car accident. Are you all right?" Maybe that accounted for the pale skin more than her surprise at running into him.

"Yes." She looked up at him again, and something inside Hunter fluttered. "I mean, not totally, considering the mess I've made." She swept a hand toward his shirt and the floor.

He glanced at Sarah, standing quietly near the counter. "I'm sorry for intruding, Sarah."

"It's quite all right, Hunter. What's the expression? No use crying over spilt milk? I suppose that applies to juice as well, *ya*?"

He put out his hand to the young woman. "I'm Hunter."

She shook it. "Annie." She gazed up at him again. She smiled. "Better you should know my name than think of me as the crazy lady who attacked you with orange juice."

This time Hunter laughed outright. A sense of humor. Good. He liked that in a woman. He jerked the thought into line where it belonged. He wasn't looking for a girlfriend—he'd been down that road not so long ago, and it hadn't ended well.

Sarah motioned to the table. "Let's start over, shall we? I will get clean glasses. Or would you both rather have coffee?"

Hunter held up his hand. "I'm good. I only came by to let you know the paint is finished in the sitting room, and I can stop by tomorrow and fix the latch on your barn door if you'd like me to."

"*Ya*. That would be *gutt*. *Denki*."

He turned to Annie. "So how does a girl happen to be in a car accident then end up at an Amish inn an hour later?"

"I found her in a ditch and rescued her." Jimmy strolled into the kitchen, his thumbs hooked in his jeans pockets.

Hunter grinned. "I could be wrong, but doesn't it take away from the heroic deed if the hero has to announce it?"

Jimmy shot him a look. "Somebody has to."

Annie looked at Hunter. "Actually, Sarah and Jimmy both came to my rescue, and I'm extremely grateful."

Jimmy sidled a little closer to Annie. "Your car has been towed to the garage. I thought you might want to know that the garage is closed, so I couldn't talk to the mechanic. But I'll pick you up in the morning and take you to make arrangements, if you'd like. You know, since I wasn't able to talk to anyone tonight."

"I can call a cab. I don't want to bother you."

Hunter shook his head, wondering if he should offer her a ride. "No cabs in these parts. Mostly buggies."

"Oh. Okay, I guess. Thanks for the offer, Jimmy. I suppose I'll need to take you up on it."

"No problem. I can't wait. I mean, er, see you in the morning."

Hunter pushed to his feet. It looked like Jimmy already had an inside track—although it was possible the kid was smitten with no reason. It wouldn't be the first time Jimmy trailed around after a pretty woman like a lost puppy. He smiled. Jimmy was a nice guy, and hopefully he wouldn't bug her too much. "I'd better be on my way. Nice to meet you, Annie. Maybe I'll see you around while you're here."

Annie's heart did a little hop-skip, then settled. "Maybe. You never know." She stared after the person who must be Sarah's handyman as he exited the room. When he'd held her shoulders to keep her from falling backward, she couldn't help but notice how strong he seemed. Plus, he wasn't too hard on the eyes, either. Short, dark blond hair covered his head, dimples touched the corners of his mouth when he smiled, and his jaw—square and rugged—unlike Scott who had a rounder, softer look.

How awful to make a first impression on one of Sarah's acquaintances by running into him and ruining a shirt—even if he claimed it was old and used for work.

He must think her a total idiot and clumsy besides.

Jimmy paused by Annie's chair and stared at her. "You look kinda familiar. Have you been in this area before?" He scratched his head. "I'm trying to figure out where I might have seen you. It'll come to me if I think about it long enough."

Concern hit Annie hard. She'd been careful, and so sure no one would recognize her. "What time did you want me to be ready tomorrow morning?"

"Oh. Right. Nine-thirty work for you? Or I can come earlier, if you'd like. The garage opens at eight."

She pushed her chair away from the table. "Nine-thirty is fine. I'm not much of an early riser. See you then."

He gave her a sweet smile and headed for the front door.

Her gaze followed him, wondering what had happened to Sarah. She scrunched her brows as she glanced out the kitchen window. Her new friend stood outside close to Hunter as he handed her what looked like a wad of bills. Sarah touched his arm, then slipped the cash into her apron pocket.

Annie turned away, not wanting to appear to stare. But why would this man be giving Sarah money? Shouldn't she be paying him for the work he'd done?

Chapter Six

HUNTER HEADED DOWN THE PATH, MORE than a little intrigued by the new visitor at the inn, and trying not to be irritated at Jimmy's obvious attempt at flirtation with the young woman. Not that he should be bothered—or surprised. Jimmy hit on anyone new and near his own age who came to town since he'd broken up with his long-time high school girlfriend. Too bad, they'd actually made a cute couple.

Annie—what? He realized he hadn't gotten her last name or learned anything about her in the few minutes they'd talked. Oh well. Guess it didn't matter. She'd accepted Jimmy's offer to pick her up and take her to the garage in the morning to check on her car. The kid had been helpful, bringing Annie to Sarah's and getting the car towed, he'd give him that. Of course, Jimmy was only seven years his junior, but he'd recently finished two years of college and had been building a decent business. But more often than not, something about the young man made him think of Jimmy as a boy.

Annie appeared to be closer to his own age. Who was he kidding? He had more than enough challenges in his life right now. She seemed nice enough. Hopefully she wouldn't be put off by the Amish way of life while staying at Sarah's.

He frowned. Even more so, he hoped she wouldn't do or say anything to offend Sarah. That young woman had enough to deal with, losing her husband at such a young age. His heart ached for her. All he could do right now was pray Annie would be a help to Sarah, not a hindrance.

Annie came downstairs after having unpacked her overnight bag and taken a quick shower. She hadn't had much time to look around her room, but it *had* seemed strange not to see a TV there or in the living area she'd walked through. Jimmy wasn't kidding when he'd asked if she'd be able to survive the lack of technology. No TV, phone, or Internet—she hadn't even noticed an old-fashioned radio anywhere. Wild. The shower had refreshed her, but she still felt a bit edgy. It unnerved her to think Jimmy might have recognized her. She didn't want paparazzi arriving at this quiet town and making her life miserable. Although why would they, if she was honest with herself.

From all indications, she'd been a flash-in-the-pan as far as her time in Hollywood was concerned. She'd thought maybe the reality show would lead to something that would give her additional income, since her catering business had been struggling. But like one radio announcer said—she'd had her fifteen minutes of fame and Hollywood had moved on.

Had she been such a terrible actress? It made her sick to her stomach to think Scott's family had hired her because Scott thought she was pretty and wanted to chase her. However, it wasn't as though she'd come to LA to act—that had only been a small part of her dream—and not one she'd planned to pursue. She loved cooking, and her start-up catering business had been more than enough to handle at the time.

She walked into the kitchen, wondering if it would be okay to make a cup of tea—assuming Sarah had any. She whirled around when a step sounded behind her, her hand flying to her heart. Sarah. Annie let out her breath in a whoosh. "Sorry to be so jumpy. After colliding with Hunter earlier, I wasn't sure if I was in for another accident. Three in one day would definitely be my limit."

Sarah smiled then reached out to give her a quick hug. "Would you care for something to eat or drink while I work? I need to make a quiche for breakfast tomorrow morning, so I can pop it in the oven and warm it. I like to do whatever I can in the evenings to prepare, so I have time for devotions before dealing with the guests."

Annie's heart had instantly warmed at the hug, and now excitement bubbled inside. "Could I help? I love to cook."

"*Nein.* I could not allow that. You are my guest. It is my job to cook."

"But I don't mind. In fact, I'm a very good chef, if I do say so myself."

Sarah's eyes widened. "So you *are* a chef. I wondered when you mentioned catering, but I did not want to pry."

Annie smiled. "It's something I love doing. You've had a long day. How about you get the ingredients out, then make us a cup of tea and sit while I throw it together."

"You are sure?" Sarah cocked her head to the side. "I do not want to take advantage."

"You'd be giving me something to do to take my mind off my car troubles. Please?"

"All right then. *Denki.* If you are sure you would like to help." Sarah opened the refrigerator door and pulled out a variety of vegetables, along with what appeared to be farm fresh eggs, then placed it all on the center island. "Here you go."

"What a lovely assortment of vegetables. Do you mind if I get creative?"

"*Nein.* I'll steep tea while you work, but you must tell me if you need help."

Annie grinned. "No chance of that. I'm in my element when I'm in a kitchen, and I'd love to make my mother's favorite quiche recipe. This is my idea of fun. Do you do all the cooking here?"

"*Ya,* but I only fix breakfast for the guests. The other meals are up to them, so it's not too hard. I am kind of basic in my skills, though. I wish I'd paid more attention when *Mamm* tried to teach me, but at the time I would rather spend time outdoors with my *Brudders* and *Daed.* Maybe I can watch you this time and learn what you mean by being creative."

Annie chopped vegetables for a moment before replying, then she looked up and met Sarah's gaze. "You do a lot of work here alone. Has it been hard?"

Sarah nodded. "*Ya.* Sometimes it has been. My Ezra passed away from cancer. He loved to cook, so I did not have to worry about that part of the business. It is the only thing he dealt with as far as running the inn, but it was a blessing to have him puttering in the kitchen. That was my favorite part of the day. 'Sarah,' he would say, 'You sit and rest. You have had a busy day, and I don't want you to wear yourself out.'" She brushed a strand of hair out of her eyes. "Of course, I did not. I helped right alongside him, as any good wife would do. And most of the time I did not let him do more than bake the desert. He was so thoughtful that way, my Ezra."

"I'm so sorry, Sarah." If only she had the courage to hug Sarah the way she'd done, but she was a guest in Sarah's home. It seemed a bit too forward, in spite of Sarah's earlier action.

"*Denki.* I miss him. He was a wonderful, loving husband." Sarah dipped her head and drew in a long breath.

Annie fumbled for words, not sure what to say. "I . . . I didn't realize Amish men cooked." It sounded lame, even to herself, but it was the best she could do. This had to be so painful for Sarah.

"Most do not, but Ezra wasn't a typical Amish man. He was interested in working wood as a boy, but he also begged to help his *Mamm* bake bread and cookies." She gave a short laugh. "Probably because he loved to eat them so much, but his *Mamm* did not mind, and his *Daed* allowed it if his chores were finished. Ezra understood me, and he did not mind that I didn't care much for cooking." Her lips tipped in a soft smile. "He teased me sometimes that I should have been born a boy, but then he would not have found a wife."

"You and I are almost exact opposites," Annie said. "I was practically raised in the kitchen with my mother. She was an incredible cook."

Sarah nodded. "Then it is no wonder you became a chef."

Annie blinked. She hadn't realized Sarah had taken her teasing comment literally, but she didn't care to go into her past at the moment. Of course, she had cooked a lot of the meals for her catering business the first year. Maybe sometime, if she got better acquainted with Sarah, she could explain a bit more, but chances were she'd be leaving town soon, and it wouldn't matter. "Time to put this thing together."

Over the next few minutes, she made the crust, whisked the eggs, and blended the ingredients, then slipped the completed quiche into the refrigerator. "There you go. Pop it into the oven for thirty-five minutes at 350 before you want to serve it tomorrow. Hopefully, you'll like it."

Sarah handed her a hot cup of tea. "I know I will

love it. Thank you, Annie. *Gott* blessed me when He sent you here."

"I'm the one who feels blessed." This time, Annie followed her heart and gave Sarah a hug. "Somehow, I feel this place is going to be good for me."

Chapter Seven

A KNOCK AT ANNIE'S DOOR SHOOK her out of a deep sleep—but barely. She cracked one eye open as the door swung wide.

"Thanks, but I have enough towels." Her sleep-fogged mind still refused to function. Was she in a hotel? How did they open a locked door? She turned over in bed and groaned. Her muscles ached. A vision of hitting the ditch in Gretchen's car brought her closer to wakefulness.

"*Gutt.* I am glad. But I was starting to worry about you." Sarah stepped into sight.

"Huh? What time is it?" Annie raised her head off the pillow and fumbled for her phone, then realized it wasn't there.

"Seven o'clock."

"In the morning?" She thumped back against her pillow and closed her eyes. "It hasn't been light long, has it? Or is it even daylight?"

She heard a chuckle from her open door. "Yes, sleepyhead, it is daytime. I have already fed my guests. We only had the one couple, and they wanted to get an early start to their day. They loved your quiche, by the way."

This woke Annie up, and she pushed to a sitting position. "Really?

"*Ya.* They even asked for third helpings, but I made sure and saved you a nice amount. Do you want to get dressed and come have a cup of coffee or tea?"

Annie nodded. "That sounds heavenly. Give me ten minutes, and I'll pull myself together."

A few minutes later, with her hair hastily brushed

and no time for make-up, Annie made it to the kitchen, still trying to dislodge sleep from her brain. Sarah bustled around the table, bringing fresh coffee, juice, and a steaming plate of breakfast. She'd changed her gray dress for a dark green one with a white apron, and her bonnet, or prayer *Kapp*, as she'd explained it was called, was firmly on her head. Annie settled into a chair at the dining table and accepted the steaming mug of coffee Sarah offered. "Do you always get up this early?"

"*Ya*. It is *gutt* to spend time with *Gott*—my Heavenly Father—before I start my day. I always have early breakfast at six for any guests who want it, and I keep food warm for those who do not want to get up quite so early. But most of my guests like to have breakfast by seven-thirty or so, and I like to be prepared. I am sorry if I woke you too soon. I forget that not everyone was raised Amish." She smiled and slipped into a chair across from Annie.

"I guess I can understand that, if you can go back to bed when they leave."

"But look what you would miss." Sarah nodded out the window facing east.

Annie crinkled her brows. "What?"

"A glorious start to the day when the sun rises and brings new life. This is the day the Lord has made—that is what the Bible says—and I hate missing any part of it, if I do not have to."

"I've seen a few sunrises, but I guess I never quite looked at it like that. Have you eaten yet?" Annie took a sip of her hot coffee.

"No. I usually eat after everyone leaves. I hope you won't mind me eating with you? Somehow you seem more like a friend than a guest."

Right then, a middle-aged Amish woman with a

man right behind her stepped into the dining room. "David and I are leaving now, Sarah, but we wanted to tell you again what a lovely breakfast that was, especially the quiche. I think it is the nicest meal we have had at your inn."

Sarah waved toward Annie. "Let me introduce you to the chef, Annie Farley. I had nothing to do with it."

The woman nodded. "It was very good, thank you." She turned and headed to the door with her husband.

Sarah turned to Annie. "Your mother must be happy that you love her recipes so much and want to share them."

"Yes, I'm sure she would be." Should she say more? Tell her that her mother was as good as dead for as much as she'd seen or heard from her the past dozen years? How did a mother decide to abandon her teen-aged daughter and go AWOL when her husband died? She shook the thought away. "She was a wonderful teacher when I was young." There, that was enough. It hurt too much to go into detail. "This is probably a silly question, but is there a way to get online here—you know—use the Internet?"

"*Nein*, but both the library and the Sweet Stuff Coffee Shop in Cave City have free Internet. If you get a ride in to talk to the mechanic with Jimmy, maybe he'd drop you off at one of those so you could do whatever you do with your Internet."

Annie laughed. "I thought I could go more than twenty-four hours, but a girl has to check her social media, you know?"

A crease showed between Sarah's brows. "Um . . . No?"

They both laughed, and Annie shook her head. "Well, this girl does, anyway."

"The library is walking distance from the garage,

and the café is another block past."

"Thanks. I have my laptop, so I'll take that with me." She darted a quick glance at Sarah then turned her attention to her food. "So, uh, Hunter . . . your handyman who I spilled orange juice on . . ."

Sarah giggled. "He is not my handyman. My Ezra worked with him occasionally when he did a housing project for an Amish family for Habitat for Humanity. That only happened once or twice, when an old farmhouse burned to the ground. The Amish always take care of their own people, but Habitat stepped in and helped a couple of times as well."

"Oh. Hunter doesn't work for you then?"

"*Nein.* He is an architect. But he became a close friend of my husband, so he worries about me. He stops by occasionally to see if I need anything. I keep telling him there is no need to do that, since I have *Brudders* who help as well." She smiled. "But he insists."

Annie put her coffee cup on the table, not sure why she felt so unsettled. "He's interested in you then? I mean, do you think you'd ever be willing to marry outside your faith?"

Sarah's eyes grew wide. "*Nein.* Hunter is only a friend. And actually, his family is part of the Amish faith."

"But he doesn't dress like any Amish man I've seen."

"*Ya.* That is because his *Mamm* left the faith before she was baptized, and she married an *Englischer.* She was not shunned since she hadn't joined the church yet. One of their children chose to join the Amish, but Hunter did not. His uncle is our Bishop, and he's been putting pressure on Hunter to reconsider and be baptized." She shook her head. "I do not think he will, though, especially after meeting you."

Annie sputtered, not sure what to say.

Sarah waved her hand. "I have no desire to marry again anytime soon, and certainly not Hunter. Although my family and the Bishop would like to see me settled again. It has been sixteen months since Ezra died. They believe that is a suitable mourning period, and they would like to see me consider another man from our community within the next year, if I am willing."

"Are you willing?" Annie wasn't sure why the answer was so important to her, but she'd started to care about this woman, and she wanted her to be happy.

"No one can take my Ezra's place. The thought of another man makes me sad, but . . ." She seemed to drift off into somewhere else.

"But . . ?" Annie touched Sarah's hand. "Are you all right? Is it something you want to talk about?"

Sarah seemed to shake herself out of her thoughts. "I saw you notice Hunter giving me money yesterday. It was for the inn. He worries I will not be able to keep it going with the low number of guests that come."

"He seems different from most men I've met."

"*Ya*, he is rare." Sarah took a sip of coffee. "And he is single."

Annie jolted. "I didn't ask that."

Sarah tipped her head. "But you wanted to."

"You know, the sweet and tender-hearted side of you makes your other side a bit unexpected."

"Which side is that?"

"The clever, intuitive, wise side."

Annie buckled her seat belt as Jimmy pulled away from

the gate in front of the Wildwood Inn the next morning. Jimmy had been talking almost non-stop since Sarah opened the door and let him in. Mostly about his life and accomplishments, with an occasional humorous story thrown in that brought a smile to her lips. "Thanks for offering to pick me up. I know it's part of your income, so I'll be happy to pay you for your time."

His grin faded, and he stared at her. "Not even. I'm doing this because I like—" He snapped his lips closed and turned his attention to the road. "So, Sarah says you're a chef, and you made a delicious breakfast this morning."

Annie sighed. "I love to cook. It's one of my joys in life." There. Maybe not saying more would put this to rest. She couldn't very well blurt that she was an out-of-work actress running from her ex-boyfriend and wannabe career. At this point in her life, she didn't want to talk about herself at all.

"Do you have anything you love doing or want to do, beyond driving customers places and helping damsels in distress?" Maybe keeping a light tone and putting the attention back on him would help.

"Yeah, besides the driving service, I'm taking classes at the community college, working with computers. I love it, but it's not what I want to do for a living. Once I'm done, I'm out of here. I only work part time, and I'll have my associates degree soon."

"That's right. I think you mentioned that yesterday." Along with numerous other details about his life that she couldn't keep track of. "What's the dream? Where are you headed when you leave Cave City?"

"Hollywood." He slowed their speed and swung the wheel, turning a sharp corner, then straightened the car and slowed even more.

Annie craned her neck and stared as they cruised the street of a quaint town. Trees lined both sides, with one and two-story businesses, several with old-style, fake fronts like something from the movies. Most of the buildings were brick, with flower boxes in front of many of the windows and doorways, creating a colorful, inviting walkway. A handful of buggies lined the street, their horses tied at old-fashioned hitching rails out front. Both Amish and *Englischers* mingled along the business area, nodding in greeting as they passed.

Jimmy shot her a quick glance. "This town doesn't get me—it's too old and out of date. I'm going to be a star someday, I can promise you that. I'll hit LA and take Hollywood by storm. You wait and see."

Annie clutched the arm rest on the car door, not liking the direction this was headed. But what could she do? If she changed the subject too fast, he might start wondering even more. "So, you want to act? Movies? A sitcom maybe? Do you plan to take acting lessons before you start auditioning?"

"No way." He slowed then stopped at an intersection, drumming his fingers against the wheel. "I don't need people writing lines for me and telling me what to do. I'm too smart for that. I plan to be a reality star."

"Really." Annie turned her face away from him, suddenly desperate to get out of this car. "That doesn't seem like it would be much fun."

"Are you kidding me? Man, that's like the new thing. Those reality stars have the life. Big money and lots of fans. They do what they want and get paid for it. It's the American dream!" He slid the car into a parking spot in front of a three-bay garage.

"Yeah, but sometimes dreams can turn into nightmares. I've heard Hollywood can chew you up and spit you out if you aren't careful."

Jimmy laughed and pushed open his door, then slid out. "No worries about that for me. All I need is an in, and I'll have it made. I'm a natural, know what I mean?" He bent to peer in at her.

Annie grabbed the door handle and all but bolted from the car. "Let's get inside and see what's up with my car, okay?" She hurried ahead of him, making a point of keeping her face turned away from his inspection.

A woman who appeared to be in her late thirties looked up from the counter as Annie entered. "Can I help you?" Her attention veered to Jimmy as he pushed through the door behind her. "Hey, Jimmy. This must be the girl who owns the sedan." She tossed Annie a grin. "Almost a classic, that one."

Her grin was contagious, and Annie returned it. "Yeah, but she's all mine. I'm Annie."

The young woman reached across the counter, offering her hand. "I'm Jules, the other half of Leo and Son." She laughed. "My dad started the business when my mom was expecting me. He was so sure I'd be a boy that he named his business *and son*. I spent most of my growing up years hanging out with him here at the garage, learning everything he could teach me. When he never had another kid, I guess he felt I fit the bill and didn't change it to *and daughter*. So, you wrecked your old baby, huh?" She gestured to Gretchen's car parked in the corner of the garage.

"Yeah, I feel bad I rammed her into a bank with a tree growing from it. How much damage did I do, and what's it going to take to fix her?"

Jimmy leaned an elbow on the glass counter. "I was telling Annie here she could be stuck in town a week or two, right, Jules? I mean, sometimes parts are hard to come by for these old cars." He gave her a quick wink.

Annie pursed her lips. What was he up to? "Uh . . . Jules. Can you give me an idea of what I'm up against?"

The woman scratched her head and glanced from Jimmy to Annie. "There's quite a bit of damage. I have to order parts, and it'll take a few days for those to arrive, then my mechanic has to get them installed. I'm guessing ten days to two weeks, tops. Maybe sooner, depending on when the parts get here."

She rattled off a list of parts and a total price then folded her arms. "Is that gonna be a problem? I mean, she's an old car, but it appears she was in decent shape before getting banged up. Not much body work besides a new bumper, headlight and housing, but the radiator is shot along with the other things I mentioned. I guess if you've got insurance, we could see if the company wants to total it."

Annie shook her head. "No, thanks. I can take care of what needs to be fixed, and I don't have full coverage on it, anyway. If Sarah doesn't mind me staying a few more days, I guess I can wait that long. I'm not sure how I'll get around while I'm here, though."

Jimmy's face beamed. "Not a problem! I'm at your service, for anything you need, whenever you need it."

Annie stared at him for a second then turned an imploring gaze on Jules. "You wouldn't happen to have a loaner, would you?"

"Yep, sure do, but she won't be available for another couple of days." Jules scratched a spot on her hip. "I'll need you to sign a couple of forms, and she's all yours when the time comes. Not as nice as your ride, but she runs and will get you around. In fact, she's pretty much a classic . . . a 1978 Gremlin. My dad bought her brand new."

Annie's heart sank. Her mind flew to her SUV, and

she heaved a loud sigh. “Right. No problem. I’ll stop by in a couple of days and see if it’s available.”

Maybe she should have agreed to let Jimmy drive her around. But one look at his eager face shut that idea down hard and fast. “Thanks again, Jimmy. You’ve rescued me twice now and taken care of my car. I’d like to pay you for all your trouble.”

“I’ve got the perfect way for you to pay me. Let’s have lunch. There’s a nice diner across the street at the end of the block. I don’t have anyone else to pick up for a while, and I could show you around town when we’re done.”

Annie weighed her options for a moment. Would it encourage Jimmy too much if she agreed? Her stomach growled. “All right. But only lunch. Then I have to go to the library and use the internet. Does that work for you?”

His face lit up like a Christmas tree with all the trimmings. “Would it ever. You want to walk? It’s only half a block.”

“Right. Lead the way. I’m famished.”

Chapter Eight

HUNTER SAT AT THE OLD-FASHIONED counter of the local diner facing the large window on the front door. He took another bite of his over-sized cheeseburger and glanced outside. Interesting. The woman he'd met at Sarah's stepped off the sidewalk in front of Jules McFee and her dad's garage and walked beside Jimmy Snyder toward the diner. He took another bite, wondering yet again about her relationship with Jimmy. Maybe he'd keep an eye on their table if they sat anywhere close.

The bell on the door jingled, and the couple stepped into the air-conditioned space. Annie looked around, her expression appreciative. "What a charming place. And it smells heavenly." Her eyes stopped moving when they met his. "Oh! We met at Sarah's yesterday. How are you?" She took a step forward.

Jimmy placed a possessive hand on Annie's upper arm and smiled at Hunter. "Hey, Hunter. Annie and I are having lunch."

Hunter grinned. "Yeah, I kinda figured you weren't here to wash dishes." He nodded at Annie. "Good to see you again."

"Let's go, Annie." Jimmy took her hand and led her to a table not far from the long counter. From the frown marring the young man's freckled face, Hunter could tell he was none too pleased there wasn't a table open at the farthest point across the room from where he sat.

What was Annie's story? He let his eyes stray her way. A jolt of awareness hit him when a glance caught her peeking at him. He gave her a slow, lazy smile and watched a rush of pink tinge her cheeks. She was more than pretty—she was downright beautiful with those big brown eyes and oval face framed by loosely curled, blonde hair. Jimmy leaned across the table, trying to get her attention. Annie pulled her gaze from his and appeared to be listening. She laughed at something Jimmy said, but a minute or two later, she shot another glance Hunter's way. Poor Jimmy.

He shifted in his chair, turning his back squarely on the couple. It wasn't fair to Jimmy to keep distracting Annie, if that's what was happening. Someone slid onto the red vinyl stool next to him, and he smiled at the woman he'd worked so hard to befriend the past few months. "Hi, Carla. You here for a cup of coffee?"

Annie hazarded another look toward the diner's counter. A woman was slumped on a stool next to Hunter, and his attention appeared to be fixed on her. Dressed in a shabby shirt, dirty jeans, and ragged sneakers with a hole in the toe, she could be anywhere from forty-five to sixty, it was hard to say. Hunter seemed interested in talking to her and laughed at something she said. Could she be a relative or good friend? Why should that matter to her? She didn't even know the man.

Jimmy cleared his throat. "You ready to go, or did you want to sit and chat with Hunter for a while?"

Warmth crept into her cheeks. "I'm so sorry. I was curious about the woman beside him. Is she a relative?"

Jimmy frowned. "Naw. That's only Carla."

"Carla?" Something about his tone triggered a less-than-attractive impression. "You say it like she's an unpleasant person."

He hunched a shoulder. "I suppose she's fine, but she's strange." He touched his forehead. "Got something wrong upstairs, if you know what I mean."

"Is she homeless?" That would account for her clothing and lack of personal care.

"She could be, I don't know. I see her around a lot standing on corners. I think she's been in town for a few months. She tried to talk to me once and rambled on about a dog she'd lost. I got away from her as fast as I could."

"Hunter doesn't seem bothered by her. Looks like he's talking to her. She can't be too dangerous."

"I didn't say she was dangerous, just strange. Not someone I want to hang around. Hunter doesn't care. He buys her coffee and pie whenever she comes in, or a hamburger if she's hungry. He's a do-gooder. Helps with Habitat for Humanity and all that."

Annie raised her brows. "There's certainly nothing wrong with doing good occasionally. That sounds like a worthy cause."

"Yeah. I'm sure it is. It's not that I have a problem with helping others, but I don't like hanging out with people who are too lazy to work. I have two different jobs. Anyone who wants to work can."

Annie bit back what she'd have liked to say and drew in a deep breath to calm herself. "I'm afraid I don't agree about homeless people. Things happen. People get fired unfairly. It's not always easy to find something else. A lot of people are hurting, and it affects their entire family. Sure, there are lazy people, but not everyone is. We shouldn't judge if we haven't been in their shoes."

"I suppose. You ready to go or did you want desert? I can show you where the library is and pick you up when you're ready to go home."

She shook her head. "No thanks."

He grabbed the check the waiter set on the table, then stalked over to the counter and paid his bill. "Want me to walk you out, or you gonna stay and talk to Hunter?"

"I'm not staying, Jimmy. I told you I want to go to the library." She stepped through the front door he held open.

Jimmy's face fell. "Right. Fine. I guess you did say you needed to work, and you could only do lunch. So how about dinner later tonight or tomorrow? There's a nicer place down the road on the edge of town. Dinner and dancing at seven. How does that sound?" He took her arm and led her to where he'd parked his van.

Annie closed her eyes briefly then met his gaze. "Thanks. I really appreciate all your help. You're a nice guy, and all, but I'm not into dating right now. Besides, it's not like I'm going to be in town long. It's only a couple of miles to Sarah's house, and it's a lovely day. I think I'll walk home when I'm done. I could use the exercise."

A red flush spread over his cheeks, and he looked like he wanted to escape. "Right. Sure. No problem." He jerked open his van door, slid in, and started to slam the door.

Annie put out her hand and stopped it from shutting. "Wait, Jimmy. Hey, it's not personal or anything. I have things I'm working through in my life right now, that's all. Like I said, you're a nice guy, but it's not good timing." She hesitated. "Maybe you can keep tabs on my car and let me know if anything changes?" She probably shouldn't even ask that, but she hated how hurt he appeared. "Thanks again for driving me in and inviting me to lunch."

He shrugged. "Yeah. Whatever. If I hear anything,

I'll let you know."

She glanced toward the diner then pulled her gaze to Jimmy. "Sure. You can point me in the direction of the library. I mean it, Jimmy, thank you for lunch."

The tension in his shoulders seemed to increase. "Sure. I get it. You have a thing for Hunter, not me. I hope you won't end up being sorry. The library is one block up the street and around the corner." He motioned that direction then slammed his door. Seconds later, he hit the gas and barreled down the street and out of sight.

Annie exited the library an hour later, wondering why she'd even bothered to go. It had felt so weird being at Sarah's with no phone, TV, or internet, and she'd longed to get in touch with the world again. Ugh. Not anymore after the stuff that continued to pour into her Twitter page and other social media.

What was wrong with people? She realized she'd been naïve thinking Scott had fallen for her, but the truth had set in—the whole *Life with the Adsons* deal wasn't real. The fans didn't seem to get that, however. They were falling all over themselves at the news she'd left and Jess would return. Maybe only one in twenty posts supported her role as Scott's girlfriend, and even they seemed intrigued to see how Jess would fit into his life.

What a sham. She'd lived a lie for close to three years and hadn't realized how much of a lie it was. Never again. She was done with that life forever.

The town bustled with people, even though the pace was slower than LA. It had a different feel. Not a brittle, fast-paced rush where no one looked at one another as they passed on the street, but somehow a friendlier, more personal feel.

And what a glorious day for a walk to Sarah's house. The sun glimmered off the grass growing along the sidewalk while birds twittered in the branches of trees dotting the residential area. She slowed her pace as a familiar figure ambled toward her, a large bag slung over her shoulder. The woman from the diner—what was her name? Carla? What did you say to someone like this, who seemed 'a bit off' as Jimmy put it? If she stopped and spoke to her, would she scare her, or would it be the right thing to do?

Then she remembered Hunter sitting beside the woman, laughing, buying her a meal, and treating her like a real person. Wasn't that what she needed? What any homeless person needed? Someone who saw them—truly saw them, rather than ignored them as they passed by? Sure, there were abusers who panhandled money who could easily get a job, waving their signs about wanting beer or being down on their luck and out of a job. Lots of them were probably scammers and lived in a nice apartment, but she doubted the Carlas of the world were like that. They were down on their luck for real.

She slowed and smiled. "Hi. I saw you at the diner with Hunter."

The woman's eyes widened, and she halted. "You know him?"

"Not very well. I haven't known him long, but he seems very nice." What did she say to this woman? How did you make small talk with someone who might be homeless? *Hi, where do you live? What do you do for a living?* She didn't want to make the woman uncomfortable. She sighed. "Do you live around here?"

Carla nodded like it was a normal question. "Here,

there, everywhere. And nowhere."

Annie scrunched her brows. What kind of answer was that?

"So you travel a lot?" It sounded lame, but it was the best she could come up with at the moment.

"Yep. I don't remember where I live, so I live wherever I want."

"Okay then." *What now, Lord?* The short prayer focused her thoughts. What would Jesus do? Nod, smile, and walk away? Not in this lifetime. And not in His. "Did you get enough to eat at the diner?"

Carla smiled, showing surprisingly good teeth. "Oh yes, Hunter sees to that. So does the women's shelter. They feed me when I'm hungry."

"Wonderful. Do you live there?"

She shook her shaggy, graying hair. She appeared to be at least in her late forties. "I don't like to stay there. Too many people who I don't trust. I'm safer sleeping in my car."

"You have a car? That's wonderful! Do you have a job in town?" What had happened to this woman who had decent hygiene and reasonably clean clothing to cause her to end up living 'here and there'?

"I scrub floors at the diner sometimes, and the owner gives me a little cash and meals when Hunter isn't there. My car doesn't run. It's an old, abandoned one on the edge of town, and I found it. Right smack dab under a big shade tree. Real pretty spot, so I stay there most of the time. I take showers at an RV park nearby. They know me and let me come in a couple of times a week. Brush my teeth there too—they gave me a toothbrush and toothpaste at the shelter." She scratched her head. "Sure wish I could remember."

Annie shifted her laptop bag to her other shoulder. "Remember what? Can I help?"

The woman looked at her like she'd seen her for the

first time. "Do I know you?" She backed away. "Don't want any trouble. I need to remember, that's all." She rubbed a spot above her right temple. "Why can't I remember? I think I had a dog . . ." She swiveled, continuing to mumble, and ambled away.

Annie wasn't sure if she should follow and try to discover what Carla couldn't remember or let her go. She seemed to have drifted into a different world in a matter of seconds. More than likely, that's what Jimmy was talking about. It was sad, for sure, but she was no social worker or psychologist. Her mind drifted back to her grandmother. Nana would have found a way to help Carla, no matter what it took. If she went after Carla, what could she say? Offer to take her to Sarah's Inn without Sarah's permission?

Annie glanced at her watch. It was later than she'd realized. She'd better pick up her pace if she wanted to get home in time to help Sarah fix supper. But in the meantime, she planned to pray about Carla.

Chapter Nine

ANNIE WALKED THROUGH THE FRONT DOOR of the inn, wondering if Sarah had started supper preparations yet. She would drop her laptop in her room then see if she could help. She shut the door behind her and turned.

Sarah stood behind the guest registry desk, a young, blonde Amish woman beside her. They both looked up from the book they'd been studying, and Sarah smiled. "Annie. Did you have a *gutt* day? I hope you got your fill of that Internet business." She nodded at the girl beside her. "Annie, this is Rebecca, my cousin and dearest friend in the world. She helps out a few hours a week, changing beds and cleaning when I need it."

Annie wasn't sure if she should offer to shake hands or only nod and smile, so she opted for the latter. "Hello. It's so nice to meet you."

Rebecca gave a half-curtsy. "*Gutt* day, Miss Annie. Sarah has told me much about your wonderful cooking skills. So, you are a famous chef, *ya*?"

Annie barely stifled a groan. How had this gotten so out of control? "Not at all famous, and really, I'm not much of a chef."

Sarah tsked. "Nonsense. You are a wonderful chef. My guests raved over the food you fixed."

"About that, Sarah. I need to know how much I owe you for a week."

Sarah's hands flew up, and she waved them in front of her face. "*Nein*, you are my guest. You helped me cook, and I will not allow you to pay."

"I'm sorry, Sarah, but I won't stay here unless you

let me pay board."

Sarah's face set in a firm expression. "You have no other place to stay."

"Then I'll have to find one." Annie stepped forward and grasped one of Sarah's hands in both of her own. "Seriously, I will not take advantage of you. The inn needs to make money. I loved helping you cook. It's something I enjoy doing, but I didn't do enough to earn my keep. I'll tell you what. How about I make a few special baked goods and print out a dozen or so recipes for you. If you want to give me a very small discount, say I pay for six nights, and you give me one free. How would that be?"

Sarah gave a slow nod and squeezed Annie's hand before she released it. "*Denki.* I will accept that, if you feel it is fair. Maybe if you want to have the recipes printed, Rebecca could take you to the store where they do that sort of thing tomorrow when she comes by."

Annie looked at Rebecca. "You have a car?"

Rebecca put her fingers over her mouth to cover a giggle. "No. I drive my buggy here from my family's farm. Would you like to take a ride in my buggy tomorrow, Miss Annie?"

"Sure. Sounds like fun. But please, it's Annie, not Miss. I feel like an old spinster when you call me that."

Rebecca grew quiet and turned her face away.

Annie looked from one to the other. "I'm sorry. What did I say? I didn't mean to offend."

Sarah glanced at Rebecca then put her arm around her cousin. "Rebecca is past the normal marrying age for an Amish girl. She is twenty-one and single. That worries her. But I tell her the right man will come along—she has to trust God. The good book says we should not worry, as that is sin, is not so?"

Annie smiled. "I could stand to be reminded of that

more often. I'm afraid I sin quite often, based on that verse. But yes, I do believe that's what it says." She turned to Rebecca. "I'm twenty-five, and I'm not married either. Maybe we should form a club for ladies over twenty and still single."

Sarah's eyes widened. "I do not think our Bishop would approve."

Now it was Annie's turn to giggle, and soon, both of the girls joined in. Sarah took a deep breath after several more chuckles. "You were joking."

"Yes. I'm going to run my bag up to my room then come help you with supper."

"*Gutt. Denki.* I'll meet you in the kitchen."

Later that night after dinner was over and the dishes were done, Annie snuggled into a stuffed chair in the living room across from Sarah. She propped her feet on an ottoman and sighed. "This feels good."

"*Ya.* Very *gutt.* I wish you wouldn't help me clean the kitchen." Sarah wagged a finger at her. "You are paying to stay here as a guest, not hired help."

"I like keeping busy. I'm not used to sitting around doing nothing. Staying busy makes the time pass faster."

Sarah nodded. "I agree. But sometimes I worry it passes too fast, if you know what I mean? I feel my life slipping past with so little to show for it. No husband. No *Bopplies.* But the good Lord knows my situation, and He cares, so I do not worry overly much. But for Rebecca, I do worry a little."

"Rebecca?" Annie shifted in her chair. "Why are you worried about her? She seemed happy enough when she was here."

"I hope she will not make unwise choices. What if *Gott* sends someone to her, and she does not listen? I think she is still pining for a man who married someone else and moved away from our district." Sarah shook her head, her eyes reflecting a deep sadness. She smoothed the folds of her skirt, then looked up. "There is a young Amish man, a widower, who is interested in her, but she doesn't seem to return his affection. I know what it's like to be alone, and I do not wish that for her."

Annie pursed her lips, thinking through what she'd heard. "And I'd hate to see that happen to you, as well. You're still very young, Sarah. I hope you'll be willing to open your heart to love if the time comes."

Sarah smiled. "Maybe. We'll see."

"There's no one in your community who interests you or who is interested in you?"

"There are two men who have shown an interest." Sarah said it as though she were asking to have the bread passed at supper. "And there was someone years ago." She shook her head. "But he decided not to join the church, and he no longer lives here."

"Sarah! Oh, my goodness. Why haven't you said anything? Tell me about them! I want to know more."

She held up her hand and waved it dismissively. "I said they have shown an interest in me. I did not say I return the feeling. I've known them all my life. Chandler is a kind man, a couple of years older than me. He and I were close friends growing up, and I think he may have been smitten with me when we were young. Then Ezra's family moved to our area to help farm the land of a relative who was ailing. I'm afraid Chandler didn't have a chance after that."

Annie bobbed her head in encouragement. "So,

who's the other guy? What's he like? Has he been in love with you for years, too?"

Sarah rolled her eyes. "I did not say Chandler was in love with me. It was a childhood infatuation, nothing more. And no, Jeremiah was not interested when we were children, but he is now."

"What's he like?"

"Serious. A hard worker. And the son of our Bishop."

"I see. And do you care for one of these men, more than the other?" Annie couldn't deny her fascination at this peek into her Amish friend's life. "Have either one asked you on a date?"

Sarah laughed. "We do not date. And no, they have not asked to court me, but I have had a feeling they would both like to. I would only be able to choose one to court."

"No playing the field? No getting to know both of them by going out a few times to see which one you'd want to have court you? Wow, that's hard. I can't even imagine. I mean, what if you agree to court one, and you don't end up liking him after all?"

"Then you do not agree to marry him. But we have social times after church, as well as singings and barn raisings where we can get acquainted without a formal courtship. I'm not ready for courtship yet. My heart still longs for my Ezra. I have told the Bishop that, as well as my parents, when they insisted I need to remarry. They are giving me more time."

"Giving you more time?" Annie sat up straight and glared. "You mean they'll force you to marry someone even if you don't want to? That's awful."

Sarah shook her head. "No, they won't force me, but it is wisdom. I'm still young. I want to have *Bopplies* one day, and for that, I must get married. And I do get lonely at times. It's not easy being alone after I've tasted what it's like to be joined to someone I love."

"But could you marry without love, just so you could have a baby and companionship?"

Sarah tipped her head to the side. "There are worse reasons to marry. I would prefer to have love, and I must at least like and respect the man. I believe love could follow if both work at it."

"Wow." Annie shook her head. "I'm not sure I could do that. But I definitely know what you mean about worse reasons to marry." She settled in against her chair, letting thoughts of Scott wash over her. She'd have married him in a heartbeat if he'd set a date and put a ring on her finger, instead of the apparent farce of an engagement they'd had.

How could she have been such a fool and thought her infatuation for a Hollywood star was real love? It couldn't hold up to what Nana and Poppy had shown every day she'd known them. Their love was genuine and shone in every little action and word they spoke. What would it be like to experience the type of love Sarah had experienced with her husband? Maybe if she asked Him, God would let her find that kind of love someday.

Chapter Ten

THE NEXT MORNING AFTER BREAKFAST, ANNIE and Rebecca stepped outside the inn into the bright, late-spring sunshine.

Annie drew in a deep breath. "It smells so glorious in the country. The fragrance of fresh cut grass and flowers are enough to make me want to stretch out in a lawn chair and drown myself in the fresh scents—not to mention the sun." She spread her arms wide. "I love spring and summer. It makes me glad to be alive." The last sentence took her by surprise. It was a far cry from how she'd felt only a week ago while still in Hollywood. It was hard to believe how much her life had changed in such a short amount of time—and how much she was enjoying it. God was indeed good. How could she have gotten so far from His presence the past three years?

Rebecca turned from where she'd walked to the end of the sidewalk and beckoned. "*Kumm*, Annie. Or did you decide to stay here instead of going to town?"

Annie moved forward and reached Rebecca as she pushed open the short gate set in the white picket fence. "No, I don't want to stay. I'm excited to get these recipes printed for Sarah. It's going to be fun to try out a few new dishes on her guests."

Rebecca untied her horse from the hitching rail on the far side of the fence, then walked to the seat and climbed up.

Annie stood and stared at the black buggy—she hadn't wanted to stare at the few she'd seen in town yesterday. This one was different from what she'd expected—not the open type wagon she'd seen in old west movies, but an almost totally enclosed four-wheeled conveyance shaped more like a box. It even had a window set in the front. She clutched the strap hanging at the perfect spot next to the door to help her up the step and inside. She settled in next to Rebecca. "Does this belong to your family?"

"*Ya.*" She picked up the reins and clucked to the tall chestnut mare harnessed to the buggy. "This is our small one for when one or two people need to run errands. *Daed* and *Mamm* have a larger one that the whole family can use. And my two older *Brudders* shared a courting buggy. My little *Brudder* will use it when he's old enough."

Annie thought fast. Sarah had mentioned courting. "Your brothers used it to take the women they courted places? Where do they go, if it's okay to ask?"

"*Ya*, it is fine. We go to singings for the youth, we take drives in the country, we visit our friends or go on a picnic. Things like that."

"Sounds like fun." And truth be told, it really did sound fun—like something she'd have loved doing when she was a young teen. "I used to go on picnics with my grandparents. They lived in the country. I think that's why I love this area so much. It reminds me of when I was a kid."

"It is *gutt* to have happy memories, *ya*?" Rebecca shook the horse's reins, and the mare broke into a brisk trot. "I have many memories I cherish from when I was young."

Annie wondered if Rebecca was thinking of the young man who'd married someone else. "Is it all right if I ask you something, Rebecca?"

Rebecca turned sparkling eyes her direction for a moment before focusing her attention between the mare's ears and the road. "I do not know, Annie. You have not asked it yet, so how can I say for certain sure?"

Annie giggled. "Right. If you don't want to answer, I'll understand. In the short time I've been staying with Sarah, I've come to think of her as something of a friend. At least, I hope we're friends. She shared with me that there are men who appear to be interested in her, but she also mentioned a man who she cared for when she was younger, who left your district and didn't join the church. I think that was before she met Ezra. Her voice was sad when she mentioned him, and she changed the subject quickly when I asked her to tell me more. Is it anything you can talk about?"

Rebecca slanted a glance at Annie and bit her lip. "Well . . . since she brought it up, I suppose I can tell you a little. But I won't go into any detail about her feelings, or anything private she has told me. You understand, *ya*?"

"Certainly. I wouldn't ask you to do that. I'd like to know more in case I can ever help her, but I don't want to pry or be insensitive."

"*Gutt*. Our Sarah was in love with a young Amish boy, Gabe, all through her final years of school, and he seemed to feel the same. He is the middle son of our Bishop, and he was quite popular with the girls. Our community thought Gabe and Sarah would marry, once they took their vows and joined the church, but Gabe wasn't sure. He held back, even after Sarah joined, then one day, he disappeared."

"Disappeared? You mean, he was abducted, or he ran away?"

"*Ya*. Ran away. He left a letter for Sarah and one for his parents. He said he wasn't ready to follow the laws of the *Ordnung*. He wanted to continue his *Rumschpringe*, and go out into the world. Gabe joined the military—the Marines, I think—and Sarah never heard from him again, other than the one letter telling her that he wouldn't return, and he couldn't marry her."

"Oh dear. How long ago was that?"

"Seven years. She was eighteen when he left. Then two years later Ezra came to work on his uncle's farm. It was love at first sight for him, I am sure. I think love grew for Sarah. I imagine it took her time to lay her feelings for Gabe aside."

The buggy slowed a few minutes later as they came to the edge of town. "Where do you want to get out, Annie? I can drop you wherever you'd like and pick you up later too."

"The library would be fine. They have a printer there, so I can check email and get the recipes printed at one place. It's such a beautiful day I may walk home. Please don't worry about me. I'm also going to stop in and see if there's been any progress on my car parts arriving. That's not far from the library." She grinned. "I'm starting to know my way around, at least in this small section of town. Thanks again for bringing me. I loved my first buggy ride."

Rebecca's brows rose. "This is the first time you've ever ridden in a buggy?" She tsked and shook her head. "You have missed out on too much of the simple life, Annie." She waited for Annie to move away from the buggy before she clucked to the mare and drove down the road.

Annie stared at her, thinking about her words. "You've missed out on too much." She was starting to think Rebecca was right. For many years, she'd longed to make her mark in the world. Then when she achieved her goal, it hadn't brought the happiness she'd expected. A simple ride in a buggy had brought her more joy than she'd experienced this entire last year.

Hunter glanced at his watch. Almost time to go to his project for Habitat for Humanity, but he had time to grab a quick cup of coffee at the diner first. When he was within sight of the building, he jogged across the street as memories of Annie returned. He hadn't seen her today, and it surprised him that he felt a small wrench of longing to do so. Hunter slowed to a stop, more than a little bothered at his reaction. He didn't even know this woman. Standing on the grassy strip between the street and the sidewalk, he lifted his eyes toward the sky. "Lord, what's going on?"

A finger tapped him on the shoulder, and he jumped. He turned to find Carla staring at him, her eyes wide.

"You do it too? You talk to yourself? I thought I was the only one who did that." She shifted her over-stuffed bag from one arm to the other. "Maybe you need someone to talk to. Want me to buy you a cup of coffee? I have a few quarters."

Hunter reached out and pulled the older woman into a quick hug, surprised that she didn't resist. This was the first time he'd attempted a hug, although he'd wanted to give her one in the past, but she'd seemed shy and standoffish. "You know what? I was talking to God, and I think He wants me to buy you one. In fact, I might even take time to buy us both a piece of pie, if you have room for dessert."

She nodded, a graying curl slipping loose from the bun she'd pulled her hair into. "Why not? Dessert before lunch is always a good thing."

"You haven't eaten yet? What do you say to a hamburger and then pie? I could sure use the company."

She narrowed her eyes. "Isn't God good company?"

He laughed and reached for the door of the diner. "He certainly is, but I can't talk Him into eating a burger or pie, so I guess you'll have to do."

Carla nodded as though that made perfect sense and walked through the door. She settled on her usual stool, the second one in from the door, and Hunter plunked onto one on the other side of her. "Jake, a burger and fries with all the fixings for Carla, plus a Coke. Peach pie and coffee for me."

His companion scrunched her brows. "You already ate your lunch? I can't eat in front of you if you're only having pie."

He winked at her. "How about you share your fries with me?"

"Yep. Will do." She reached for the glass of Coke and took a long sip from the straw. "Now that's what the doctor ordered."

The door jingled as it opened, and Hunter glanced toward it out of habit and curiosity. "Annie! Are you here to meet Jimmy?"

A mystified look crossed her face. "No. Was he looking for me?"

Hunter took a drink of his coffee. "Not that I'm aware of. But the last time I saw the two of you . . ." He waved toward the table where Jimmy and Annie had sat the day they'd had lunch. "I thought you might have something going."

Her cheeks tinged with pink. "I'm afraid I might have hurt his feelings. He asked me out for dinner, and I didn't want to encourage him. I'm not looking for a relationship, and I told him that. I haven't seen him since."

"Ah, I see. How about friendship and dinner? Would you be open to those if they went together?" His heart pounded. Where had those words come from? They slipped out before he'd realized it.

She smiled. "I guess it depends on who's offering."

"I'd take both." Carla popped a couple of fries in her mouth and looked from one to the other.

Annie chuckled. "How about I take you to lunch or dinner sometime while I'm in town, Carla? I'd love to be your friend, if you'd let me."

She shrugged. "Maybe. I'll think about it. I'm still trying to remember something." She rubbed her forehead and sighed. "It'll come to me one of these days. I know there was a dog. A German Shepherd. A big one."

Annie slipped onto the stool beside Carla. "Did it scare you or chase you?"

"No. Nothing like that. I think I liked the dog and it liked me. But that's all I remember. I'll keep trying."

"How long have you lived in Cave City, Carla?" She glanced at the waiter who hovered over a coffee mug with a pot and nodded. "Cream and sugar, please. Thanks."

Carla finished chewing and swallowed. "Not sure. Maybe a year. Don't remember how I got here, either. I might have walked, but I don't think so. My head hurt, I know that."

Annie glanced at Hunter, but he shook his head and shrugged. He didn't know much more about Carla than she did, but he was enjoying seeing how kind Annie was while interacting with the woman.

Carla finished the last bite and took a final draw from her glass. "Thanks, Hunter. I'll get that pie another time. I need to take a walk now. Maybe it will help me remember what I've forgotten." She slid off the stool and headed for the door without looking back.

Annie watched Carla leave, not sure what to think. She swiveled on her stool and faced Hunter. "Is she always like this? How much do you know about her?"

"I don't know much. I've never gotten any more information from her than she gave you. In fact, that's the first time I've heard her say the dog liked her. I met her a little over six months ago, and at the time I assumed she'd been a fixture in town most of her life, and I simply hadn't seen her. I didn't find out until recently she'd only been here a year."

"No one knows where she came from or anything about her?"

"Not that I've talked to. But a lot of homeless people have deeper problems than simply not having a place to stay. I haven't been able to uncover what put Carla on the streets, and she can't seem to remember—or she doesn't want to say. I'm not even sure which one it is."

Annie poured cream into her coffee and dipped in a spoonful of sugar then stirred. "This coffee is exactly what I needed." She drummed her fingers on the counter. "I think I'll dig into her story on my own. I could use more to do than helping Sarah with meals." She looked at him over the rim of her cup. "You were saying something about dinner and friendship. Or was that meant for Carla like she thought?"

He laughed. "No, I was hoping you might be interested in dinner tomorrow night."

She lifted one brow. "Not a date. Dinner only, right?"

"Right. A friendly face in a strange town. Someone to help you pass the time, and we can even go somewhere besides the diner."

She glanced around the room at the juke box playing soft sixty's music and the checkered table cloths covering the square tables. "I'm getting kind of fond of the diner. Do they serve anything besides burgers?"

"Yep. They have excellent steaks and fries, but I know another place that I think you'd like as well. Are you game to give it a shot?"

Annie nodded. "Sure. Why not? I'd like that if Sarah can spare me for the evening." She glanced at her watch. "In fact, I've been gone longer than I expected. I promised to bring her a batch of recipes I printed, and I want to make a pie for her. Maybe I'll do that tomorrow."

"Hmm. My favorite dessert, if you haven't figured that out yet." He pointed at his now empty plate with his fork. "What's your specialty?"

"Pecan. It was my mother's favorite recipe."

"Sounds great. Maybe you can make me one sometime."

She smiled. "You never know. Oh, man." She blew out a breath. "I totally forgot I needed to check something on the Internet and send an email to a friend. Guess I'd better get back to the library."

Hunter stood and beckoned toward the door. "We can go to my office. It's closer than the library, then I can run you home if you'd like."

She looked up at him, surprised and intrigued by the warmth in his eyes and the laugh lines around his lips. "Sure. Sounds good. Lead the way."

"It's only about a block." He held the door open and waited for her to go through, then followed. "How's the progress on your car?"

"Not great. The parts aren't in yet, and Jules says it could be a full week from now before she has it running again. I guess they got delayed."

"Wow. You think you'll be able to handle living without all your technology for another week?"

"Funny you should mention that. It has been kind of strange not having a phone, TV, or Internet, but I'm learning to appreciate the peace and quiet, and Sarah's wonderful. But I'll admit it's been hard not being able to pull up my email or get on the Internet anytime I want to."

"You can always watch TV at the far end of the bar in the diner. They have a small one up over the bar. You didn't notice it?"

"Uh. No. I sure didn't." Her steps slowed. What were the chances they'd tune into *Life with the Adsons*? She shook her head and quickened her steps to keep from falling behind. No use borrowing trouble when it hadn't arrived. Most diners and bars played sports or news, and more than likely, this one did too.

Glancing forward, she noticed an older Amish man with a gray beard and stern expression walking slowly toward them. Annie leaned in closer to Hunter. "Of course, if I go much longer without any connections to modern America, I might turn gray like him."

The man slowed as he neared them, then came to a halt. "*Hallo*, Hunter. *Vee bisht du hight*?"

"I'm doing *gutt*, Uncle Abraham. Thank you." Hunter nodded to Annie. "This is Annie Farley. She's visiting our town and staying at Sarah's inn."

"*Ya*. I heard. *Gutt* day, Miss Farley." The older man leveled a stern gaze on Annie. "I hope you enjoy your stay there." He nodded then moved forward, his strides purposeful and strong.

Annie grabbed Hunter's forearm. "Oh, no. That was your uncle? I'm so sorry. That was such a thoughtless remark I made about going gray. Please forgive me. I don't know what came over me. He didn't seem to like me, did he?"

Hunter smiled and tucked her hand through the crook of his elbow. "I knew you were joking. He's always a bit stern, so please don't take it personally and don't think any more about it. Now let's get to my office before those gray hairs start sprouting."

Chapter Eleven

ANNIE WAITED UNTIL HUNTER SHUT HIS office door to give her a bit of privacy before she pulled out her laptop and booted it up. She was glad Hunter gave her his wifi password so she could get in touch with Gretchen. She couldn't believe she'd been gone from home close to a week and hadn't thought to check in with her friend. Poor Gretchen must be frantic.

She signed in to Facebook chat first. Yes! Gretchen was online. Annie sent her a quick private message and waited, rocking back and forth in the leather desk chair.

Finally, her reply came. *Where have you been? I've been so worried! Social media is on fire with speculation about where you are. I thought you'd call me before now. I was worried my old car conked out and left you stranded somewhere. I've been texting and calling nonstop.*

Annie chuckled as she wrote. *I'm afraid it's worse than that. I ran your poor baby into a ditch after I threw my phone out the window. That's why I haven't answered any texts or calls.*

WHAT??? Gretchen typed in all caps. *Why would you toss your phone? Are you crazy???*

I was sick of all the tweets coming in about me leaving the show, as well as Scott's texts and voicemails, but I do kind of miss it. I'm staying at an inn owned by a sweet Amish woman. I'm not going to tell you where, in case Scott or Veronica try to pressure you to find out.

Annie paused and watched the screen, hoping Gretchen would hurry before Hunter returned. *Oh, they've already done that, big time. Scott almost had a heart attack when he pulled up behind me at a gas station.*

Gretchen put smiley faces across the screen then started typing again. *He demanded to know where you were. I told him I didn't know, you gave me the car to use while you're gone. He acted like he was going to rupture a blood vessel. I had to show him the title you signed over to prove I didn't steal the car and dump your body.*

Annie rolled her eyes. *Sheesh. I'm sorry he put you through that. So, you're okay now?*

Yeah, they grilled me like crazy, but I didn't lie. I hadn't heard from you since you left and said so, and said you told me to use your car and signed the title to keep me out of trouble. They were crazy worried about you, especially Scott.

Annie laughed as she typed. *Right. He's so worried since I turned down his marriage proposal, broke his heart, and ran out on him? Ha!*

You heard about that, huh? I hoped it wouldn't get back to you. I'm so glad you're somewhere safe, but don't tell me where!!! That way I don't have to lie if they grill me again.

No worries. My lips are sealed, Gretchen. I'm glad you didn't get in trouble.

Me too. I'm building my travel blog on the side in case they decide to fire me. I'll keep working for the show until they decide to dump me or until I can afford to quit. My guess is they're keeping me on hoping you'll contact me so they can get to you through me. How are you?

Annie glanced at the door, hoping Hunter would give her another few minutes to finish. *I'm the same. It's been wonderful not being caught in the crazy life of the Adsons since I left. Thanks for covering for me.*

No problem. I'd do it again in a heartbeat.

Annie raised her head. Had she heard something out in the hallway? Maybe Hunter was returning. Her fingers flew over the keys. *I'd better go, Gretchen. Thanks again.*

Wait! One more thing. Since they brought Jessie onto the show, it's been bumpy around here. Veronica decided to spice things up by making a mystery out of where you might have disappeared.

Huh? What's that supposed to mean?

There was a long pause while Gretchen must have been typing. *I'm not sure, but I know Scott's desperate to find you—I think he'd do anything at this point to get you back. Veronica is all over social media, trying to make the most of it. I think they're hoping a fan will call in and tell them you've been spotted. You know how much she loves drama. I'll keep my eyes and ears open and contact you if anything comes up I think you need to know.*

Right. I'll be in touch when I can. I still need time away. Thanks so much.

The words came fast. *I'm glad you're okay and contacted me. What do you want me to say if anyone asks if you've called?*

Annie thought for a moment before returning to the keyboard. *If they only ask if I've called, you can say no. I didn't. But if they ask if you've heard from me, I guess you'll have to tell them the truth. I told you I'm fine and happy, but I didn't say where I'm staying. That's it.*

Good. Hey, I'm loving your car, by the way. Thanks again. Gretchen put another smiley face after her remark.

Your car, not mine. Annie smiled as she typed. *You've been a wonderful friend. I'll keep in touch when I can. Gotta run. Somebody's coming.* She switched over to check news headlines, only to see a picture of herself on an entertainment section with the headline, *"Where's Ann Stanway?"*

The door slid open, and Hunter came in.

Annie gave a small gasp and shut the lid of her laptop. No way did she want him to see her picture.

Hunter chuckled. "Sorry about that. I should have knocked. Next time I'll ring a bell or something. In fact, maybe we should borrow cow bells from my uncle's farm and wear them so we don't crash into each other or startle one another anymore."

Annie laughed, and it felt so good. Something about this simple life and this town—or could it be this man—seemed to suit her.

"Hey, I had another idea." He leaned against the doorframe, his eyes warm as they met hers. "I'm working on a house for a local family tomorrow. Mostly painting in a couple of rooms, installing baseboards and other finishing touches in the rest. Want to swing by and see it sometime? I could pick you up unless you want Jimmy to drive you?"

Annie's smile faded. "I don't want to give Jimmy any ideas, but yes, I'd like to come."

Hunter slipped into a chair across from his big mahogany desk and cradled his coffee mug. "Tell me a little about yourself. You aren't from around here originally, right?"

"No. I grew up in Pennsylvania, but I've never visited your lovely town before my car broke down."

"You should try to see more of the area while you're here."

She took a sip of her coffee and smiled. "You make a mean cup of coffee."

He laughed. "My assistant made this batch. You can float horseshoes in mine."

"Nice. I think I love your assistant's brew. So yeah, back to what you were saying. I like what I've seen of this town already. The main street is so picturesque. I've never seen an Amish buggy in real life before arriving here. Pretty amazing and very old-school—quaint." She suddenly put her hand over her mouth. "I'm so sorry. When will I learn to keep my mouth shut? First I offend your uncle and now you."

"I'm not a bit offended. I get it, don't worry. And you didn't say it in a mean way at all. Now come on, I'll drive you to Sarah's if you're finished in town."

She straightened. "I'm sure you've got plenty to do. I planned on walking."

"Nonsense. Even the boss gets to take a break occasionally." He ushered her outside, wondering why he didn't want to release the light touch on her elbow. This woman was getting under his skin way too quickly, but somehow, he didn't mind.

He turned the corner and almost ran head-on into Uncle Abram. "Uncle. Forgive me, we didn't see you."

His uncle barely glanced at Annie, giving her only a slight nod. The Bishop wasn't a big fan of *Englischers*, but it wasn't like him to be rude, either. Had Annie really done or said something to offend the older man that Hunter wasn't aware of? Maybe they needed to tread lightly.

"Good day, sir." Annie held out her hand. "It's good to see you again so soon."

The bishop tugged at the brim of his hat then shifted his attention to his nephew. "Hunter, I have come to tell you. I have spoken to the committee as you've asked. We will do what we can, but I cannot promise you anything since you are dealing with *Englischers*. God's will be done."

Hunter's heart lurched. Would his uncle stand against the work he was trying to do in the area? "Thank you, Uncle. That's all I can ask."

He stood without moving as the older man strode down the sidewalk away from them, then turned to Annie. "I'm sorry he didn't speak to you. He still holds it against my father that my mother didn't join the church and left the Amish way of life. I'm afraid it's reflected in his treatment of many *Englischers*. He doesn't want the fancy way of life intruding on their simple life. He worries it will corrupt his people."

Annie sputtered. "Corrupt? I'm not corrupt. I mean, I've done a few things I wish I hadn't in my life, but haven't we all? After all, the Bible says that none of us is without sin, and we all need forgiveness. I haven't been the Christian I should be the last three years, but I'm trying to change that now."

Hunter tried not to laugh as he placed his hand lightly on her shoulder. "Shh. It's not personal, and I'm not calling you a sinner—and I don't think he is, either. He simply doesn't approve of the fancy lifestyle most of us live, and he doesn't want that rubbing off on his people and making them dissatisfied. It's understandable, from his perspective."

"Oh." Annie drew in a deep breath. "I suppose you're right." She tipped her head, her eyes inquisitive as she gazed up at him, making his heart pound. "You act differently around your uncle. Is it strange, having an Amish man as a relative? Do you wish you'd been raised Amish?"

He tucked her hand into the crook of his elbow. "Come on, let's head to the car, and I'll answer that as we drive." He escorted her the rest of the way, then helped her into the car, waiting to shut the door until she was settled. He walked around and slipped inside, then started the car and moved carefully into traffic, keeping an eye on the buggy up ahead. "To answer your question, being raised 'part' Amish has been difficult. My mother wanted to instill some of the customs and beliefs in my life, but the Amish kids in the area were told not to play with me when I was young. The *Englisch* kids were leery, because I had a mother who used to be Amish, so they thought I was weird." He shrugged. "It was hard figuring out who I was and where I belonged."

"What did you do?" Annie clasped her hands in her lap and looked at him.

"I finally figured out it's not about whether I'm Amish or an *Englischer*. It's what I believe. It's who I am. I'm a child of God, and He is my father. So are many of the Amish—at least, the ones who truly believe in Him and have chosen to trust Him. Not all of them have. Many still cling to the old ways, and they don't read the Bible for themselves or understand what faith means. They simply follow the *Ordnung*, thinking that following the rules will get them to heaven. They don't realize they need something more beyond themselves—a personal relationship with God, not just church membership."

Annie nodded. "That makes sense. It's the same with many people in our world who attend church and think they're Christians as a result. So you decided you're a child of God, and that's it? I mean, I realize that's enough. I was raised in a Christian home by godly grandparents after my father died. I clung to my faith until I moved away, then somehow it seemed to slowly disintegrate."

Hunter nodded as he put on his turn signal and hit the highway toward Sarah's inn. "I get that. The world has tugged me in different directions in the past. I decided that having a solid real relationship with God was what defined me as a person, not my earthly heritage. Ever since I made that decision, I've been at peace." He shot her a quick glance, wondering if he'd been too preachy and how she'd take it.

"Thanks for sharing that. I think I needed to hear it. It's hard sometimes, deciding who is the real you and where you belong. What did your uncle mean about the committee deciding something and him trying to help? Is it anything you can talk about?" She waved a hand as he pulled into the parking area at the inn. "Hey, we're at Sarah's already. That was a lot faster than walking."

As she reached for the door handle, he touched her arm. "If you want to wait a second, I'll answer that question."

She swung toward him. "Sure thing. Is it a secret?"

"Not at all. My company donated the plans for a new house for a local *Englisch* family who lost their home in a fire. But we're short-handed right now. That's the house I invited you to come see. I asked Uncle Abram if any of the Amish men might be willing to spare a few hours to help. They have a couple of times in the past, so I didn't think it would hurt to ask again. He said he'd see what he could do, but he couldn't promise. That's about the best I can hope for, since I can't very well go door-to-door among the community myself."

Her brows drew together. "Why not?"

"My parents are still considered outcasts. Mom wasn't shunned since she never joined the church, but she keeps her distance most of the time. It would be awkward for me to try to solicit help for *Englisch* families."

"Oh. I see. That's too bad. Maybe I could help paint or something?"

He cocked his head to the side and smiled into her wide eyes. "Are you any good at it."

"I can swing a mean paintbrush." She laughed. "I helped my grandmother paint growing up, so I'm not a total amateur."

He straightened. "You're on—I'll pick you up around ten tomorrow and take you to Sarah's when we're done, in plenty of time for you to rest and change before dinner."

Veronica tapped her pen on her desktop waiting for everyone to be seated, although she could have done without Jan and Tanya. Doyle should have passed the word to his underlings, but he insisted they tag along. Whatever. When her dynasty grew to the place it should be, she'd get people who were true movers and shakers who could get things done.

The silence in the room grew louder as the three stared at Veronica. Exactly as it should be. She was the boss of this operation, not Doyle, or Scott, or anyone else. She slowly raised one brow, then spat out her next words. "Jessie is a mess. She's turned into a total train wreck."

Doyle had the nerve to snort. "She was your idea, Veronica. So what do you propose to do about it?"

Veronica pinned him with a hard stare until he squirmed. That was why she'd insisted this meeting be in her office, not his. She would not let this man get the best of her, sitting behind his big desk and lording it over her. "We don't have time to point fingers. We need to decide what we're going to do."

Doyle hunched one shoulder and mumbled. "We?"

She ignored him. "Tanya? What have you got?"

The door opened, and Scott strode in. "Mother? You called a meeting without letting me know?" He looked from one face to the next until he settled on her again.

"Oh, hush." She waved her fingers. "No time for that now. Tanya is going to tell us the results of the research she's done on Jessie. Sit down and listen." She didn't have time for her son's whining. Greater things were at stake. Things that could make or break their future.

The young woman stared at her iPad a moment then looked up. "Our test audience has been using words like . . . 'mean girl' . . . 'stuck up' . . . 'arrogant' . . . 'condescending'."

Scott leaned forward in his chair. "We have zero chemistry."

Doyle cleared his throat. "Exactly what do you plan to do about it, Veronica? The network is not going to like this at all."

Veronica looked at Tanya again. Why didn't the girl speak up? Did she have to snatch that tablet out of her hands and do her work for her?

Tanya's eyes widened. "Oh. Right. Well, the tide seems to be turning. They don't care for Jessie, but now it appears they're missing Ann."

Veronica almost purred. "Absence makes the heart grow fonder."

Doyle jolted upright in his chair. "What? Now you're thinking about bringing her back after you made such a big deal of getting rid of her?"

"We don't even know where she is." Scott scowled at

his mother, but she ignored him.

“Then we’d better find out where she is. And quick.” She resumed thumping the end of the pen on her desk.

“And exactly how do we do that?” He leaned back, his scowl still in place. “I’ve tried everything I know to do, and nothing has worked.”

She allowed a small smile to slip out. “I think I may have an idea.”

Chapter Twelve

ANNIE WAS UP IN TIME TO see the sunrise Sarah had been talking about, and it was every bit as glorious as she'd promised. Not that she'd never seen one before—they'd had more than one early-morning shoot on the set—but paying attention to the sky hadn't been a priority at the time. Now Annie wanted to take in everything about her surroundings.

Besides, she didn't think she could have slept much longer, anyway. Hunter would be arriving in a couple of hours to take her to the job site. Why had she agreed to help? It wasn't like she'd ever worked on a project this big, and painting her bedroom years ago certainly didn't make her an expert. She sighed as she walked through the kitchen door.

Sarah looked up and smiled. "You are up early. I didn't even have to knock at your door this morning. Are you all right?"

Annie nodded. "I thought I'd check out that sunrise you mentioned. I agree. It's worth getting up for. Besides, I wanted to help with breakfast, if I'm not too late."

"I would like that, *denki.* There is not much left to be done, as I did most of it last night, but you could carry the plates to the table and pour the juice. We still have a little time before the first guest comes to the dining room. No one wanted breakfast until after seven this morning."

"How about I start helping you every day? I need to do more to keep busy. Going to the library occasionally isn't enough."

Sarah wiped her hands on a dishtowel. "I would

only agree to that if I do not charge you for your room."

Annie held up her hand. "No way. We had a deal with one free day. I'm not poor, Sarah. I still have money saved from my last job. I want to help cook, truly I do."

Sarah narrowed her eyes and stared at Annie for a full minute then gave a deliberate nod. "One more day free, and I'll agree."

Annie laughed. "You drive a hard bargain, but fine. I'll go nuts if I don't have something to do."

"*Ya*, but you're helping Hunter today and having dinner with him tonight. That will keep you very busy."

"About that." Annie busied herself with the chores Sarah had asked her to do. "I offered to help at his project today. I mean, help as in work. I'm afraid I didn't think this through. I've never even been on a construction site, much less worked at one. What if I mess up or do something wrong?"

Sarah took a hot dish out of the oven and put it into the warmer. "What did you offer to do?"

"Paint. I probably can't make too big of a mess out of that, can I?"

"It's not too hard. Will you be using a paint roller or a brush?"

Annie's shoulders slumped. "I have no idea. Does it matter?"

Sarah shook her head, and the loose strings on her *Kapp* swung. "Probably not. Follow directions, and you'll be fine." She looked up, a sly smile tugging at her lips. "You like him, don't you? Hunter?"

Annie bit her lip. "I'm not sure. I ran into him yesterday. I told him I've painted before and could help. I don't know why I did that. I haven't painted since I was fifteen."

"You don't need to try to be someone you aren't,

Annie. Be yourself. That's all any of us can be."

She gripped the plate she was holding to keep from dropping it. Did Sarah know who she was? Had she guessed or been told? But how could she? Most of the people Sarah knew didn't own a TV or ever go online. Maybe she'd guessed Annie wasn't a chef and was giving her a chance to confess. "About that, Sarah. I'm *not* a famous chef. I'm not really a famous anything at this point in my life. I'm not sure who I am anymore, or where I belong."

Sarah reached over and squeezed her hand. "Whomever you are, I like her. Please don't worry."

"I'm not sure why I'm even drawn to Hunter. My last relationship with a guy was a disaster. I promised myself I wouldn't get drawn into anything like that again. But he seems different, somehow. I'm so confused. I don't know what I want or what I should do with my life."

The sound of a man clearing his throat swung both Sarah and Annie toward the front entry hall. Bishop Swarey stood with arms folded, his mouth pulled into a tight line. "Sarah. I would speak with you alone. *Kumm* with me to the parlor please." He turned and strode that direction without waiting to see if she'd follow.

Sarah's eyes widened, but she nodded. "Bishop. *Hallo.* Of course I will *kumm.* Please excuse me, Annie."

She stood rooted to the spot knowing she couldn't go with them, but for some reason Annie didn't quite understand, that man made her nervous. As Sarah followed him out of the room, Annie edged closer to the door, hoping she might be able to hear into the next room.

The Bishop's deep rumble carried clearly, as though he didn't care—or even wanted—her to hear him. "*Sind Sie ein Englischer*? Are you an *Englischer* now?"

"*Nein.* I apologize if I've done something wrong."

"Why is one working in your kitchen and staying at your house? She is clearly a woman of the world, and you are spending too much time with her."

"Her car broke down outside of town, and she had no place to go. Does the Bible not teach us to give hospitality to strangers in need?"

Annie's lips parted. She hadn't known Sarah would be willing or able to stand up to the bishop—especially on her behalf. She prayed her friend wouldn't get into trouble on her account.

"It also teaches us to keep ourselves separate from the world so that we do not become lured by its ways. When we gave you permission to open this inn, it was with the understanding it would be used for our people as they traveled through the district. Then we gave permission for you to take in a few people each month who were travelers to our area, after your husband died. We knew you needed the extra income. However, we cannot condone you allowing modern *Englischers* to corrupt you or your home with their ways."

"It will only be for a week longer, sir. Until her car has been fixed and she can go home. Surely it cannot hurt to help a person in need?"

There was a long silence. Annie wanted to edge closer in case they'd lowered their voices, but she didn't dare. The last thing she needed was to get caught spying, but she also wished to help should Sarah require it.

The Bishop's gruff voice started again. "I suppose we can allow it. But I do not want any trouble to come to this inn or our community because of this decision. It is time you remarry, Sarah. You have had a sufficient time of mourning."

"*Ya.* I am still considering Jeremiah's proposal. I do

not see a need for hurry."

"You were made to be a wife and mother, not an innkeeper. It is time you think about closing this place and following *Gott's* plan for your life and future."

Annie heard footsteps and jumped away from the doorway. She heard a gruff, "*Gutt* day," before the front door opened and closed. Whew. She had to admit she was thankful he hadn't come through the kitchen. It would have been hard to keep her thoughts to herself. The nerve of that man telling Sarah she needed to close her inn and follow God's plan for her life. Who was he to decide that for someone else? She was working up a temper when Sarah returned to the kitchen.

"You heard all of that, Annie?"

"Wha-at . . ?" She wanted to deny it, but staring into Sarah's honest eyes, she knew she couldn't. "Yes. I'm sorry. I was worried about you, and I listened. Please forgive me."

"*Nein*. You must not worry."

Annie sank onto a kitchen chair. "But why, Sarah? Why is he saying all that? Have I done something terrible that's made him angry? Should I leave?"

She shook her head and plucked the whistling teapot off the stove. "It is complicated. You are not Amish, so it is hard for you to understand our ways."

"But he wants you to close the inn and marry his son."

Sarah poured the tea into the two mugs she brought from a cupboard. "It is our way. Women do not often run a business and stay single. Especially not if there's at least one eligible man who wants their hand. The inn has not been profitable, and Jeremiah is a *gutt* man. He may not understand like Ezra did, but he's a *hutt* man, in spite of that. It's not that I don't love my community and want to do my part. But sometimes I'm not sure I even understand myself. So how can I expect Jeremiah to do so?"

Annie nodded. "Trust me, I get that. So sometimes, do you feel like you're not who everyone thinks you are, or who they want you to be?"

Sarah blew a soft breath on her hot tea. "A person cannot be Amish and of the world at the same time. But when I pray, I often feel that God is telling me I am supposed to be running this inn. Maybe it's part of a ministry to travelers, *ya*?" She shook her head. "However, maybe I cannot run this inn and be a good wife. The Bishop does not believe they can go together. I think only Ezra understood it was possible, but he is gone."

Annie reached across the table and covered Sarah's hand with her own. "I don't know anything about being Amish, but I do know you can only go so long not being true to yourself before you start losing who you are. That's not a good thing, believe me." She placed a hand over her heart. "You start losing something inside."

Sarah squeezed Annie's hand. "Perhaps this is why *Gott* sent you here—to help me understand these things and find my way."

Annie's eyes filled with tears. She hadn't been this real with someone in a long time. "I'm not sure how to even say this, but . . . would you like to pray together? I haven't done that very much lately, but it might help both of us."

Sarah's eyes widened. "I would like that. Thank you." She reached out her other hand and took Annie's, as a gentle peace enveloped the room.

Chapter Thirteen

HUNTER JUMPED FROM HIS PICKUP AND headed up the walk to Sarah's, surprised at how eager he was to see Annie. The woman was getting under his skin. He'd had to remind himself more than once that nothing they were doing today was a date—friends only, working on a project together, per her request.

It was refreshing to meet a woman who was so honest that she actually said what she meant and spelled out what she wanted. His last relationship had been exactly the opposite. Gloria had played games—she'd been a master manipulator, determined to get what she wanted even if she had to lie to accomplish it. He'd learned to hate lying almost more than any other vice, especially after that experience. Besides, even though his mother didn't stay in the Amish faith, she raised her children with the same values and morals she'd been raised with, and lying was definitely *verboten*, or forbidden, by any person of faith.

He rapped on the door then pushed it open, knowing Sarah had an open-door policy during daytime hours. "Sarah? Annie? Anyone here?" He spoke quietly, not wanting to disturb anyone who might be resting. He waited but didn't hear so much as a giggle or a whisper. Had Annie forgotten he was picking her up?

He strode through the foyer, across the dining room, and into the kitchen, then stopped. Annie and Sarah stood together, holding hands, their heads bowed. He couldn't hear what Annie was saying, but her lips were moving. Backing up a step, he waited, not wanting to intrude. Had something happened to upset Sarah?

"Amen." Sarah's strong, vibrant voice carried to where he stood. "You may come in now, Hunter."

His eyes widened. "How did you know I was here?"

She released Annie's hands and turned toward him, laughing. "Your feet say it all. You do not tiptoe when you walk across wooden floors. And since we knew you were coming to pick up Annie sometime this morning, who else would it be?"

"Oh. Right." He felt a bit foolish, then grinned. "Everything okay in here?"

Annie nodded. "We were praying for more guests for Sarah's inn. I have an idea how to help, but we both thought we should pray first."

"An idea?" He quirked a brow at one then the other.

"Nothing I can share yet. I still need to discuss it later with Sarah and another friend. But when I'm free to tell you, I will. If Sarah says it's all right when the time comes."

Sarah lifted the coffee pot and held it where Hunter could see it. "This all sounds very mysterious. Jimmy will arrive any minute to take me to town. I need to get a few more baking supplies. Oh, and I want to pick Annie up in my buggy in a couple of hours, after I return from shopping, if that's all right. I thought she might enjoy a little tour of our countryside from the slower pace of a buggy. Hunter, would you like coffee before you leave?"

"No thanks. And sure thing—I should stay at the project longer than a couple of hours, so if Annie wants to go for a ride with you, that's cool. I need to head out, if Annie is ready." He glanced at her, surprised to see she wore a pair of new jeans, a short-sleeved t-shirt that looked brand new, and low-heeled shoes. Not the type of clothing he'd expect from someone who'd offered to help paint, but maybe she hadn't brought any old clothes on her trip. He gave a mental shrug.

"Ya, as Sarah would say, I'm ready." Annie gave him a cheeky grin. "Let's go."

Jimmy trudged to the door of the Wildwood Inn and lifted his hand to knock, his mind still on the brush off Annie handed him when he'd asked her out. He'd sat at the diner immersed in a stupid TV show for way too long. He'd promised to drive Sarah to town for groceries. The door swung open before he got in the second rap and Hunter almost walked into him.

The other man grabbed the doorframe and stopped himself from running over the top of Jimmy. "Whoa. Sorry about that, man. I guess I was talking to Annie and didn't hear you knock. You here for Sarah? She's getting her list from the kitchen. She said to tell you she'll be right out."

Jimmy clenched his jaw. Here to get Annie, huh? So, the two of them were getting cozy. Not what he'd hoped for, but what could he expect? Hunter had everything. Good looks, a growing business, and a great reputation in town. He, on the other hand, had very little—only his van and a small apartment. But that would change if he had anything to say about it. "Yeah, I'm here for Sarah. Thanks."

He stepped aside to let Hunter pass then swiftly blocked Annie's way. "Hey there, Annie." Keeping his eyes fixed on her face, he waited. Would she even notice him this time, or brush him off again? And what was it about her face that kept niggling at his mind?

Her eyes widened, and she moved back. "Oh. You startled me. How are you, Jimmy?" She took a step to the side.

Jimmy stepped the same direction. “Oh, sorry.” He stepped the other way at the exact same time she did, never removing his gaze from her face. “There’s something about you—and at some point, I’m going to remember.”

“Excuse me, Jimmy, but I need to get going. I’m helping Hunter on a project today.” She lifted her hand in a small salute then walked around him and straight to Hunter’s car.

Jimmy stared after her, anger swelling in his throat to the point he thought he would choke.

Annie climbed into Hunter’s car, trying to calm her rapid breathing. She kept her face turned away from him as she snapped her seat belt closed, hoping he hadn’t heard the exchange with Jimmy or noticed her trembling hands. Did he know anything, or was he simply being the somewhat obnoxious Jimmy she’d come to expect?

“Annie?” Hunter touched her arm.

She jolted and turned to him. “Yes?”

“Everything all right? You’ve been staring out the window like you forgot something. Did you need to go in the house or speak to Sarah or Jimmy?”

“No!” Panic almost overtook her at the thought of seeing Jimmy again. What might he say to Sarah or Hunter? “I’m fine. You’re ready to go, right? I’m rarin’ to get to painting. Time’s a wastin’, as they say.” She tried to keep her voice bright and cheerful, but from the look in his eyes, he wasn’t fooled.

He turned the key in the ignition and pulled out

onto the road. "If you say so. Hey, I was kind of wondering . . ."

She pulled her attention to Hunter again. "Hmm?"

He waved a hand. "Your clothes. Are you okay with getting paint on them?"

Her lips formed a little O. "Why would I get paint on them?"

He laughed. "You did plan on painting today, right? Or did I misunderstand your offer to help."

"Oh, that. Right. Sorry I'm so distracted. I guess I was thinking about what happened at the house a little earlier." Should she tell him about Jimmy or turn the discussion to Sarah? Was it even right to mention Sarah's problems to him? Or did he already know? "Of course, I plan to paint. But I'm very careful. I'm sure my clothes will be fine." She looked at her new jeans, high-end slip-on shoes, and new t-shirt through his eyes, remembering the old t-shirt Grandma insisted she wear years ago when they painted her room. "Or not?"

This time Hunter laughed. "I'm guessing you got so busy talking and praying with Sarah that you forgot to change?"

"Uh. Yeah." Relief filled her that she could honestly direct the subject away from talking about Jimmy. "Something like that."

"No problem. I have a couple pair of coveralls at the job site and old shirts of mine that would probably come down to your knees. You should be fine. Everything else okay?"

She turned to give him her full attention this time. As far as Sarah was concerned, everything was definitely *not* okay. "Not really. Your uncle wants Sarah to marry his son, Jeremiah."

Hunter's brows rose. "You know about that, huh? Is that what the two of you were really praying about?"

She shook her head. "Yes, kind of. Well, maybe Sarah was, I'm not sure. I had other things on my mind, and we'd been talking about how to help her inn succeed. Oh, hey, I didn't even realize. Jeremiah is your cousin, right?"

"Yep." Hunter turned into a parking area riddled with stacks of what appeared to be left over scraps of lumber, a refuse pile of sheetrock pieces, and other odds and ends showing the job must be nearing the end. "My cousin is a good guy, even if he is a little like his father. He's more flexible in his beliefs, but he's firm about not following the ways of the *Englisch* or spending too much time with them. Sarah sees things differently, but I don't think he judges her for it. He's secretly been in love with her for years. At least since Ezra died, if not back in school."

He got out of the car and strode around to her side, then opened the door and helped her out.

"Thanks. But I don't understand. If he loves her, why would he agree with his father and insist she close the inn if they marry?" Ann shook her head. Women should be able to marry who they want and choose their occupation. Why should Sarah be any different? "It doesn't make sense, Hunter."

He tilted his head. "You weren't raised Amish, so you wouldn't understand. It's not their way."

Chapter Fourteen

SCOTT SAT IN FRONT OF HIS laptop in the perfect position for the small camera mounted on the top rim to catch his image at the best angle. Not that he had any bad angles, but hey, a guy couldn't be too careful when he was going to be doing a live stream to his adoring fans in the next few minutes. His hand hovered over the keyboard then paused and looked at his mother. "You sure about this?"

She arched a plucked brow. "We have to do what's best for the show, Scott. There's more than our family involved." She glanced at Doyle and Tanya hovering nearby. "Other people's livelihood rests in you making this believable." She flicked her hand toward the computer screen. "Now get to it, and make our viewers ooze with sympathy at your terrible plight."

He tapped a key that activated the screen then another to start the live feed. One glance at the small screen to the right showed the running tally of how many viewers had tuned in. Looked like tens of thousands after all the media coverage of the big announcement they planned for today. Good.

Scott drew in a deep breath and mustered the most dejected expression he could manage.

Jimmy sat at the counter in the diner, trying to tune out the TV hanging right above the bar as he mulled over what he was going to do with his future. He had at least an hour to kill while Sarah finished her shopping, and he could take her home. He took a sip of his coffee. This driving people around gig was getting old. He had to find a way to get into the Hollywood scene.

"And now, in Hollywood news, we're bringing you a live stream from Scott Adson, the famous reality star of *Life with the Adsons*."

Jimmy groaned. Just what he needed. Some dude who'd already made it big gloating on TV. He took another drink of his coffee, wishing he hadn't had it refilled. Maybe he'd head home as soon as he dropped Sarah off, even if he didn't have another job lined up yet.

"Scott Adson here. Hey, *Lifers*! So glad you tuned in." The guy's cocky smile lit up the screen. Jimmy curled his fist, wanting to smash it. "Besides this live stream, this broadcast is also being carried on TV. How's that for success?" His expression instantly sobered, almost like a curtain had been pulled. Definitely practiced. Jimmy turned his head in disgust. This guy got paid big bucks. He could do the same thing if given half a chance.

The voice on the TV returned. "We promised an announcement, and I wish it could be a happy one, but it's not." He waited a heartbeat, as though waiting for that statement to sink in, then drew in a deep, soulful breath and continued in a melancholy tone. "I have some bad news to share."

Jimmy perked up. Bad news, huh? Maybe everything wasn't going perfectly in pretty-boy's world, after all.

"I know there are rumors that Ann is missing, and I have to admit, we didn't part on the best of terms." Scott leaned into the camera. "I want you to know, I miss Ann and care about her more than anything in the world. I couldn't live with myself if something happened to her." He held up his phone to the camera. "I've had this picture as my background photo for a couple of years now. Whenever I look at it, I miss her more than ever."

He looked at the phone and swiped it, then touched the screen and held it up again. "And how about this one? We were on our first date together. She's pretty cute here, don't you think?"

Jimmy moved closer to the TV and almost choked on his coffee. A picture of Scott with a woman who looked like it could be Annie was captured on the phone.

Scott settled back in his chair. "Even then I knew Ann was special. Help me find her? I need her to come home."

Jimmy leaned forward to get a closer look, but Scott lowered his phone. A niggling suspicion started to grow. He couldn't be sure the woman was Annie, since the picture was taken in the shadows and she wasn't a blonde, but there was something about her smile and the tilt of her head . . .

"I'm offering a reward of ten thousand dollars to anyone who spots her and calls this number. Ask for the producer or contact me via Twitter or Instagram." Scott rattled off a name and a number that scrolled across the bottom of the screen. Jimmy scrambled to find a pen and napkin to write on before the camera returned to the smiling announcer.

Jimmy climbed out of his van and sauntered into Leo and Son's garage. Hopefully Jules wouldn't be here, as Leo was easier to get information out of, if he could get the old guy into a talkative mood. He leaned on the beat-up laminate counter then pulled in a deep breath. "Hey, anyone home?"

"Ya don't have ta shout. Ain't none of us deaf around here. What'cha need, Jimmy?" Leo Newman stopped long enough to shoot a stream of tobacco into a nearby can before he made his way to the counter. "Ya need a cup of coffee whilst you're here? I got a pot simmerin' on the hot plate." He beckoned behind the counter toward a partial glass wall that housed a small office.

"No thanks. I need to pick something up for one of your customers."

Leo scratched his head. "Yeah? Who might that be?"

"Annie Farley. Hey, how's her car coming along? You think it's going to take much longer before she can be on the road?" He sure hoped so. He'd like to uncover the truth and collect the reward Scott Adson offered before Annie split town.

"Still waiting on a couple of parts, but we're gettin' there. Now, what else did ya need?"

"Something out of her glove box. Okay if I grab it for her? That would save her a trip into town, since she's staying out at The Wildwood."

"Yeah, yeah." Leo waved toward the car. "You help yourself while I go get that cup of coffee. Sure you don't want one? I can probably scare up a clean cup somewhere."

Jimmy barely suppressed a shudder. "I'm good, but thanks. I'll find what she needs and get out of your hair. Thanks, Leo."

"No problem. See ya, kid." He walked around a greasy table with an assortment of parts strewn across the surface and went into the office, closing the door behind him.

Jimmy released a long breath. Good. But he'd better hurry before Jules came in and started asking questions. She was a lot nosier than her father. He slid in the passenger side and opened the glove box, his heart pounding. He couldn't imagine why a big reality star would drive a beast of a car like this, but maybe it was part of her disguise. Her name on the registration was all the proof he needed. He was breathing hard by the time he found it among all the other junk in the compartment.

He withdrew it and quickly opened it, all the while trying to keep an eye out for Jules. His gaze darted to the signature line at the bottom, then he jerked in shock. Gretchen Simms. Who in the world was Gretchen Simms?

Chapter Fifteen

ANNIE BRUSHED A LOCK OF HAIR from her face with her knuckles, praying she hadn't smeared paint on her forehead or turned her hair a rich beige. Returning to anything even remotely close to brunette, even if it was through the use of paint, would probably trigger even more questions from Jimmy. That was the last thing she needed. What had set him off, anyway? Was he simply fishing because he thought she looked familiar, or had something happened she wasn't aware of? Whatever the case, she needed to watch her step. She put her roller into the pan and moved back, surveying the wall.

"I thought you were supposed to be painting the trim." A catty voice behind her made her swing to face the door. "What are you doing painting the walls?" A young woman with shoulder-length auburn hair and a perfect figure strode into the room, planting her hands on her hips and scowling. "I figured when Hunter showed up with you in that get up—" she gestured to the skinny jeans showing beneath the long shirt Hunter had loaned her— "you didn't have a clue what you were doing. Now it seems I'm right."

Annie's mouth dropped open, trying to take in the deluge of words and sort out what she'd heard. Who was this woman and why was she being so critical? "Trim? Uh—I'm painting what Hunter told me to paint."

"Nope." She flicked her fingers toward the windowsills. "That's what you were supposed to paint. The boards around the windows, doors, and along the floor. See, it's even masked off so you can't make a mistake." She pointed at the boards at the bottom of the wall. "*Those* are called baseboards. I guess you didn't know that, either."

Footsteps sounded outside the door, and a second later Hunter appeared, his smile fading as he looked from the woman to Annie. "Jennifer. Is there a problem? I heard you saying something to Annie about painting the wrong thing? What's up?"

Jennifer's smirk turned into the semblance of a smile, and she moved close to Hunter's side. "I'm all done with my job, Hunter, but Annie still has a lot of work to do. I was thinking it would be nice to take a break. Want to go grab a Coke?"

He shook his head. "I'm good. You go ahead. And don't worry about trying to tell Annie what to do. I'll take care of things here while you're gone." He waved toward the door.

Annie bit her lip to keep from grinning as Jennifer glared at her before flouncing out the door. "Thanks. But I'm really sorry if I messed up. I guess I didn't hear you say to paint the trim. I thought I was supposed to paint the walls."

"You are." He walked to the far wall and peered from the ceiling to the floor. "Not sure where she got her information, but it's wrong. This room was supposed to be beige, and the trim will be white."

Annie had her own idea what Jennifer had hoped would happen—she'd start painting the trim only to be told later by Hunter she'd messed up. But thankfully, he'd come in time to keep her from following Jennifer's instructions. No doubt the young woman had a crush on him and had hoped to make her look stupid. Not that she hadn't done a good job of that on her own by wearing the most inappropriate clothes possible for painting. Oh well, live and learn. "Whew. Glad to hear it." She looked down at his shirt covering her new t-shirt. "And I'm sorry about the paint I got on your shirt. I can buy you another one if you tell me where you got it."

He laughed, making his eyes crinkle and Annie's heart lurch. "Nope. No need for that. It's why it's called a paint shirt. If you look closely, you'll see other colors mixed in there besides yours. Glad I had another one hanging around you could use."

Her cheeks warmed at the look he gave her, and she turned her head. "Yeah, me too. Well, I guess I should get back to work."

"It's almost time for Sarah to come, and in a couple of hours, I'll wrap things up for the afternoon. Hey, I want to make sure. Are we still on for dinner tonight? It's the least I can do as a thank you for the work you did today."

She cocked her head. "I thought this was a volunteer project and no one got paid."

"Yeah, well, occasionally we do pay people, and it's not like you're on our list of volunteers. You'll have plenty of time between now and then to get ready." He chuckled. "And wash the paint off your face. Does six-thirty sound good?"

Her eyes widened and she scrubbed at her nose until he laughed again. "Sorry, I couldn't resist. Don't worry, there's nothing there."

She punched his arm. "Thanks a lot! Actually, I've been looking forward to going all morning. But not because I helped. I would have done that anyway. Just . . . because."

He met her eyes and held her gaze for several seconds longer than needed. "I like the sound of that." The words were soft, and they brought another wave of warmth to her cheeks, but this time she didn't turn away.

Sarah clucked to her horse, and the animal moved forward, causing a slight jolt to the buggy. Annie smiled. There was something about traveling this way that she could get used to. The rhythmic clip-clop of the horse's hooves and the gentle motion of the buggy almost lulled her to sleep. Funny, the first time she'd ridden in it she hadn't understood how people could travel so slowly and take so much time to get where they were going. Now, the idea of slowing her world down a bit appealed.

Sarah settled deeper into her seat, allowing the mare to go at her own pace. "You look lost in thought. Did you have a good time helping paint the house, or did it not go as you had hoped? It does not appear you are covered from head to foot in paint, so something must have gone well."

Annie laughed at the twinkle clearly showing in Sarah's eyes. "That's because Hunter has paint shirts and coveralls, as well as old tennis shoes and boots for people like me who come, uh, unprepared. He was very sweet and said I must have forgotten to change clothes because we were praying."

Sarah's brows rose, then she flicked the reins as the mare tried to steal a bite from a bush growing along the side of the road. "Ah, he heard us, then? Hunter was raised in a *Gott*-fearing family, so I'm sure he was very comfortable hearing us pray. Did that bother you?"

"Not at all, but I wasn't sure what to tell him at first. Since the Bishop is his uncle, I figured Hunter knows how the Bishop feels about you running the inn. I hope you don't mind that I told him I was helping you pray about it. I mean, not that we specifically prayed about Jeremiah or the inn, but I guess I kind of thought, you know, that's what you were praying about."

"*Nein.* Not at all. And yes, I pray about that often, but I was also praying for you. I know there's something on your heart that you might not want to share yet, and I'm fine with that. I'm sure Hunter will pray for me as well, if he isn't already, now that you've mentioned it to him."

"Oh." Annie didn't know what else to say. Her new friend could see too much. Why wasn't she digging and asking questions? No one in her old life would say they were fine with her not sharing what was going on, not even Gretchen. Most of her old crowd were gossips, and every one of them would judge her and whisper behind her back if they knew the lie she was living now.

"Sarah?" Annie drew in a deep breath then blew it out.

"Hmm?" Sarah gave her a small smile but didn't press when Annie didn't respond immediately. She reached over and squeezed Annie's hand. "Do not worry, my friend. When the time is right, God will find a way for you to know your own heart."

Annie blinked and stared. "How do you know . . . what do you mean . . ." The words almost stumbled across her lips. "Thank you. Now, may I talk to you about something else? Not about me, or even about you?"

"Certainly. Now you have me very curious. Is this about Hunter?"

Warmth stole into Annie's cheeks. "No. I mean, he knows about this, but it's not directly about him. It's about Carla. The homeless woman in town."

"Ah yes, Carla." Sarah nodded wisely. "She has been on my heart the past few days. I recently saw her in town, and she appeared thinner than the last time I saw her. I wish there was something I could do to help. I offered her a room when I first met her, but she said no. She found an old car, and she doesn't want to be in a house with a lot of people."

"Oh, I didn't know she'd feel that way about a regular house. She told me she won't stay in the women's shelter because there are too many people she doesn't trust. What I don't understand is why doesn't she remember how she got to town, and what it is she's always trying to remember?"

Sarah slowed the mare and moved her to the shoulder as a fast-moving car approached. "I have wondered that as well. When anyone asks her, she stumbles around but cannot seem to come up with an answer. Like you said, the shelter helps all they can, but you cannot force someone to move in or accept help."

Annie bit her lip, wishing she could do more. The older woman's plight tugged at her heart. "I've seen a lot of homeless people in L.A., but somehow she's different. She's not really panhandling, although she accepts the occasional burger or piece of pie from Hunter." She chuckled. "And he doesn't seem to mind. Carla has a lot of pride too. At times she's very lucid, then she says something that doesn't quite make sense. Like remembering a dog—a German shepherd—and not knowing why."

"I suppose it could be a childhood memory. Do you think maybe she has been on drugs and it has damaged her mind?"

"I'm not sure what to think, but I want to try to help her. I just can't figure out how. I guess more than anything, I'd like to find a way to help her remember, but I'm not sure that's possible. Not, if like you said, she has damage to her brain."

Sarah drew back on the reins. "You might consider praying about it, Annie. Maybe *Gott* will show you what you need to do. I think it's a worthy desire to help Carla, and I am sure *Gott* would agree with that. Ask Him, and see what He tells you."

Chapter Sixteen

HUNTER HELD ANNIE'S CHAIR FOR HER then slid it forward a bit as she settled into it. "I hope this is okay. I brought you to the Blue Moon Restaurant to give you a taste of the local ambience. They have great food and a quiet atmosphere, which makes it easier to talk."

Annie gave him a warm smile, and his heart jolted. "Quiet is a nice change from what I was used to in L.A.. I get tired of loud music and people trying to talk over the top of each other. This is very nice. Thank you for thinking of it."

The waiter stopped next to their table, laid the menus in front of them, and took their drink orders before departing. A few minutes later he returned with water and two Cokes, took their order and then disappeared. Hunter looked around the room, trying to see it through Annie's eyes. A cozy fire flickered in a fireplace at the far end of the room. Small tables were clustered around the room, their tops draped in white linen with a candle centerpiece ringed by greenery. The bar off at the far side of the room wasn't boisterous and only featured a big screen TV but no hard liquor.

Yes, it was definitely the right place to bring Annie for a quiet chat. He'd like nothing more than to get better acquainted with this lovely young woman who continued to mystify him the longer he knew her. Or didn't know her. That was part of the problem. "I thought with all the cooking you've been doing helping Sarah, you might enjoy not being in the kitchen tonight."

Annie shrugged. "It's a nice change, but I love cooking, so it's not a hardship." She looked up as the waiter set a steaming plate of grilled salmon in front of her and a medium-rare steak at his place. "Hmm. Smells delicious. I guess I am kind of glad I'm not cooking tonight." She looked at him, her glance shy. "Would you mind saying grace? I've gotten back into the habit since staying with Sarah, and now it feels strange not to." She sucked in a shallow breath. "But I don't want to put you on the spot—if you'd rather not. I can pray silently."

His heart warmed, and he reached across the table. "I'd be happy to. Remember, my mother was Amish, and that's one custom she clung to. My father agreed, as he was raised in a solid Christian home." He bowed his head and gave a short, but heartfelt thanks for Annie's friendship and their meal, then he raised his head and smiled. "How's Leo coming with your car repair?"

Her fork paused on its way to her mouth. "Good, I guess. Jules is supposed to call me when it's ready, although she warned me it could take a while."

"That's too bad. The people you were headed to visit must be disappointed at the delay." He tried to keep his words casual and not too intrusive, but he couldn't help the slight edge of curiosity that laced his words. She'd been shy about sharing anything about herself so far, and hopefully this wouldn't send her scampering the opposite direction.

"They understand." She carefully put the bite in her mouth.

"You never talk about any of that stuff. You know, friends, family, home."

Annie's eyebrows arched. "What do you mean?"

"You have no phone or steady Internet connection at Sarah's, but you have a business at home. I would think it would be hard to keep up with what's going on, unless of course, you have a very good manager. You don't seem overly worried. I suppose it makes me a bit curious, is all."

She chewed slowly before she answered. "I'm afraid it would be a very long, very mortifying story that wouldn't interest you."

"Mortifying?" He smiled. "That's a thought-provoking choice of words. You might be surprised at my level of interest, but I sense you aren't too anxious to share the details. Am I right?"

She bit her lip. "Is that all right? You aren't offended that I'd rather not talk about myself?"

"Nope." He grinned. "But tell me one thing."

Her eyes widened, looking a little like a startled fawn. "What's that?"

"Why does Jimmy keep staring at you like you're his lost puppy?" He jerked his head toward the bar where Jimmy swiveled away from them before Annie could turn.

She shook her head. "I'm clueless. I didn't even realize he was here."

"I think you have a fan."

"What? No. Jimmy's a friend. I think. I mean, I don't even really know him." She placed her hand over her heart as though to quiet its beating.

If he didn't know better, she almost appeared to be frightened. Had Jimmy said or done something to upset her? Hunter cast one more glance toward Jimmy then stood. "Would you like another Coke? The server is busy, but I don't mind going to the bar and grabbing a couple." He didn't wait for her to respond but strode to the bar. Something told him he needed to dig a little deeper and discover what was going on. He'd noticed Jimmy's interest before and assumed he had a crush on Annie, but somehow this felt different. More intense.

And Annie's reaction had spurred him to find out why.

He slid onto a stool and waited for the bartender to finish with another customer. The young man had his back to Hunter and seemed absorbed with his phone. Hunter rose a few inches and tried to peek over his shoulder, mystified. One minute Jimmy acted like he couldn't stare at Annie enough, and now all he could do was stare at his phone. "Hey, Jimmy. What's up?"

Jimmy swiveled his stool, his eyes wide, then stuffed his phone into his pocket. "No—nothing. Hanging, that's all."

"Right. I thought maybe you were needing to talk to Annie." Hunter gestured toward their table.

"Annie?" Jimmy's eyes widened. "Oh, is she here? I was busy looking up info to help my business. Nope, I don't need a thing. In fact, I probably should scram. See ya." He almost bolted from his stool and hit the door with the palms of both hands, jarring it open.

Hunter waited for the two Cokes then returned to his table. What had happened here? Jimmy had acted odd in the past, but this was beyond his normal eccentric behavior.

Annie reached for her glass then took a sip. "Thanks. I'm a little tired. When we finish these, do you mind if we head home?"

His heart took a nosedive. "Sure. Come on, we can head out now." Was she in a rush because he'd questioned her, or did it have something to do with Jimmy?

She stood, then hesitated. "You're sure you don't mind?"

"Not at all." He left cash on the table then walked her to the door. "Hey." He held it open, then reached down and grasped her hand after she exited. "I want to apologize."

She tipped her head to the side. "For what?"

"Being nosy. I'm not usually like that. I like you, and I enjoy spending time with you—a lot—in fact, I'd like to get to know you better. I guess I've been worried. I wanted to make sure you aren't in some kind of trouble you need help with."

She gave his hand a squeeze and then released it. "Mysterious stranger shows up in town with no story about her past, no cell phone, and doesn't want to talk about herself."

He rolled his eyes. "Yeah. I guess it does sound kind of stupid when you put it like that."

She smiled. "Sarah's right. You are one of the good guys."

Hunter chuckled. "It must be the Amish in me." He stopped next to her side of his truck and met her eyes. Everything seemed to still around them as he waited, then he leaned down and kissed her—so gently he wasn't sure it could be called a kiss—then stepped back. "Come on, I'll drive you home."

Jimmy ducked down in his van as Hunter's truck drove past. Hopefully they'd been too busy smooching to notice him parked right across the street from the pickup. He'd have to be more careful after this.

He glanced at his phone, then punched in the code to wake up the screen. Ha! He'd done it. Gotten a good one. He grinned. A perfect shot of Hunter's lips brushing Annie's upturned ones blazed from his screen. It couldn't be a better picture of Annie.

Chapter Seventeen

ANNIE SETTLED BEHIND HUNTER'S DESK WITH her laptop in front of her as early morning sunlight shone through the window facing the street. "Are you sure you don't mind? You have work to do, and I don't want to boot you out of your own office."

His eyes crinkled at the corners as he smiled. "I could use a break. How about I get us both a coffee? I can walk across the street to the coffee shop if you'd like. I'll see if there's anyone to chat with for a bit and promise to give you at least thirty minutes of privacy."

"Perfect. Do you think you could help me do a little sleuthing a little later?"

"Yeah? What about?" He leaned a shoulder against the doorframe, his face holding a quizzical look.

"Carla. I want to see if I can figure out how she appeared in town. It's still such a mystery."

He straightened. "Interesting. And how do you propose to do that?" As soon as her lips parted, he held up his hand. "Never mind. I'm eating into your personal time for emails or whatever you need to get done. Enjoy. I'll be back."

She waited until the door closed behind him, and she heard his footsteps retreating down the hall before she opened Skype and typed in Gretchen's name. "Come on, Gretchen. Be there." She waited a full minute while it rang on the other end, praying her friend wasn't in the middle of work with other people around.

Right as she was ready to disconnect, Gretchen's freckled face appeared on the screen, a grin stretching her cheeks. "Ann! You caught me at the perfect time.

I'm in the office, and no one else is around. How are you? Are you coming back? Do you need me to ship your car to you?"

Annie laughed, wondering how she'd stem the tide of questions. "Good. No. And no. I only have a few minutes before Hunter returns, so I can't chat too long."

Gretchen's brows rose. "Hunter? Sounds yummy. Is he as tall, dark, and handsome as his name sounds?" She clapped a hand over her mouth. "You're blushing! No way! He is handsome and yummy, isn't he? I knew it. So how long have you been dating? What's he like? What does he do for a living?"

"Gretchen. Seriously, I don't have time for all the questions. I wish I could sit and chat for an hour, but I can't."

"Oh. Sorry." Her friend's face sobered. "How can I help?" The old Personal Assistant tone had crept into her voice, leaving it almost flat.

"Oh, honey, I'm sorry. I didn't mean it like that. I wish you were here, and we could curl up with a glass of iced tea and talk all day. I'd tell you everything about Hunter. And yes, he's yummy. But I'd better keep my voice down, as I don't want him hearing I think that."

Gretchen's eyes lit with a happy glow. "Gotcha. So, what's up? You calling to get the scoop on what's happening around here?"

"Nope. Honestly, I don't care. I'm calling to see how your travel blog is doing?"

"Huh?" Gretchen pushed her unruly curls out of her face. "Whatever for? I mean, don't you have more important things to think about or talk about than my blog?"

"Not at the moment. You see, I have this Amish friend who runs an incredible inn here in town—it's where I've been staying. She needs more business and, well, I thought maybe with your blog . . ."

Gretchen clapped her hands and bounced in her chair. "Great idea!" She quickly stilled. "But an Amish inn? Why would anyone want to stay there? They like, don't have electricity and cook over a fireplace, right? And outhouses. Ugh. I can't send people to a place where they have to use an outhouse."

Annie laughed so hard her eyes teared. "They don't have outhouses or cook in the fireplace. They have a generator for things like electric lights, but they don't have TV's, phones in the house, or the Internet."

Gretchen's eyes bugged out. "Seriously? So that's why you have to go to this Hunter's office to use the Internet? No wonder. But what's the draw? Why would anyone want to stay there?"

"Peace and quiet. And the most amazing sunrises. Good cooking. A sweet, quiet atmosphere, all for starters. This would be a getaway for the technologically overloaded person who needs to unwind and truly rest. Ever heard of sitting on a porch swing and reading a book? It has its merits."

"No way. That's what you've been doing? I can't believe it. Not after the hectic life you've lived here in L.A. the past three years." She twisted her lips to the side. "Of course, simple does sound kind of good. I think I could even go for that for a few days."

"Exactly." Annie nodded, her heart swelling with excitement. "Would you be able to put together a little article, maybe a description if I send it to you, with the name of the town and Sarah's phone number?"

"I thought you said they can't have phones."

"Yeah, but if you have a business you can have one outside in the barn or in a little phone kiosk outside your house. Since Sarah has a business, she owns one.

Plus, she has voice mail through the phone company in case she misses a call."

Gretchen looked incredulous. "She has a land line? Not a cell phone? Who does that anymore?"

"Believe it or not, Gretch, lots of people who don't live in the big city. Out in the country, life is a lot slower, more laid back. Most people have cell phones, but yes, land lines do still exist." She leaned forward. "What do you say? If I get the information to you in the next day or two, can you put something on your blog about it?"

"Sure thing. Sounds like a place I'd like to visit sometime. For a day or two. I don't think I could handle it much longer." She smiled. "But hey, I thought you didn't want to tell me where you're staying."

Ann nodded. "I've thought of that. But I assume no one's been quizzing you lately?"

"Nope. Not a peep. I guess they finally believed me after the first three or four times they tried, that I truly don't know where you are."

"Then I trust you, and I'm not going to worry about it. I'll shoot you an email with the details as soon as I can get where there's Internet service. Hey, I hear someone coming. Better run. Love you!"

"Love you too. This is going to be fun."

Right as the final word was spoken, there was a quick tap at the door. It swung open, and Hunter stood there, his gaze swinging around the room.

As she started to shut the laptop, Gretchen's voice came through with a desperate note. "Hold it! There's something I forgot to tell you. Veronica's up to something—"

Annie slammed it shut before Gretchen could say more. No way she could let Hunter overhear anything about her previous life, even if she was dying to know what Veronica was up to now.

Hunter eased the door shut behind him, wondering who Annie had been talking to. Must not be a boyfriend. It had sounded like a second female voice in the room as he'd come through the door. She sure shut down quickly, though. Was she hiding something, or had she simply finished working at the exact time he walked in? "Do you need more time to chat with your friend?" Maybe he shouldn't be fishing, but Annie had been a bit mysterious in her actions since arriving in town.

"Not at all. I've finished." She sat up straight. "I was trying to help a friend, but I think we said everything we needed to say. I'm ready to brainstorm now, if you have time? I can always come back later if you need to work." She started to stand.

"No need." He grabbed a chair and spun it around to sit next to her at the end of the desk. "This works. We can chat here. You said you wanted to try to help Carla. Are you thinking of doing research?"

Annie nodded. "You don't happen to know her last name, do you?"

"I wish. She's given several different ones and always says she's not sure if it's right, but that she's pretty sure Carla is her first name. That's going to make it hard to check on her, right?"

"Let's start with what you do know." She leaned her forearms on the desk. "Can you remember the date she showed up in town?"

He settled into his chair. "Hmm. About a year ago, I think."

"Jimmy thought she'd been here a few months, and Carla told me she thought it might be a year. Do you happen to remember the season?"

"This is mid-summer, and I think it was a little later—fall maybe? It wasn't very hot, just pleasantly warm the first time I remember seeing her. She was walking down the road into town, looking a bit lost and bedraggled." He cocked his head to the side. "In fact, now that I think of it, I asked if she needed to see a doctor. She had a cut on her forehead that was dried and not bleeding anymore, but it looked like it might need stitches. She refused and didn't want a ride. She asked if I knew of any houses that had a German shepherd. I thought that was kind of strange, but I let it go and headed home."

"She's mentioned the same dog to me at least once, and said it wasn't a bad memory, but a good one. I wonder if wherever she came from had a dog like that? Maybe her old home?" She flipped open her laptop and powered it on. "Can't hurt to try."

An hour later, Annie closed her laptop again and leaned into her chair. "I'm frustrated. We didn't find a thing." She raised a brow at Hunter. "Should I give up? I mean, she's probably a homeless woman who's been wandering for years, but there's something I can't quite put my finger on. I wish I could figure it out."

Hunter crossed his arms over his chest, the muscles tightening in his biceps. "Don't give up. I agree with you. I've felt drawn to her since I first met her. Maybe it was God's way of trying to get my attention, and I was too thick-headed to figure that out."

"I doubt that." She shot him a playful glance. "You seem to have a brain or two in that handsome head of yours, from what I've been able to tell."

He leaned a little closer until their arms touched on the desktop. "Handsome, huh? That does sound a little better than thick-headed, thanks." He reached out and tweaked a lock of her hair. "You're pretty cute yourself."

As much as she'd love to continue flirting, she wasn't sure she was ready for where it might lead. After all, hadn't her relationship with Scott started in a similar way? Laughter, teasing, compliments, dinner out, a first kiss, then spending day after day together until she landed her part on the show. By that time, she was beginning to believe his feelings for her were real. Now she knew his actions had all been for the sake of the program. No way would she fall for that kind of line again.

Of course, Hunter didn't seem to have anything personal to gain from a relationship with her, but how well did she know him? How well did she want to know him? It was too soon to get involved with someone else. Besides, when her car was finished, she was moving on. Where, she wasn't sure yet, but it wouldn't be this town. Her life and catering business were back in L.A., if she could get over her heartbreak and ever return to start her business up again. She was foolish to have let it go and believed Scott's lies. She had to admit, the man sitting so close beside her had certainly helped ease that heartbreak over the past few days.

She sucked in a deep breath and pushed to her feet. "I'm not going to give up. In fact, I'll tackle it again the next time I come to town, if that works for you? Or I can go to the library, if you'd rather not keep on slogging through the Internet on what might be a wild-goose chase. But right now, my brain is tired, and I think I'll head to Sarah's. I promised to help her cook."

"Ah, that's right." He pushed to his feet and stood less than a foot away, making her heart rate speed up.

"You're a chef. She's lucky to have you staying there. Cooking has never been Sarah's strong suit."

Annie's head spun. Should she tell Hunter her idea? Would he shoot it down or support her? She'd never know unless she tried. "Hunter, if I tell you something, will you promise to keep it to yourself and not get upset with me?"

His brows rose then he gave a slow nod. "Of course, on both questions."

"It's about Sarah."

"Okay. But why don't you sit down and relax for another minute or two. I'm not in a rush, and I'd like to hear what you have to say."

"Thanks." She settled into her chair and drew a deep breath, still unsure what his reaction might be. He'd been very protective of Sarah and her Amish beliefs in the past, and she had a feeling he might be again when he heard her idea.

Hunter leaned back, lacing his fingers, but his gentle smile urged her to continue.

"So—I want to help Sarah expand her business at the inn. She's barely getting by with mostly the Amish who stay there when they travel through on their way to visit family in another town or district. It's not enough, Hunter. I know a way to bring in more people at a faster rate, so she's not always scrimping. I hate that for her."

"I know. I hate it too. What exactly do you have in mind?" A smile tugged at his lips.

"I contacted a friend." Excitement stirred inside Annie as she leaned forward. "She has a travel blog that's taking off and getting noticed nationwide. I asked her if she'd do an article about the Wildwood Inn, highlighting the peace, lack of distractions, and beautiful countryside. Once we get things rolling, we can link to the State Tourist Office. They get thousands of hits per week. Of course, we'll need a few good reviews, since those are more valuable than almost anything, but I'm sure they will come."

"Annie, hold on a second. I want to help Sarah, but I'm not sure about this."

"What isn't there to be sure of? Sarah needs a solid start, and this will give it to her. All I need you to do is to take pictures of the house and maybe a couple of Sarah that we could post on the blog. That's simple, right?"

Hunter's hands dropped to his lap. "I'm sorry, but that's not possible. You don't want her to lose the inn, do you?"

Shock coursed through her at his cool tone. "What? Why? I can't believe you won't agree to take a few pictures to help Sarah. Posting pictures on a travel blog is not going to make her lose it, it's going to allow her to keep it."

"That's just it. It won't. It will hurt her. The Amish don't believe in allowing anyone to take their pictures. Putting Sarah's picture out on the Internet would make life very difficult for her, and she would probably be disciplined by the elders."

Annie's hand slipped up to her throat. She felt sick to her stomach. "No way. That doesn't make sense to me at all. People have their photos taken all the time. You mean they don't have pictures of their kids growing up?"

"To them, it's a form of pride and vanity, and it's not allowed. You need to understand, Annie. Your world is different from theirs. You have one set of beliefs; they have another. In the Amish community, the needs of the whole outweigh the needs of the one. If the rest of the community comes to believe she's forgotten that, she could be shunned. At the least, they may pull away from her."

She wanted to rant and yell, but it would do no good. However, she had to try one last time. "It's not pride. It's wanting to share with family or keep a memory alive. That philosophy is antiquated and out of date with the world."

"But she's not *of* the world, Annie. That's the whole point. She joined the church, which in essence means she's taken a vow to turn her back on the world and live a simple, plain life. By trying to change Sarah, you will only bring confusion and pain into her life. Is that fair?"

That last question about finished her. She hung her head, ashamed she'd come so close to hurting her friend. "No," Annie whispered the word. "I guess not."

"Annie, look at me."

She raised her head, and he reached over, touching her cheek with the tip of his finger, so light she almost thought she imagined it.

Annie sat frozen for what seemed like a millennium but couldn't have been more than three seconds. More than anything, she wanted to lean into this man, to be held in his strong arms, to soak in his quiet steadfastness.

Then reality hit her harder than the fakeness of the show she'd been on for three long years. Could any man be trusted to be honest and trustworthy, or were they all like Scott under the surface? She leaned back, breaking the moment. There was no way she'd risk her heart again to find out. "I'll try to remember everything you've said. I don't ever want to hurt Sarah." But her mind continued to spin between Hunter's gentle touch and her need to help her new friend succeed and keep her business. If photos of the Amish people were against the rules, so be it. She'd find a way do it without the use of Sarah's photo. Somehow, someway, she needed to help Sarah save her inn without causing her to lose favor with her community.

Chapter Eighteen

ANNIE COULD BARELY KEEP HER MIND on what Sarah was saying as they finished working in the early afternoon. She prepared dishes for the next day's breakfast while her friend sat at the table going over her ledgers for the inn.

What had Gretchen been about to say? Annie kicked herself for the hundredth time for tossing and breaking her phone. It could be a good thing, though. She wouldn't put it past Veronica to put a P.I. on her tail who might track her using the embedded GPS or whatever that gadget was that detectives on TV used when they found someone by tracking their phone.

She shivered. The last thing she wanted was to have Veronica show up in town—worse yet, on Sarah's doorstep. She'd come in like a tornado, destroy the peace of Sarah's home, and turn this town on its ear.

Somehow, she had to get to the library or Hunter's office and find out what was happening in LA. Maybe she should ask to use Sarah's business phone. She could offer to pay the long-distance charge. But if Sarah overheard her, that could raise questions she didn't want to answer. At least, not yet. She trusted Sarah, probably more than she'd trusted anyone since her grandparents died, but was she ready to let her new friend know she hadn't been totally honest about her past?

"Annie?" Sarah waved a hand in front of Annie's face and gave her a playful smile. "Is everything all right? You seem a bit pale and distracted today. If you would like to lie down, I can take care of the preparation. Remember, you are a guest."

Annie jerked to attention. "Sorry. I guess I've been wishing I had my car. It's been kind of hard depending on everyone else for rides into town when I want to use the Internet."

"*Ya*, I can see how that would be difficult."

She placed the last covered dish in the refrigerator and turned. "All done."

"*Denki*. So sad. All this wonderful food and not many people to share it with."

"How's that going?" Annie gestured at the ledger as Sarah closed it with a snap.

Sarah shrugged.

"That bad, huh?"

"We believe we are in this world, but not of it. However, for me the difficulty comes down to keeping the home I love and the business which I believe ministers to weary hearts and souls as they come here to rest. I wish it wasn't so hard to make it succeed."

Annie squeezed Sarah's shoulder. "You work so hard. I don't understand why the Bishop won't help you and why he'd expect you to close this place when you love it so much."

Sarah sighed. "It is complicated."

"You mean, if it were to succeed, then you'd be able to provide for yourself and would have no need to remarry, and he doesn't like that idea."

"It is not said in those words." Sarah raised weary, sad eyes and stared at Annie.

"That's not fair. I don't care what he says, it's not fair!"

"Please understand, Annie. I do care for Jeremiah. But it is hard to choose between a life with him on his farm and one here, doing what I loved with my Ezra."

"What if I helped?" Annie slipped into the chair across the table from Sarah.

"You have already done so much. I cannot allow you to do more."

"No. I don't mean give you money or cook. There's a lot that could be done to bring new people here. Advertise, put the inn on a website or travel blog. Things I could help with, if you'll let me."

"I know nothing about those things. Besides, that would bring in more *Englischers*, and I do not think the Bishop would approve."

Excitement started pushing out the sadness in Annie's heart. "But that's a good thing. Not about the Bishop, but bringing in more people. They'd love your home. They'd pay top dollar to get a taste of the real Amish life and stay here, even if it were only for a night or two. You'd be full all the time. Think of it, Sarah. You wouldn't have to give up your home or be forced to marry, if you didn't want to." She paused for a moment to give Sarah time to take in all that she'd said. "I have friends who could do it for you. It would only take a day for it to be finished and go live, if you give the word. People from all over the country could find out about you."

Sarah's eyes grew wide. "Is this true?"

"Absolutely."

"But—I cannot ask this of you."

"You didn't ask, I offered. Besides, it's not a big deal, and my friend would love to add your business to her blog."

"Blog?" Sarah's forehead crinkled.

Annie waved her hand. "Never mind, that doesn't matter. It's a place on the Internet where people can find new places to stay when they travel."

Sarah smiled. "I knew God brought you here for a reason."

"It's kind of starting to feel that way, isn't it? So

you'll let me do it?"

"I'd like to try. Thank you, Annie. Now, you need to go to town again? I have grocery shopping I could do, if you don't mind another slow trip in the buggy."

Annie nearly hugged her until she realized Sarah was probably only being kind. "I don't know. Since you haven't mentioned needing to go until now, I'm guessing you only want to help me. It takes a lot of time to hitch the horse and drive to town and back. Maybe I'll start in the morning while it's cool and walk. I haven't gotten enough exercise since I arrived. Then I could stop by Leo's garage and see if there's been any progress on my car."

"Nonsense." Sarah pushed her chair away from the table. "It is no trouble at all. I love spending time with you, but I truly do need a few things. Not so many that I must call Jimmy, but I'm low on fresh produce, milk, and coffee. I am afraid we would have very grumpy guests if I don't serve them coffee each morning."

"All right, if you're sure, I'd love to ride into town with you. It doesn't feel nearly as slow in your buggy now that I've ridden in it a couple of times. In fact, I've found I enjoy the time as I notice the scenery so much more going at a slow, sedate pace." She grinned. "And I loved when you allowed me to drive. Think you'd be willing to chance letting me handle the reins again for a short time?"

Sarah chuckled. "I think we may survive if I allow you to drive, *ya*. You get whatever you need together while I hitch my mare."

A few minutes later they climbed into the buggy, and Sarah guided the horse down the driveway, stopping to look both directions before easing onto the road. "It is a quiet day with very little traffic. Do you need me to remind you of anything before you take the reins?"

Annie shook her head. "I don't think so. Thank you for trusting me."

"As long as my mare trusts your hands on the reins, that is what matters. Steady, gentle, but firm, and you will do fine."

Annie's mouth suddenly went dry. "Maybe I'd better not. I didn't realize your horse would know someone else was driving. What if she doesn't like me or won't listen if I ask her to stop or turn? I don't want to confuse her or cause an accident."

"You will do fine." Sarah held the reins toward Annie. "*Kumm.* Take them. I am sorry I said anything to make you nervous. My old mare knows the way to the market even if no one is driving."

"All right." Annie took the two long, leather straps and clutched them so tight her nails bit into her palms. "Steady. Calm. Gentle. Firm." Her breathing accelerated as she started repeating the words in her mind after she'd said them out loud the first time.

"Annie." Sarah's fingers rested on her arm. "Relax. You must not be stressed over this. Look at my mare. She hasn't so much as flicked her ears after you took over. She is relaxed and not a bit upset. Now, tell me, is there something that's very important you must do in town? How much time will you need? I should be at the market and another store about an hour. Will that be enough?"

Annie drew in a long breath then released it slowly. "Yes. I'm sure it will. If you can drop me at Leo's, I'll talk to him or his daughter, then go to the library and use the Internet for a few minutes afterwards. Will it work for you to pick me up there, or shall I walk to the market and help you load groceries?"

"*Nein.*" Sarah waved her fingers in the air. "The

grocer's boy loads everything for me, and there's a hitching rail in front of the library, so that is fine."

"I'll be sure and be outside before the hour is up, so you don't have to wait. We're coming into town now. I think I'd be more comfortable letting you drive the rest of the way."

"*Ya,* that is fine." Sarah maneuvered the horse and buggy around a corner and another two blocks until she pulled to a stop in front of Leo's garage. "I hope your mechanic has good news for you, although I will be sad if the car is finished early and you leave town sooner than you'd planned."

Annie stepped down from the buggy then turned and looked up at Sarah. "You know what? So will I. I'm not sure I've found the answers I'm searching for yet, so I may decide to stay a little longer even if the car is finished early. If that works for you, of course."

Sarah beamed. "I would like nothing better. Now I should get to the market and let you run your errands. I will see you in an hour." She lifted a hand and waved then clucked to the horse.

Annie pushed open the door of the garage and stepped inside, allowing her eyes to adjust to the dimmer light for a few seconds. Seeing no one at the counter, she walked to a door and pushed it open enough to poke her head through. "Hello? Anyone here?"

"Just a sec." A voice drifted from somewhere near the floor. The sound of wheels squeaking preceded a flat mechanic's dolly as it rolled out from under a jacked-up pickup, with a man in a mechanic's uniform lying flat on his back. He pushed to his feet, then wiped his hands on a rag before stuffing it into his pocket. "My daughter's on her break, so I'm mannin' the desk and workin' on the cars. I'm Leo. How you doin'? You're the one who owns that Ford sedan we're workin' on, right?"

"Yes, sir." She stepped to the counter as he strode behind it. "How's the work coming along? Almost finished fixing her?"

"Gettin' close, missy. Most of the parts are in. I'm waiting for one more, then I can put it all back together. It should arrive in a couple of days. It was on backorder all this time, or I'd a been done with it by now. Probably figure a day to do the work, seeing she's all tore down already. Then button her up, and she should be right as rain. That goin' to work out for you? Sure sorry it's taken so long to get her on the road for you."

"No problem, although I can't believe I've been here so long. I appreciate that you made time to work it into your schedule. I've enjoyed staying with Sarah, and I might even stay in town a few more days once the car is finished, although I'll admit it will be nice to have wheels again." She turned to leave then remembered. "Do you mind if I look in my car? I think there's a phone number in the glove box I might need."

He rubbed his chin. "Sure thing. She's on the far side of the garage, help yourself. But I thought Jimmy did that for you already."

She froze with her hand on the door leading into the shop. "Jimmy? I'm not sure what you mean."

He scratched his head, his face crinkling in confusion. "He came in not long ago and said you sent him to get somethin' out of your glove box. Figured since he dropped you off here and introduced you to my daughter, it was okay. I'm sure sorry if I did wrong by lettin' him look. He said he found it, then went on his way. Didn't have nothing in his hands, though, so I don't think he took anything."

Annie eased back into the office, her desire to find

Gretchen's phone number gone. "No problem. You're right. Jimmy did bring me by. Please don't worry about it. I really don't need anything else out of there right now." She had no way to call Gretchen at the moment anyway.

Jimmy. No wonder he'd been asking questions and looking at her so strangely. Then another thought hit her, and she almost laughed out loud. The Ford didn't have her name on the registration, it had Gretchen's! Maybe he hadn't figured out who *Annie* was yet, but he had to be curious, and he certainly was digging. She'd better be on her guard.

Leo cleared his throat. "I can give you a discount on my labor since you've had to wait so long."

"No need for that. You gave me a fair quote, and I'm guessing you might even find other little things that are needed to put her in tiptop shape. If it ends up coming to more than you expected, I'll understand."

"Nope. A quote is a quote. Won't be a cent more, but I do appreciate your offer. Anything else, missy?"

"Thank you, I think that's all. I'll check in with you again in a few days." She waved then headed out the door, swinging her laptop case, feeling lighter than she had since she'd driven the car into the ditch. Now she could face Gretchen again with a clean conscience when she got home. She'd been dreading breaking the news to her friend that her car was totaled if Leo hadn't been able to fix it.

Home. She halted abruptly on the sidewalk, thankful no one was behind her to bump into her. Was L.A. home anymore? Was that even the life she wanted to return to? She wasn't positive anymore who she was or what kind of life she wanted. A caterer, an actress, a reality star, or a small-town, country girl wanting to start a new life. What would her grandparents say?

More than that—what would her heavenly Father say?

She resumed walking, consumed by the thought. When had everything else in her life become more important than finding God's will? Had she ever prayed about dating Scott or his possible proposal? Certainly not that she remembered. Thinking about it, she doubted he was a Christian. At least, he'd never talked about a personal relationship with God or finding meaning in life through Jesus. Why hadn't she noticed that before now? How could she have become so hardened to God's voice and where He might be leading her?

Something about this town drew her in a way L.A. never had. She was finding more contentment helping Sarah bake and fix meals for her guests than she'd ever done with her own catering business. Hunter—well, Hunter was another story. The man intrigued her. Calmed her. Drew her with his depth and strength of character, as well as his tender heartedness toward Carla and willingness to help families in the community through Habitat for Humanity. Somehow, Scott couldn't measure up in any of those areas. That might not be fair to Scott, since he traveled in different circles and lived in a different world, but his idea of volunteering to help someone was to write a check—he'd never consider doing manual labor or getting his hands dirty. She couldn't imagine him sitting next to a homeless woman in a diner and buying her a meal, or swinging a hammer to help build a house.

Annie sighed as she pushed through the door of the library. Best to shelve these thoughts for a more appropriate time. She needed to find out what Gretchen was talking about with Veronica, in case she needed to put a plan into action. What kind of plan she had no idea, but maybe something would come to her once she knew what the danger might be.

Chapter Nineteen

VERONICA, DOYLE, AND GRETCHEN ALL sat around a table in the conference room. Gretchen glanced from one face to the other, wondering if this was when she got fired. Most people who were given their pink slip were called into Doyle's office, so maybe it wouldn't go that far. The place had been abuzz for days with the effort to find their missing star. She hated that she'd been drawn into the search and was going to be forced to help.

Doyle thumped his fist into his palm, making her jump. "I think the guy is legit. Tell Veronica what he said, Gretchen. In fact, start from the beginning, so she doesn't miss anything."

"Right." Gretchen tried to stall for time, hoping a brilliant plan to divert the conversation would come to her, or someone would blast through the door with urgent news, but nothing happened. "This guy called, claiming he knows where Ann is living."

Veronica's top lip curled. "How many calls does that make since Scott made his dramatic announcement with the offer of a reward? That was a bad idea. Not one of them have brought us any results; they've only cost us money to track down dead-end information. How is this guy any different?"

Doyle steepled his hands under his chin. "Tell her, Gretchen."

"He won't give his name, and his cell number is blocked. But he claims Ann was in a car accident and—"

Veronica sat upright, her eyes wide. "Was she hurt? Did it do any damage to her face or speech?"

Disgust filled Gretchen at the direction the woman's thoughts had gone to first. She wished she could get up and walk out and never look back. But she'd said too much already and couldn't retract any of it without looking like a fool or a liar. Another PA had overheard her conversation with the guy on the phone and reported it to Doyle before she could get rid of him and pretend it didn't happen. He'd questioned her in front of the PA, then dragged her in here. There was nothing to do but tell the truth. "No. The car was banged up, so she's stuck in a very small town in Kentucky while she waits for it to be fixed."

Veronica shook her head. "That makes no sense. Why doesn't she simply fly home?"

"I'm guessing she doesn't want to." Doyle arched a brow. "She'd be easily recognized on a flight. Maybe not so much in a small hick town in the middle of nowhere. Driving makes it easier to not be recognized."

Veronica gave an unladylike snort. "How do we even know it's her? Does he have any proof?"

Gretchen nodded. "He says he has photos, but he'll only show them to Scott." She prayed Veronica would dismiss the whole idea and ignore it like she had with several other reports she didn't believe.

"Interesting." Veronica drummed her fingers on her desk, then picked up her cell phone and hit speed dial. "Scott, honey? Would you come in the conference room for a minute? We need to speak to you."

Annie settled into a chair, then slipped her laptop out of its case. She drummed her fingers on the table waiting for it to boot up and connect. At least she'd been here one other time so it would recognize the network and connect automatically. There. Done. She checked her email first in case Gretchen had written. Nothing. But knowing how busy the production company kept her, it wasn't surprising.

Strange. No new emails from Scott, either. She'd thought he'd have filled her inbox again like he did not long after she left. No doubt her cell phone would have a couple dozen text messages stored in the cloud waiting to be delivered when she replaced her phone. Funny she hadn't felt a need to race out and get another one.

Her fingers hovered over the keys. Check for any new gossip or news centered around her name, or try to connect with Gretchen? Facetime on her phone would be so much quicker and easier, but Skype would have to do—that is, if Gretchen were at her desk.

She logged into her Skype account and sent a request for a video call. It rang at least six times before saying the person on the other end wasn't available. She rolled her eyes. Great. Now what? This was one of the times she'd love to be able to pick up her phone and call or text her friend. Gretchen practically had her phone attached to her body. She'd hear a ping and answer as fast as she could, if she were free. No use crying over the lack of a phone. What was done was done, and part of her was enjoying the freedom she'd had since tossing it.

She hit the video request again with the same result. Looked like the best she could do was send an email and check in again the next time she got to town. She'd meant it when she told Sarah she'd walk. Not knowing was going to drive her crazy if she waited any longer than tomorrow. She wanted answers now.

She exited the screen and opened her browser, then did a quick search for her name. Thousands of results popped up, but most of them were old or repeats. Her eyes scanned the top ten, looking for anything new. One jumped out at her, and she gave a soft gasp.

Reality star Ann Stanway missing. Boyfriend offers reward for information on her location. Has foul play met Stanway or is she hiding from the world and from love?

Hunter pulled his car to a stop in front of Sarah's inn and waited, still wondering if he was doing the right thing. He raised his eyes toward heaven. "Lord, help me not to mess up here." A few seconds later, he strode up the walk and tapped on the door.

It swung open, and Annie gazed at him for a second before her face broke into a wide smile. "Hunter. What are you doing here?"

"I was hoping to talk for a few minutes. Actually, would you take a drive with me? I'd like to show you something, as well."

She looked down at her jeans and tank top covered by a light, lacy thing he presumed passed as a sweater but couldn't possibly be warm. "Am I dressed all right for wherever we're going?"

"Perfect."

"Great. Let me tell Sarah. How long do you think we'll be gone?"

"Maybe an hour."

"Okay. Give me a minute." In less than that, she arrived at the door and slipped outside. "Ready. Where are we headed?"

"It's a surprise. It's super close, but I thought it would be nice to drive." He led her to his truck, his heart rate accelerating as he took her hand and helped her up into her seat. This woman was affecting him way too much for his comfort. What would he do when she decided to leave town? He didn't even want to think about that. Maybe he could find a way to convince her to stay.

He pulled out onto the road. "Before we get there, I want to tell you something." He glanced at her. "I've been doing a lot of thinking about what you said about helping save Sarah's inn."

She held up a hand. "Wait. I want you to know what Sarah told me. She said she feels like God might have brought me here to help her. I know you don't agree, and you think it's a terrible idea to use the Internet to bring her business, but what if she doesn't agree?"

"I do think it's possible God brought you here for a reason." He wanted to retract the words before she got the wrong idea. "I mean, for more than one reason, not only Sarah."

She gave a short laugh. "Yeah, and I've been trying hard to believe that since Sarah suggested it, but I'm struggling with the entire concept. My car went in the ditch. I guess that's the real reason I'm here. I'd like to think I could help Sarah or Carla, but look where my search for info on Carla went. I didn't find anything to uncover who she is or where she might be from. I talked to Sarah, though, and she likes the idea of the travel blog, but you said it would hurt her with her community. I've even tried praying about it, and I didn't get any answers at all. You said it was a terrible idea, so I probably shouldn't have gotten Sarah's hopes up by talking about it to her." She turned her head and gazed out the side window.

"Wow." He reached over and placed his hand over hers. "I don't think I've ever heard you so cynical before. So ready to give up. What happened to Sarah saying you were brought here to help her?" He couldn't believe he was switching over to the other side, but something had been prodding him since she first talked to him about the idea. "Maybe I was too quick to shoot down your suggestion."

"What?" She faced him, her eyes wide. "You know, I'm not even sure who I am anymore, or what I'm supposed to be. Sometimes I don't even like who I've become these past few years."

He swung his gaze back to the road, then navigated down a narrow stretch and parked. "We're here. But before we get out, I want to finish talking. I like who you are, even if you aren't sure who that is yet. So does Sarah. And even more important, you've helped her. When Ezra died, Sarah lost a part of herself—for a while I was afraid she might even walk away from her faith. You were right in thinking she'd be losing something precious if she gives up her business and home. It would be a little like losing Ezra again, since he was such a big part of it all. Since you arrived, I've seen a new faith building. She seems stronger. More at peace. So yes, I do believe God brought you for a reason, and it has much to do with Sarah."

She placed her hand over her heart. "Seriously?"

"Seriously. As for Carla, we'll tackle that again soon. In fact, when we finish here, we can go to my office and do more digging, if you'd like. I think we can discover a clue if we keep at it. She didn't drop out of the sky and appear here a few months ago. There has to be a trail."

"Thank you so much. I don't know what else to say."

"All I ask is that you tread lightly with Sarah. The travel blog might work, if it's done right. But start out slow and easy, okay? So she's not overwhelmed, and it doesn't come back to haunt her. Remember, no pictures of Sarah, but using one of the inn should be fine. Maybe have your friend say limited reservations available, or only open on weekends or something for now. Do you think that would work?"

She bobbed her head, her eyes dancing. "Yes. Oh, yes. I'll make sure it does. I won't get her in trouble. I promise."

Annie walked beside Hunter down a dirt trail leading nowhere that she could see, the afternoon sun shining its warmth on her shoulders. She was so overjoyed at his response in the truck that she didn't even care if what he'd brought her to see was nothing more than a pretty walk along a peaceful path in the woods. She wanted to repay his kindness and let him know how much she appreciated him. Besides, she'd always loved the woods, and she was getting used to so much peace and quiet. The way she felt now, she wasn't sure she could ever return full-time to the noise and pollution of L.A.

"It's pretty here. Are we going to walk far?" She looked around, still not seeing anything until he stopped.

He pointed. "See that ahead? Look lower. Yeah, that's it."

"What is it? A hole in the rock wall with bushes around it?" She moved forward toward the hole placed somewhat low in the rock face. As they drew closer, she saw the hole was bigger than she'd thought. Big enough for her to walk through upright, although Hunter would probably have to duck. "There's a light glowing inside.

Is this a cave?"

"Sure thing. I want you to see what's inside."

"Inside? How far do we have to go?" She shivered. "I'm a bit claustrophobic."

"The cave system extends for miles, but we won't travel the system."

"Have you ever gotten lost?"

He turned a sober expression her direction. "Only once or twice. But I eventually found my way to the mouth." Hunter waited a full five seconds before he burst out laughing. "No. I've never gotten lost. It's well marked and well used. In fact, I'm surprised we have it to ourselves. Some of the Amish community come out from time to time, and an occasional tourist visits."

He extended his hand. "Come on, I'll show you." He stepped inside the mouth of the cave where a lantern emitted the soft light she'd seen from outside. He plucked two unlit, old-fashioned lanterns off a ledge, then took a box of matches from beside one. "This particular cave entrance is on Amish land, and they prefer the old oil lanterns. They've been kind enough to allow visitors here without charge, but some day that could change." He slid the box open then struck a match, lighting both lanterns with the globes raised. As soon as the wick burned at a good height, he put the globes on and handed her one. "There. That should do it. You take this, and I'll keep the other. We'll have plenty of light that way."

She tucked her hand into his, loving the way he enveloped it in his larger, strong one. The touch brought comfort as well as something more—something she didn't think she was quite ready to face yet. But soon, maybe. If she could only bring herself to tell him the truth—who she was and why she was here. Keeping secrets from someone you were growing to care about couldn't be a wise thing to do.

Then fear slammed into her, and she almost pulled her hand away. He'd reject her if he knew she hadn't been honest with him from the start. She had to wait. Find the right time and words, so she didn't blow this.

"Annie?" He stopped and tugged at her hand. "Everything okay? You slowed down and were almost dragging me backward. If you're afraid, we don't have to go any farther. I don't want to upset you or scare you."

She removed her hand from his, feeling lost as soon as she did. "No." She rubbed her upper arms again and hugged herself. "Just cold, I guess. This is open enough I'm not afraid. I assumed it would narrow down, and we might have to crawl, but the ceilings in here are tall and amazing." Stalactites and stalagmites hung and grew from the floor and ceiling, while water dripped from above and puddled along the path. "These rock formations are amazing! It was so warm outside. I wasn't expecting this temperature change."

Hunter set down his lantern then took off his long-sleeved shirt, leaving him wearing a white T-shirt. He held it out so she could slip her arms into the sleeves. She stared at him for a moment before setting her lantern down and complying. "How very kind, thank you. I've never had anyone do that for me before."

He smiled. "Then maybe you're hanging out with the wrong people." He held out his hand again. "Ready?"

"Yes. Let's go. I want to see this." She gazed around, awed by the immensity of the rock formations, but a bit intimidated by the dark fingers clawing toward them from beyond the lantern lights' reach. "It's so quiet."

"Yes, that's one of the things I love about coming here. Wait. Do you hear the running water?"

She hesitated, straining her ears. "Yes." They

continued forward. "It's getting louder."

"We're almost at our destination."

"What is this place, and why are the lanterns here?"

"I came by earlier and lit the one inside the entrance, but there are always lanterns here for visitors who come unprepared. Many years ago, this underground river was the water and power source for the town. Cave City was almost built around it. There are other entrances to this system and other caves in the area. The tunnels and caves, as well as the underground water, run beneath the edge of town, so it was easy for them to sink a shaft and tap into the pure water. We're almost there."

He took three more strides then stopped. He held his lantern up, seeming to get his bearings, then he placed the lamp on a rock formation with a flat top.

"What are you doing?" Annie stared around her, trying to figure out what she should be seeing. The sound of water was closer, and she held up her light. A narrow river ran not more than a dozen feet away, not rushing, but quietly moving as though with a purpose and a plan.

"Wait. Let me adjust the wick. Here, give me yours."

She did as he asked, hating to part with the light, but knowing she could trust him. The glow intensified. Suddenly, the entire cavern sprang to life. The walls, ceiling, and even the floor sparkled with an iridescent glitter. She gasped. "The light reflecting off the rock is beautiful! What's making it do that, Hunter? It's like a perfect light show, courtesy of Mother Nature."

He dropped his voice to a whisper. "No, courtesy of a Holy God who loves us enough to place something of such beauty here that we could enjoy it. It's called vitreous luster. Better known as quartz. It's all over in these caves. Oftentimes gold is found with quartz, but thankfully none was ever found here."

She turned to him. "Thankfully? Wouldn't the town want to find gold?"

He shook his head. "Some things are more valuable than gold." He took a step closer and placed his hands on each of her shoulders. "Still cold?"

"No. In fact, I'm quite warm . . . now." She smiled up at him, loving his strength and peace.

He drew her a little closer, wrapping her in his arms. The beat of his heart came through his shirt, and she sighed. She hadn't even known this was what she'd been longing for.

"Annie?"

"Hmm?" A sweet dreaminess stole over her, and she didn't want this moment to end.

Hunter drew back a bit and tipped up her chin. "I care about you very much. I hope you believe that." Slowly, he lowered his head and gave her a sweet kiss. One that was altogether too short to her way of thinking. He lowered his hands, his eyes wide as light reflected off his handsome features.

"Hunter." She breathed his name, not wanting to break the spell.

He reached out and pulled her to him again, holding her in a strong embrace, then met her lips. His kiss was longer, sweeter, but with an insistent urgency that almost took her breath away. She slipped her arms around his neck, wanting to prolong the kiss. Not wanting to think through the ramifications or the what-ifs. Simply longing to savor every wonderful second and pray it wouldn't end.

Jimmy sat at the counter of the Blue Moon Diner,

bouncing his knee and staring at his phone.

Linda, the older lady on shift at the moment, leaned forward, holding the coffee pot. "Refill, Jimmy?"

"Sure." He looked up and tried to smile, but there was a hard knot in the pit of his stomach. Was he doing the right thing? Had he blown it big time, responding to the reward offer for information on Ann Stanway? The people he'd talked to earlier certainly didn't sound too grateful. "Expecting a call."

"Ah. Business, right?"

"Yeah. You wait. I'm going to hit the big time soon. You'll only see my tail lights leaving town." At least, he hoped that was the case.

She leaned her forearms on the counter. "Good for you! I hope it all works out. You deserve a break."

"Thanks." His phone's ring tone jangled, making him jump. He glanced at the screen and gulped. "Sorry, gotta go." He held it up to his ear as he dashed for the door. He answered before it hit the third ring, trying to quiet his breathing. No way could he let this guy know he was nervous or having second thoughts. "Hello?"

"This is Scott Adson. Who am I talking to?"

Jimmy pumped his fist in the air, adrenalin surging as he saw a successful future looming ahead, after all. He couldn't worry about Annie. This was what was best for her, anyway. She was a star and didn't belong in their small town. One day, she'd thank him for helping her. "Hey, man. Good to talk to you. It's a pleasure."

"Who is this? Your name, please." The voice on the other end was anything but warm and friendly.

Jimmy sobered. "Jimmy. Uh, James. James Snyder."

"Fine, Jimmy. Let's cut to the chase. You told one of our PA's that you have info on Ann Stanway. What makes your claim any different than the couple of dozen dead ends we've gotten from other losers hoping to get the reward and get their name in the paper."

Jimmy halted under a tree to the side of the gravel parking lot. "I told you. I have pictures to prove it."

"Right. Pictures can be faked."

Jimmy's hackles rose. The nerve of this guy. "They aren't fake. She's right here in this town."

"How do I know that? How do I know you aren't only after the reward?"

Jimmy gritted his teeth and tried to answer with a civil tone. He didn't want to blow this opportunity. It was too important for his future. "Because I don't want a reward, that's why."

Silence met his ears for several seconds, then he heard a short laugh on the other end. "So you're calling out of the goodness of your heart. If you don't want a reward, then what do you want?"

"I'm a big fan of your show, Mr. Adson. I know how all of this works. I want a piece of the action. I don't want money, but if you want to know where Ann is, I want your word I'll get a part on your show."

Chapter Twenty

HUNTER SAT IN FRONT OF HIS computer, with Annie beside him, trying to shake the memory of that kiss from his mind so he could concentrate on the quest for Carla's past. Nearly impossible with Annie sitting so close and peering at the screen. Had she felt what he had there in the cave? The drive to his office had been nearly silent, with only a quiet thank you for showing her the hidden beauty, then she asked if they could still do the research on Carla.

Who was this woman who had dropped into his life such a short time ago? Was she exactly what she appeared to be—a woman who had a catering business in L.A., traveling to visit friends or family somewhere beyond their little town? Or was there another story he'd yet to hear—the one that made her keep commenting on not being sure who she was or where she belonged. Somehow, he had to convince her she belonged here. With him. Or at least with Sarah, so he and Annie would have time to get better acquainted. It about killed him to think that she might leave after her car repairs were finished, and he might not see her again.

"Hunter." She nudged his arm. "Are you going to boot up your computer or stare at the blank screen?" She gave what sounded like a nervous laugh. "I don't want Sarah to worry about me."

"Oh. Right. Sorry." He hurried to comply then opened a browser. "I had an idea. I'm going to do a search for missing persons, female, in Kentucky, around the time period we know she came to town. If that returns no results, I'll widen the search to surrounding states."

She bumped shoulders with him. "Have I ever told you how brilliant you are?"

He grinned, liking the lighter note that had crept into her voice. "Nope. And I sure don't mind if you tell me again."

She punched him this time. "Once is enough, mister. Now start typing."

"Hey, Ms. Pushy! All right, all right. I'm typing." He tossed her another grin and hit the keys, entering a search for reports of missing persons in the state of Kentucky in the last year. Several popped up, all with pictures, but none were even close to what Carla looked like now.

They spent several more minutes scouring the Kentucky results, then Hunter turned to Annie. "Think it's time to broaden the search?"

Annie nodded. "But which state? How many states touch Kentucky's border?"

He pulled up a map of the state and studied it. "Looks like seven. Missouri, Ohio, Indiana, West Virginia, Tennessee, Illinois, and Virginia. That's a lot of territory to cover."

"She doesn't have a southern accent, although that might not mean anything, since she could have been raised anywhere. But regardless, let's start with Illinois, Indiana, and Ohio."

"Sure. Sounds like good reasoning to me. If we strike out there, we can go to the next two until we hit them all. Hopefully, we'll find a clue in one of them."

Annie sat back in her chair and sighed. "Unless she's not missing. Her family may know she wanders around and not care. It's possible no one has reported her as missing. What then?"

"I'm not sure. We can't exactly take it to the police,

as she's not a child and hasn't committed a crime. If she's ever been fingerprinted, she'd be in the system, but that wouldn't necessarily tell us why she's here and doesn't remember her past. But we'll want to keep that option open though, since the police department has resources we don't have."

"I'm worried it could be drug related—that her mind has been destroyed over the years. If that's the case, I'm not sure we can help her, other than try to convince her to live at a shelter."

Hunter shrugged. "I've tried numerous times. She's not open to that idea. But hey, let's not give up before we finish searching."

"Right." She sat forward. "Hit it."

They plowed through the records for Indiana and Illinois with no results. Hunter poised his fingers over the keys. "You have enough time to check Ohio, or should I take you home?"

She looked at her watch. "Let's do it. We've come this far, and I hate to quit until we've checked at least half of the states."

"Here we go." His fingers raced over the keyboard, then he hit enter. A screen came up with a list of names reported missing the past year, with ages and links to see a photo. "Let's narrow it down to women above the age of thirty-five, since some of these are teen runaways." He narrowed the search and hit enter again. Three names popped up along with descriptions, contact numbers of family and sheriff or local police offices, as well as the last photo the family could provide.

They stared at the screen. A picture of a blonde woman wearing make-up, her hair neat and tidy, stared at them. It was a much more put-together version of Carla than the one they knew, but definitely Carla.

Annie leaned forward, her heart racing, and read out loud. "Missing: Clara Blackwell. Age 50, went missing after going shopping in Oak Hill, Ohio. Her wrecked car was found off the road a few miles from town, with no sign of Clara in the vicinity. Please contact the local police office and her husband at the following numbers if you have information. Reward offered."

Hunter reached out and pulled Annie into a hug, laughing and patting her on the back as he embraced her. "We did it! Someone *is* looking for her. The town she came from is nearly three-hundred miles from here, and across a state line. Maybe that's why she hasn't been found. The police and her family expected she'd still be in Ohio, not Kentucky."

Annie pulled away and wiped her fingers under her eyes trying to stem the tears. "I can't believe I'm crying. I barely know Carla—or Clara, since that's what it says her real name is—but I'm so happy I can't stand it. Now, what do we do?"

Hunter exhaled a loud breath. "I'm not sure. My first inclination is to call her husband, but I think proper protocol would be to call the sheriff and ask him to contact her husband. They might want a picture of her or some other proof it's really her before they tell her husband. I mean, what if we're wrong, and she only looks like this woman? I'd hate to get his hopes up."

"I didn't think of that." Her excitement shriveled a little as she peered at the picture again. "It is hard to imagine Carla could have looked so put together and well-groomed, but if that's not Carla, it has to be her sister. That's too strong of a resemblance to not be her, don't you think?" She clasped her hands, hating the idea they might have hit yet another dead end.

"Let's not assume anything until we talk to the authorities. Did you need to check your email or anything while you're here? I can step into the other room and call him if you want to do that real quick."

"Oh. Yes! I'd forgotten I need to. I sent a note to a friend this morning, and I've been wondering if she's answered. It'll only take a minute. Thanks." Annie's pulse throbbed in her ears. What if Gretchen still hadn't responded? How could she find out what Veronica was up to? As soon as the door clicked behind Hunter, she opened her mail account and searched the new entries. Bingo. Gretchen's was the third one down, and as usual, it was full of exclamation points and all caps. She skimmed it quickly, then read it again as her stomach almost catapulted into her throat.

Ann—you need to WATCH YOUR BACK!! Some guy named Jimmy called saying he knows you, and he plans to talk to Scott. He says he has pictures of you as proof!!! He won't talk to anyone but Scott, and he's taking the call right now!!! Maybe you need to leave town??? Like, NOW! I don't know what Veronica will do, but I wouldn't put it past her to send Scott out there. Call me if you can. YOU NEED TO GET ANOTHER PHONE, GIRL!!!

Hunter stuck his head back into the office. "I talked to the sheriff. He thinks it's worth talking to Clara's husband. I gave him my number and asked that he keep in touch." He stepped inside then closed the door behind him. "You okay? You look kind of pale."

Her mind spun, racing back and forth between Hunter's good news about Carla and Gretchen's upsetting report about Veronica and Scott. What now? Should she take Gretchen's advice and drop everything and run? She closed her email account, wishing she'd had time to reply to Gretchen's note. "I'm okay I guess.

And that's great about Carla. I hope her husband or the officials call you soon to follow up. I had a little unsettling news from my friend, is all. Nothing I can't handle."

He walked to his desk and held out his hand. "Anything I can do to help?"

She placed her hand in his and allowed him to pull her to her feet. She tightened her grip and moved a step closer. "Not a thing, other than being you." Maybe it was time to tell Hunter the truth about why she was here and why she'd run away from L.A. But she didn't know where to start. How had it all gotten so complicated? Could she tell him the truth without causing him to view her differently? She wanted him to like her for herself, not because of the name she'd made for herself in Hollywood. Was that so terrible? But what if he got angry she hadn't told him the whole truth?

He grinned. "I'm afraid I can't change that, so you've got it. Ready to go home?"

"Yes." She gave a slow nod. "I believe I am."

Hunter darted a glance at Annie as they rode in silence to Sarah's. What had that email contained that had upset her to the point she'd lost most of the color in her face? He'd thought she'd be exuberant over the fact they'd found a family member who was looking for Carla, but that had taken a backseat to whatever news she'd gotten from her friend. Was the friend sick or in need of help, and Annie didn't know how to respond? Maybe she wanted to go visit the person, but with her car not finished, it wasn't possible.

He cleared his throat and reached across the seat,

taking her hand. "Annie?"

She turned a distracted gaze on him. "Hmm?"

"I can loan you my truck or get you another car to drive, if you need to go see your friend. I mean, if she's in trouble or something, and you feel you need to go. I don't want you to feel you're trapped here because you don't have a working vehicle yet."

"Oh. Right." She nodded, but he could tell her thoughts were still a thousand miles away. "I might take you up on that. I haven't decided what to do yet, but thank you." She edged a little closer to him and squeezed his hand. "I appreciate you, Hunter. I truly do."

His heart sank. 'Appreciate.' Was that all there was to her feelings for him? Appreciation? Only recently he realized he'd been hoping for more. Every time he saw her, she grew more important to him, someone he wanted to keep in his life and hold close. But maybe she only saw him as a friend—someone to appreciate. He mustered a smile and squeezed her hand in return. "Whatever you need, Annie. I'll be here. Always. Just let me know how to help, okay?"

She nodded as he pulled up in front of Sarah's house. He exited the truck and ran around to her side to open her door. "Looks like Sarah has a guest." He pointed to a car. "It has rental stickers on it, so the person must have flown into the airport and driven here. Amish don't rent cars, so it's got to be an *Englischer*. Has your friend mentioned the Wildwood Inn on her travel blog already?"

Annie stared at the car, her eyes wide, then slowly shook her head. "No." The word came out as a whisper. "I have no idea who it might be."

He walked beside her up the path and opened the door, allowing her to go first. "Sarah? You here? Annie and I are back."

"In the kitchen, Hunter. Annie has a friend who's come to visit."

Annie halted in the hallway, and her hands started to shake.

Hunter moved beside her. "Are you all right?"

"Yeah. Sure." She gave him a brittle smile. "Guess I need to see who my company is, huh?"

He stepped close, wanting to comfort her but not knowing how, or what she needed. Something appeared to be wrong, but he couldn't imagine what.

Chapter Twenty-One

ANNIE HEARD A STEP AND FROZE. As soon as Sarah had said there was a visitor here, she'd wanted to run.

"Ann? Is that you?" An all too familiar voice spoke in the hallway that led to the kitchen.

Annie stayed rooted to the spot, willing her mind to engage and figure a way out. "Scott?"

The man she'd once thought so handsome stared at her. He looked the same, his clothing perfect and his hair scruffy. Why hadn't she ever noticed that he always looked like his hair was badly in need of a cut—but that was the way he liked it. His face was clean shaven, and his eyes appeared rested—definitely not those of a man worried about his missing girlfriend. He strode toward her and wrapped her in a hug.

She pulled part way out of his embrace, but he slid his hands down her arms and grasped her fingers. "What are you doing here, Scott?"

His eyes widened. "What am I doing here? Looking for you, of course. You ran off without a word. No one at the office knew where you'd gone, and we've been sick with worry. I was afraid something happened to you."

"I'm fine." She struggled to get free and peek over Scott's shoulder at Hunter.

He squeezed her hands. "You have every right to be mad at me. But I want you to know that I've learned my lesson. I'm a changed man. I want you to come home. I'll make things right, Ann."

"Scott . . ." She gently tugged at her hands, not wanting to make a scene with Hunter watching, but Scott refused to release her. What must Hunter be thinking? His expression was almost neutral, but she was certain she'd seen a flicker of frustration or anger cross his face before he schooled it.

"I want to make things right. That's why I had to find you. So I could tell you that letting you go was the worst decision of my life."

"I think it was the other way around. I seem to remember I let you go."

"Fine, but I'm here now, and that's what matters. I know we can work this out because I still care about you. I always have."

She glanced at Hunter again, and this time, her tug caused Scott to release her hands.

However, it also made him aware of the silent man standing nearby. He pasted on his most conciliatory smile. "Hey, man. I'm Scott Adson, star of *Life with the Adsons*. I'm trying to have a moment with my girlfriend, if you don't mind."

Annie gasped and opened her mouth to reply, but Hunter raised his hand and forestalled her, then he pivoted and swung open the foyer door.

"Hunter, wait!" Annie lunged toward him, but Scott grasped her arm. She tried to shake it loose as Hunter turned one last inquiring gaze on her.

Hunter froze and stared at Scott's hand. "Get your hand off the lady. She may be your girlfriend, but that's no way to treat a woman." He stepped close, looming over the shorter man.

Scott loosened his grip and raised his hands. "Hey, I wasn't hurting her. I was excited to see her, that's all. Not that it's your business."

"It's always a man's business if a lady is being treated with disrespect. Annie, are you all right with this guy or do you want me to send him packing?"

"Please stay, Hunter. I should talk to Scott since he

came all this way, but I don't want you to leave. And he's not my boyfriend, no matter what he says."

"Sorry, I can't do that, Annie. I'm afraid I've been lied to before, and I'm tired of being burned. Enjoy your time with your . . . friend." He stepped outside and pulled the door shut behind him.

She ran down the sidewalk as Hunter closed his truck door and started the engine. "Hunter, please! Don't leave."

He lowered the window and gave her a soft smile. "It's all good. Have a nice day . . . Ann." He put the truck in gear and drove off.

Annie swung around to find Scott standing close behind her, wearing a half-amused, speculative expression. "Hey, I recognize him now. He's the guy from the photo."

She stared at him, wondering what he could possibly be talking about now. Hadn't he done enough damage, showing up here and chasing Hunter away? "What photo?"

"The ones someone sent me of you and that—that person who just left. Some local guy from this two-bit town called the studio and claimed the reward." He waved his hand toward where Hunter had driven off. "Nearly ten days since you walked off and left me, and you've already moved on." He shook his head. "I'm surprised. I thought what we had was more special than that. I didn't expect you to find some new bozo to play with as soon as you left town."

He reached for her again, but she pushed his hands away. "Leave, Scott. Go back to L.A. where you belong. You aren't wanted here."

He grimaced. "Right. Sorry. I guess I deserved that. But I want to point out that I'm here alone. No cameras, no crew, in the hope we could talk, just the two of us.

Don't you think you owe me and the show that much since you left town without so much as a word? You have to realize the spot you put all of us in at home."

She gritted her teeth, hating to admit that he might have a point. No doubt he wouldn't leave until she talked to him anyway. "Fine. No cameras. What do you want?"

He took a step closer, but she held up her hand, and he stopped. "I want us to be together again. I miss you. I had no idea how much until you disappeared. I hoped you'd give us a chance again."

She looked into his eyes, searching for the shallow man she suspected him to be, but saw only truth. "You really mean that?"

"Yes. Very much. I can't believe you don't know that I love you. My life doesn't feel right without you."

Annie's resolve didn't weaken as she examined this man she'd once believed she loved—and not that long ago. But she did need to be fair. Had the network's decision to put Jess in her place been his fault, or was all of this on his mother's shoulders? Had she judged him too harshly, not giving him a chance to talk it all out before she left home, as well as refusing to return his calls and texts? This man who stood before her seemed like the old Scott—the one she'd fallen for in the first place—the gentle, caring man who wanted to put her first. She shook off the thought before it could take hold, remembering the Scott he'd become and how disillusioned she'd been.

She had to be sure. "What about the show?" She held her breath, wavering between wanting him to prove his love hadn't been a lie and hoping he'd let her go. She hated the thought she'd been a complete, naïve fool to believe he'd loved her, only to discover now every part of her last three years had been a lie. Had all of it been about the show as she'd come to believe, or did a small part of this man honestly care?

His forehead scrunched. "What *about* the show? Of course you'd come back. We'll get rid of Jess and give you your old role. It can all return to the way it was."

She was surprised how little that hurt, but deep inside, she'd known. His trip to Cave City *was* about the show. It had never really been about them, no matter what she'd tried so hard to believe. "That's exactly what I thought. No way, Scott. It can never be like it was before, because *nothing* was real. Don't you get that? That's why I left. I can't pretend to live in a fairytale any longer."

"No. That's not true. Maybe some of the show was for the fans, but not my feelings for you. Those were real the entire time. Besides, I plan to get more involved with the production side of the show. I'm not going to allow my mother and Doyle to call all the shots anymore. We can change things—make it more like you wanted from the beginning. I'll have more power to run it the way I want. I love you, Ann."

Annie stood on the path to the house, wondering if Sarah was worried or watching from the window. What must she think of this man who'd barged into her world and into her home? And Hunter . . . she didn't even want to think of the damage done there. "I know you think that. I believe you mean well, but my returning to the show won't happen. You fell for an inexperienced girl that the fans see through a soft-focus lens, but that's not me. That's not the real Ann Stanway. I'm not who you think I am, and I no longer want to be that phony girl."

He stared without speaking for several long seconds, then slowly nodded. "So, it's over. You won't come home with me?"

Relief flooded her in waves and boosted her courage. "That's right. I'm sorry if that hurts you, but I don't think our relationship ever really began. What we had was an illusion, nothing more. You're a nice enough guy, and I know you think you love me, but it's over. I don't feel the same. It's time to move on."

His lips parted, then he snapped them shut, turned and headed to his car without looking back.

Annie waited until he drove out of sight, wondering. She'd never seen Scott give in so easy—unless it was to his mother. But he'd always gotten his way when he and Annie disagreed. What made him accept her decision and leave? She shook her head, not able to figure it out, but thankful he'd seen fit to give up.

She ran up the path and slipped inside the door. Sarah stood by the window where she must have been looking out. Annie couldn't blame her. Her friend had to be confused about what she'd witnessed, and no telling what Scott had said to her before she arrived. "Sarah, I'm so sorry. I'm not sure what to say."

Sarah shook her head. "That man said you're a famous actress, and he was here to take you home to Hollywood. Is that true?"

"No. I'm not really an actress, but I did work in Hollywood."

"I do not understand." Sarah beckoned toward the kitchen. "I have a pot of tea on. *Kumm.* Sit. Tell me what has happened if you would like to."

Sarah's gentle spirit and quiet tone went a long way toward soothing Annie's bruised heart. How freeing to realize it wasn't bruised over Scott, but more for the damage he'd caused to her new friends and her peace of mind. "I was on a TV show for three years, but *I* didn't think I was acting—at least, not where my feelings were concerned. It was something called a reality show, meaning the cameras follow you all the time, filming parts of your life. Scott was part of that life, but something happened recently to make me realize it wasn't reality at all, but a sham. I needed to get away."

Sarah poured tea into two cups, then handed one to Annie and slipped into the chair across the table. "So, you came here."

"Yes. The producer changed things on the show, and it woke me up—made me realize what a fool I'd been, believing any of it was real. I wanted to run as far from that place as I could. When I ended up in that ditch and met you, I was transported to my childhood—meeting you and Hunter, living a simpler life, all helped me remember what reality truly is. Not a fake, glitzy world where people chase you for autographs and pictures, but a peaceful one, where people are known for their strong values and kindness. I didn't know until I got here how much I missed that." She shook her head. "Somehow, I lost myself, and it took coming here to figure out who I am and who I truly want to be."

Sarah tapped her fingertips together. "I see. Well, I suppose I don't really, but I am trying to understand. What about your cooking? Your catering business and being a chef?"

"I was never a true chef, although I did have my own catering business. In fact, that's how Scott and I met. I was catering a party he attended, and he struck up a conversation with me, then asked me out to coffee the next day. I was impressed that he didn't try to hit on me and take me out that night for drinks. He was the perfect gentleman, never presuming or pushing. I think that's why I fell for him in the first place."

"So, you fell in love with him?" Sarah's voice was soft with no hint of censure.

Annie bit her lip and thought for a moment.

"Looking back, I'm not sure I was ever in love with Scott. Maybe in love with the idea of being in love with someone so popular, or having someone notice me in a town where I'd felt like such an outsider. I was drawn to him because he was so different from what I thought Hollywood personalities would be. Within a few weeks we became an item, then he asked me to be on his show, *Life with the Adsons.* I couldn't believe someone like him—a famous TV star—would even notice a small-town girl with a country background, much less show a serious interest, so I agreed. But it was never my dream, even though I came to L.A. in the first place half thinking I might land an acting job. After I went on the show, I missed cooking and catering. It was hard to walk away from that part of my life, especially when I wasn't totally satisfied with my new life."

Sarah took a sip of her tea then smiled. "*Gutt.* Because I will need your help."

"Huh? I'm not sure I follow?"

"Whatever your friend did on the Internet, it must have worked." Her eyes sparkled as she leaned forward and touched Annie's hand. "I already have two different couples who have contacted me, wanting to come soon. One arrives tomorrow. I have you to thank for that."

"Oh, my! That's great, Sarah! I didn't realize Gretchen had the information up already—she'll add a picture of the inn and grounds after I have time to send them. I only gave her basic info, so I didn't expect it to get done so fast. I know your inn will be a success. I'll help in any way I can."

"*Denki.* So, should I still call you Annie? Your friend called you Ann."

She shook her head. "No, I'll always be Annie to you and everyone I've met here. I'd like to think I left Ann behind in Hollywood."

"That is *gutt.* But what about Hunter?" Sarah's warm eyes studied Annie over the rim of her cup as she took another slow drink.

Annie's heart sank. "I'm afraid it's too late. He saw Scott hug me and heard him call me his girlfriend. Ugh. Hunter probably hates me."

"*Nein.* He couldn't hate you. But you must go see him. Tell him the truth. You cannot keep secrets any longer. It is not good for your soul or for your friendships."

Annie bowed her head for a moment, then she met Sarah's eyes. "I know. But I don't know if he'll forgive me."

"He cares for you. The same way you care for him."

Annie felt heat surge into her cheeks. "Is it that obvious? I mean, we haven't known each other long. We don't have any kind of understanding, and he doesn't owe me anything."

"*Ya,* it is obvious to anyone with eyes to see. It does not matter if you are Amish or *Englisch*; matters of the heart are all the same." She started to rise. "I will go outside to the phone and call Jimmy. He can drive you to town."

"No. Please don't. I've left two messages for him lately, and he hasn't returned my calls or come to see me. He's definitely avoiding me."

Sarah arched her brows, her eyes wide. "Why would he do that? Jimmy might be a little eccentric at times, but he has a *gutt* heart."

"That may be, but a friend in L.A. told me he's the one who contacted Scott and told him where to find me. The studio was offering a reward, and he sent them pictures and gave them your address."

Sarah pushed to her feet. "Then you must go see Hunter. I will take you to see him first thing tomorrow morning."

Chapter Twenty-Two

HUNTER SAT AT HIS DESK, BARELY able to take in that it had been less than twenty-four hours since the guy who apparently was Annie's ex showed up. He'd thought—or at least hoped—that a lasting relationship with Annie might be possible. After the trip to the caves and the heart-jolting kiss they'd shared, his hope had fanned into something like a solid belief, only to be snuffed out when that Hollywood guy showed up at Sarah's inn.

Time to put it behind him. Obviously, Annie—or Ann, as the man had called her—would be leaving town and reuniting with her boyfriend soon—no matter what she'd claimed. If she hadn't already left. He didn't know what to think or believe anymore. He'd thought she might be hiding something, but no way had he guessed she'd have lied to him about her past—allowing him to think she was a country girl who'd become a cook in the city but never saying anything about being a reality star.

He knew all about her now. It hadn't taken much searching on the Internet to find out the whole, sordid story of her escape from Hollywood. No doubt this was another stunt for the show. Run away from the show and have the boyfriend follow. No doubt the cameras would show up next.

A tap sounded at his door. Not the bold, confident one of a friend or client, but a timid, hesitant one. His heartbeat accelerated. "Come in." He tried to clear the gruffness from his voice, but it didn't work.

Annie walked through the door and closed it carefully behind her. "We need to talk."

"No." He shook his head. "We don't. I think everything has been said—or at least, been made clear."

She twisted her hands. "Scott Adson is not my boyfriend. It was all an act."

He lounged back in his chair. "Sorry. But it didn't look like an act when he pulled you into a big hug and didn't let go. Although I believe the act part—from the time you arrived in Cave City you've been acting." He shook his head. "Besides, that's not the half of the problem, and you know it."

Her hands dropped to her sides. "I didn't know he was going to show up like that. I haven't returned any of his calls since I left Hollywood. That life wasn't real. None of it. I didn't realize that at first, but I certainly do now."

He steeled his heart against her, not wanting to get sucked in again. "You mean the reality show you're a part of, what happened at the caves, or what happened at Sarah's?"

Her face lost some of its color. "You knew about the reality show?"

"No. I didn't have a clue. Totally blindsided me. I watch very little TV and never those shows. But that guy looked familiar even to me, so when he introduced himself as Scott Adson, I did a little digging on the Internet. Your name and his, as well as your pictures, were splashed pretty much everywhere. It wasn't hard to figure things out from there. Especially when I saw a notice for a reward for the missing Ann Stanway posted on every site." He tried to laugh, but it came out more like a grunt. "Ann Stanway, huh? So, you changed more than your hair. Nice job on that, by the way."

She stared at him without moving, then motioned toward the chair. "May I sit? I'd like to talk about this. Please? I know I should have told you."

Hunter wanted to stride around his desk, grab her in his arms, and show her what a real hug felt like, but he pushed down the desire. "I'm not sure there's much point in talking. Besides, tell me what? That all of this was a game to you? Part of the show? Where were the cameras, hiding in the bushes so they could get the whole reunion scene?" He hated himself for his snide tone, but a deep hurt kept him going. "I'm glad I know now that nothing was real about your time here, Ann."

She stiffened. "Yes. It was." Her voice was a mere whisper, but it still sent chills up his arms.

"Was what? Real? It's all over the Internet. How you broke up, and how you ran off. They've been searching for you, and apparently, the show's ratings have soared since your stunt. You did a great job of making me believe you cared. As far as I'm concerned, we'll work together to finalize this deal to help Carla get home, if she wants to go, but that's all. I heard from her husband, and he's coming tomorrow. If you want to be at the diner at two o'clock so you can meet him and see if she recognizes him, you're welcome to come. Then we're done."

"You think all of this was an act for me? That everything I did—our kiss—wasn't real? But that's not true."

"I can't think of any other reason you'd do what you did and not tell me the truth."

She looked at him with tears brimming in her eyes. "Maybe because for the first time in years I felt like you—and others—actually cared about me—for me. For who I am, not due to my supposed fame. Maybe I was afraid of ruining that if you or anyone in town knew." She flicked her hand in the air. "And look what happened—the first person to recognize me sent for Scott and got a reward for his information." She waited, as though hoping he'd relent and forgive her.

"Fine. I guess I can buy that, but where was the trust, Ann? If you cared about me, you wouldn't have lied to me. You should have been able to trust me. I grew up with honest, trusting people who didn't hide things. And not so long ago, I had a very bad experience with a woman who loved playing games. Sorry, but I can't think of it any other way."

"But I didn't lie, I just . . ." She hesitated, deep longing in her eyes, then turned and slipped softly out the door, letting it click behind her.

He'd been honest when he said he didn't understand why she couldn't trust him, but something inside died a little as the door shut behind her. But in his world, if someone lied, even by intentional omission about one important part of their life that impacted a relationship, then there could be no *real* relationship. He'd learned that the hard way with his last girlfriend, and he wasn't going there again, even if his heart screamed with pain at the thought of letting Annie leave without racing after her.

Chapter Twenty-Three

ANNIE CRAWLED INTO HER BED THAT night and snuggled under the comforter, thankful the heat had abated at least for the evening, and a cool breeze had sprung up. She'd held onto her emotions since arriving home, answering Sarah when she spoke to her without much thought. Bless her; Sarah seemed to understand and didn't push to have a conversation. One of the couples who'd seen her ad on Gretchen's travel blog had arrived, and the second couple would come tomorrow. She was happy for Sarah, but right now, even that small victory felt hollow and meaningless.

How could Hunter think all of her actions were lies or merely acting? Didn't he know her better than that? He said it was a matter of trust, but if she'd told him sooner, she was positive his actions and attitude toward her would have changed. Everyone treated her differently as soon as they figured out who she had been in her other life. And that was the last thing she wanted from Hunter.

Thankfully, the truth didn't appear to have affected Sarah. But her friend was different. She'd never been part of the outside world, and she had no real concept of what a reality star was, or how it might have impacted Annie's life.

She threw off the comforter as a wave of remorse turned her body hot with shame. Trust. She'd had trouble trusting Scott in the past, when she'd seen him flirting with another woman and thought he might have strayed. She'd allowed herself to be convinced he was only acting, but now she wondered. How faithful had he been since they'd started dating? Had she been a fool to ever trust him, based on the life he lived and the way he'd treated her over the past few months?

How could she expect Hunter to trust her, when she hadn't been any more honest with him than Scott had been with her? Even worse, she hadn't trusted her heavenly Father. She'd been trying to hide the truth due to her own fears and insecurities, not knowing who she was anymore or what direction her life should take. Why hadn't she thought to give this over to the Lord and allow Him to take control? If only she'd done that before she ever left L.A. Even more so, she should have asked for His guidance before ever taking the part on *Life with the Adsons*. She covered her face with her hands, trying to hold in the sobs that threatened to erupt, but a soft wail broke free.

A few moments later, a knock sounded on her door, and Sarah peeked inside. "Annie? I heard you. What is wrong?" She took in Annie's tear-stained face and walked forward, then settled on the edge of Annie's bed and stroked her hair like a mother would a child. "It would help to talk about it, maybe?" She pulled out a tissue from the box on the nightstand and tucked it into Annie's hand.

"I don't know. Maybe." Annie sniffed then blew her nose. "I guess it might. It won't change anything, but I appreciate that you care enough to listen."

"Always. It is Hunter, *ya*?"

"*Ya.*" Annie smiled as the word came out so easily. "But it's not only Hunter. It's so much more. Thank you for driving me to town to see Hunter and not pushing me to talk about it on the way home. I needed time to think and sort through my feelings."

"That is as I thought. Did you sort out your thoughts, or are you still working on it?" Sarah laid her hands in her lap, the picture of perfect peace.

Annie gave her a longing look. If only she could have that kind of peace and hold onto it. It had become so elusive the past few years. "I think so, but I'm not sure. I guess talking would help. Hunter doesn't believe me; that I care about him. For him. That I wasn't living a lie the whole time I've been here."

"*Ach.* I am so sorry, Annie. You have told him it's not so, *ya*?"

"I did, but he thinks all of it was an act for the show—that cameras were somewhere filming it all." She waved a hand in the air. "I don't think he really believes that, but I understand what he meant. He said it's a matter of trust for him."

"Trust?"

"That I didn't trust him enough to tell him the truth."

"May I ask why you did not tell him? Or me? I have to say, I have wondered since you told me yesterday."

Annie gripped the sheet and pulled it under her chin, hating that she'd hurt Sarah too. "I wasn't trying to hurt anyone. At first, I was hiding. But once I got to know you, I wanted to be loved for who I am, not because I was on a stupid reality show that means nothing in real life."

Sarah gave a slow nod, a contemplative expression on her face. "I can see why you would feel that way, if I understand the concept behind the program you were on. I imagine it would always feel as though you are living a lie and being pulled between two worlds, *ya*?"

"Exactly!" Annie pushed herself higher on the pillow as relief swept through her. "I hoped you'd get it. I think you're the only one who does. I've been trying to figure out who I am for longer than I'd realized, and being on the show with Scott only muddied the waters. It didn't bring me clarity. I guess I've only begun to realize God wants us to be true to who we are—to trust Him with our past, present, and our future. I guess that's one reason I was crying when you came in. It hit me pretty hard that I've failed Him as well as you and Hunter."

"*Nein.*" Sarah touched Annie's hand as it rested on top of the sheet. "You have not failed me, *Gott*, or Hunter. You only failed yourself by forgetting who you are for a time. But you can change that. You are the one who must decide what path you want to travel. *Gott* can lead you if you decide to trust Him with everything, holding nothing back."

Annie nodded. "Yes." The word came out in a whisper. "That's what I want. I haven't had peace in so long. I want to make things right."

"But it cannot center around not hurting me or even trying to become what Hunter would want. You must search your heart and make the choice that's right for you. Can you do that? Can you allow the Lord to lead you?"

"I think so. I hope so. Maybe I need to spend time listening for a change, instead of trying to make everything happen on my own. Thank you, Sarah. You have become more of a friend than anyone I've ever known."

Sarah pulled her into a long hug then pushed to her feet. "And you are my friend as well. Now I will leave you alone so you can find your way onto the path that will bring you peace." She walked to the door and out into the hall without looking back.

Chapter Twenty-Four

HUNTER PULLED TO A STOP OUTSIDE the diner a full thirty minutes before the meeting with David Blackwell. Hopefully, they'd be able to find out more about the woman who might or might not be his wife. He'd called the homeless shelter yesterday afternoon and asked them to send someone to find Carla and bring her to the diner at lunchtime. He asked that they not say anything other than Hunter wanted to buy her lunch, so she wouldn't get spooked and refuse to come.

He'd barely slept the night befor, thinking about Annie, as well as the hope and excitement over helping Carla find her family. Even though he knew Annie's real name was Ann, he had a hard time thinking of her that way. Part of him felt guilty for not hearing her out or using a softer tone when she'd come to his office, but she'd hurt him—deeply. He couldn't get past the fact she'd allowed them to start getting close and had kept the truth from him. However, he couldn't think about it now. There were other things that had to be dealt with first.

He glanced out his car window. Would Annie be willing to face him again after everything that had happened between them? She was the one who started the search to uncover Carla's past, so he couldn't imagine she'd stay away, but maybe she'd lost interest now that her old boyfriend had come to town. It was possible she'd decided to resume her life, regardless of what she'd claimed. It was hard to believe she'd walk away from a starring role in Hollywood or could ever be happy with a small-town guy.

A car pulled into the parking spot beside him.

Hunter pushed open the door, recognizing the older model wagon as belonging to the director of the homeless shelter. He lifted a hand as she exited the car. "Hi, Kathy. Any problems getting here?" He inclined his head toward the passenger seat where Carla still sat, unmoving.

She shut her door and walked around the front toward him. "Not when I told her you were buying lunch. But for some reason I don't understand, Carla doesn't want to get out of the car. Think she might have a sense something is going on?"

He shrugged, mystified at the woman's behavior. "Hey, Carla." He leaned down and spoke through the closed window. "May I open the door?"

She shook her head, her eyes wide as she looked around the parking lot. She lowered the window an inch. "Where's Annie? I haven't seen her around town for a long time. She didn't leave, did she?"

He drew in a breath, ready to answer, when a clopping of hooves drew his attention to an Amish buggy that had rounded the corner and was headed into the parking lot. Sarah held the reins, and Annie sat beside her, looking directly at him. His heart lurched then moved into a rapid beat. She'd actually come. It had to be for Carla's sake alone; regardless, he couldn't help but rejoice that she'd stayed in town another day before returning to her old life.

Maybe he wasn't being fair. Annie had said she didn't care for Scott Adson anymore, so why not trust her word on that much? Because he'd trusted before and gotten burned. Part of him wanted to believe Annie was being completely honest this time, but what chance did he have against the draw of the bright lights, a rich boyfriend, and the fame of Hollywood?

"Whoa." Sarah halted her mare in front of the

hitching rail positioned for Amish buggies and smiled. "*Guder mariye*, Hunter."

"Good morning, Sarah." He dipped his head at her passenger. "Annie. I see you decided to come. Carla was asking about you."

"Oh?" Her gaze finally moved from him to Carla. "Is anything wrong?"

"She doesn't want to get out of the car. We're not sure why." He gestured toward the director. "This is Kathy Mason, the director of the shelter, who drove her here."

Annie climbed down from the buggy and walked toward them, then turned to Sarah. "Are you sure you don't want to stay?"

She shook her head. "It looks like Carla is already a little nervous. Too many people may make things worse. I will go to the market and pick up a few things, and check here in an hour, *ya*?"

"*Ya*." Annie grinned up at Sarah. "*Denki*."

Sarah beamed at her, then clucked to the mare and turned her away from the hitching rail and into the street.

Annie walked to the station wagon and stood next to the passenger door. "Hi, Carla. Are you hungry?"

The older woman nodded but didn't speak.

"Hunter and I were going to get something to eat in the diner. Want to come with us?" She shot him a glance, hoping he'd understand she wasn't trying to trap him inside with her. He gave her the barest of nods.

Carla stared at her, then swung her gaze to Hunter then back to Annie. Then, she jerked her thumb at Kathy. "She's not coming, is she? I think she's trying to force me into living at the shelter, and I don't want to." She bit her lip and rolled the window all the way down.

"I want to go home. I wish I could remember where that is. I miss my house. It was so pretty. It had a big green lawn and a front porch where I used to sit in a rocker." Her eyes widened. "I remembered." She rubbed her forehead and scowled. "Now if I could remember about that dog."

Annie reached for the handle and opened the door. "I don't think Kathy is staying. She has a lot of work to do. I'm sure she'd never force you to live at the shelter."

Kathy shook her head and smiled. "You can stop by anytime you want to, but we won't make you stay."

"All right." Carla swung her legs out of the car. "I'd like a burger and a Coke and a piece of pie." She stared at Hunter. "You gonna buy?"

He laughed as joy flooded his heart. If life could get better for Carla, maybe it might turn out okay for him, as well. "You bet. Come on. I'll buy for all three of us."

"Good." She headed toward the door of the diner with Hunter and Annie trailing behind.

Annie followed Carla inside as Hunter, ever the gentleman, held the door open for both of them. Anxiety settled in her stomach, making her wish Sarah had chosen to stay—she would have been an excellent buffer between Hunter and herself. She settled onto a stool next to Carla, half hoping Hunter would take the seat next to her, but he chose the one on Carla's other side. She glanced at him, only to find him studiously avoiding her gaze. She released a soft sigh. He hadn't forgiven her, that was obvious. "Hunter?"

His head jerked up and around almost as though he'd forgotten she was there. "Yeah?"

She motioned toward the door. "Were we expecting anyone else?"

Carla accepted the Coke the waitress set in front of her and took a sip. "Is your Amish friend coming back? I like those people. They're always kind to me. They make my heart feel peaceful whenever I talk to them."

Hunter patted her shoulder. "Sarah will be back a little later. We have something we'd like to talk to you about, Carla. But how about I order for us first, okay?"

She nodded, and he placed their orders and waited for Annie to give hers.

Annie wished they were sitting in a booth or at a table that was a little less public. She gestured toward a nearby empty table with four chairs. "Carla? I wonder if you'd mind if we sit at a table this once? Um . . . it's so much nicer to have something to lean against, don't you think?"

Carla arched a brow. "Yeah, these things hurt my back. Chairs are so much better. I'd love to move. I'll bring my Coke. I never did like sitting on these stools, anyway."

Annie laughed as Hunter's mouth gaped open.

He snapped it shut and followed them to a table. "I thought you preferred the counter. Why didn't you ever tell me you'd rather sit here?"

Carla stared at him. "You never asked me." She jerked her chin toward Annie. "She did. I guess she has more manners than you, huh?" Her eyes sparkled, and a smile tugged at her lips. "My mama always used to tell me to sit up straight and use my manners."

Annie reached out and touched the older woman's hand where it lay on the table. "You're remembering quite a bit today. That's good. You mentioned your house and the rocker on the porch and the nice lawn. What would you think if we told you someone is coming who might remember your house and maybe even the dog you've mentioned? Would you want to meet him?"

Carla's brows scrunched together. "Maybe. Is he nice?"

Hunter nodded. "I talked to him on the phone for quite a while yesterday, and he seems very nice."

The waitress set their orders in front of them, and Carla reached for it with eager hands, then she paused. "Maybe we should say grace. I think I always did at home. I pray every night before I go to sleep and ask God to help me remember."

Annie reached across the table, her heart warming at the request. "May I hold your hand while we pray, Carla?"

"Sure." She grasped Annie's hand then reached for Hunter's who sat in the chair beside her. "You have to hold Annie's other hand. The circle can't be broken, you know. That's the way you do it when you pray. Three cords are stronger than two."

Hunter hesitated then reached across the table, his hand outstretched. "Do you mind, Annie?"

Her heart hammered. He'd called her Annie. Not Ann. She willed her hand not to shake as she extended it. Her eyes closed as his warm embrace enveloped her fingers, and she bowed her head, wishing this moment could last forever.

"Dear God." Carla's voice was calm and strong. "Thank you for this food and these friends. Please bless them and help them to be happy together. And show me where I belong, so I don't feel so lost anymore. In Jesus's name, amen." She lifted her head, released Hunter and Annie's hands, and immediately picked up her cheeseburger and took a big bite. "Mmm. Good. Thanks, Hunter." She spoke with the food tucked into her cheek, then leaned back and chewed contentedly.

"What were you saying about someone coming who might remember my house? What makes you think that?"

The bell on the door jingled as a man with steel-gray hair at the temples and serious blue eyes walked inside. He stopped and looked around. His gaze landed on Carla, and he gasped. "Clara!"

Chapter Twenty-Five

HUNTER SET HIS BURGER DOWN AT the sound of the man's voice then pushed to his feet to greet him. "Mr. Blackwell. I'm Hunter Lewis, the man who called you about Carla. Uh, Clara. Would you like to sit by Miss Farley?" He indicated a chair beside Annie. "She's been helping with the search. In fact, the entire thing was her idea from the start, so I guess I'm the one who was helping." He waited until the man seated himself. "I think we might want to take this slow. There is a bit of a memory issue, as I mentioned on the phone."

"Thank you. Of course. I forgot myself for a moment. And please, call me David."

Carla stared at him from across the table. "Who are you? You can't be a friend of Hunter's and Annie's, or they wouldn't have introduced themselves. I don't trust strangers. They steal from people like me. I'm only friends with the right kind of people."

He leaned his forearms on the table. "What kind of person is that, Cla. . . Carla? And to answer your question, Hunter is a new friend, and I hope Annie and you will both be, as well."

"Good people who are kind and try to help me. Not just buy me food like Hunter does, but listen to me, like Annie. She cares that I'm lost."

David sucked in a sharp breath. "Do you know how you got lost? How you came to be in this town?"

"I can't remember, and it really bothers me. I want to remember so bad. It feels like I'm lost and can't find my way home." She rubbed her temple and frowned. "Sometimes I think my memory will return. I've dreamed that I drove here, but I don't remember driving, and I don't have a car. Sometimes I sleep in an abandoned one out in the woods, but it isn't mine. So, what does that mean? Do you think I have a home somewhere? Or will I be all alone forever?"

Hunter blinked the moisture from his eyes, but David wasn't even trying to keep the tears from falling. The man appeared so choked up he couldn't speak. Good. He'd worried this guy might not be the real deal, or that Carla had run away from a man or a family who didn't love her, but that didn't appear to be the case. "Carla, what would you think if I told you I know someone who does care about you and knows where you used to live? Would that make you happy?"

She gave a quick nod. "Yes. It would. At times it seems like my brain is almost clear, and I get little glimpses. Like that German shepherd and the house with the porch and the rocking chair. I wish those pictures were clearer and wouldn't leave so quickly."

David brushed his sleeve across his eyes then reached into his hip pocket and drew out his wallet. He opened it and removed a picture. "Take a look at this, and tell me if it looks familiar." He handed her the picture, his hand shaking as he held it out.

She looked at him, a wary expression on her face, but she took the photo with a quick grab. "What is it? Why do you want me to see it? I don't know you." Pursing her lips, she raised the photo in the air and stared at it. Her eyes widened, and she sucked in a sharp breath. "This is it."

Annie leaned forward. "What, Carla? It's what? Do you recognize something?"

Carla turned the photo around so Annie could see it, then flashed it at Hunter. "This is the house I keep dreaming about. And look, there's a dog in the front yard, just like the one in my dream. Isn't she pretty?

She looks exactly like Amira." Her mouth formed an O. "Amira. Is that the dog's name? How did I know that?"

David gave her a soft, encouraging smile. "Yes. The dog's name is Amira, and she misses her owner very much. And that's the house where she lives."

Carla shook her head as though trying to clear it. "What happened to her owner? Did she die?"

"We were afraid she might have, when she went to the grocery store one day and didn't come home. We've hunted and hunted for months, and kept holding onto hope that she was still alive and might someday come home to us. Would you like to see another picture?" He withdrew another one from his wallet and held it.

She nodded. "Yes." This time her hand trembled as she extended it and reverently took the photo. "Who is this? It looks like a family, and Amira is with them." She peered more closely at it. "Is that you? Your hair is more brown than gray here. You must have been a lot younger. Who are the kids and the woman?"

"That's me. My hair wasn't as gray a few months ago, but it turned this way when my wife disappeared. That's her with our two children standing next to me. My wife is Amira's owner. Look closely, Carla. Do you recognize her at all? Or the kids? They're seventeen and nineteen-years-old now, and their names are Jennifer and Joey."

She ran her finger over the picture, mouthing the names as though trying to taste them and see if they fit. "Jennifer and Joey. Jennifer and Joey." Tears welled in her eyes. "I should know them, shouldn't I? And the lady, she looks a little like me."

"Yes, she does, but that's an older picture." David pulled out another picture. "Here's another I want you to see. It's of the same lady, my wife, with me, and it was taken a month before she disappeared." He stood, then walked to Carla's side and dropped to his knees next to her chair. "Look at it, then take a long look at me. Look into my eyes and tell me what you see there. Can you do that? I promise not to touch you or do anything that would upset or scare you."

She bowed her head and stared at the photo for a full minute, then raised her head and peered into his face.

Hunter's heart almost quit beating. He chanced a glance at Annie. She must be feeling the same. Her hand was over her heart, and her lips were parted as she stared at the couple beside him. He quietly scooted his chair a little way from Carla, not wanting to intrude on this moment.

Carla blinked a few times then took a quick, hard breath. "David? Is that you?" She reached out and tentatively touched his cheek with her fingertips, then his hair where it had grayed at the temples. "You used to have such dark hair."

David's face crumpled, but he didn't move. "Yes, sweetheart, it's me. Like I said, worrying about you so much made my hair turn gray. Your name is Clara, not Carla. Do you remember that? Amira, the kids and I all miss you very much. That's your house in the picture. Your porch and your rocker."

"I recognize the porch and the rocker. They've been in my dreams too. And you look familiar. I knew your name when I looked into your eyes. Everything was clear for a few seconds, then it went dim again." She rubbed her forehead again. "I've had headaches since I came to this town. I think a nice person brought me after I walked for a long, long time. I'm not sure, but that's what I have dreams about sometimes. I figured it was only a dream, but maybe that was my mind trying to help me remember." She dropped her hands and placed them on the table. "Something is wrong with my head. It doesn't work like it should most of the time."

"We can try to find a way to make that better. Do you think if you saw your own house and Amira again, it might help some of it return?"

Carla shrugged. "I don't know. Maybe. I remembered you for a little bit." She tipped her head to the side. "Do you want me to come?"

"Very much. It's your home. It's where you belong, and I want to see if we can't make the headaches go away and find a way to make your memory return." He pushed to his feet and slipped into the chair across from her. "I think when you wrecked your car, you must have hit your head pretty hard. You probably suffered a serious concussion with partial memory loss. There are good doctors out there, Clara, who specialize in that sort of thing."

Her eyes widened. "You won't put me in an institution and forget about me, will you? I won't go with you if that's what you're going to do."

"No, honey. Of course not. I want you to come home, and we'll find the best doctors we can to figure out how to make everything better. If you have to go anywhere for tests, I'll be with you every minute. You never have to be alone or feel lost again."

"All right." She pushed to her feet. "Let's go."

His eyes widened. "Now? You want to go now?"

"Yes. I want to see Amira and Jennifer and Joey. I want to see that house with the porch and the rocker. I'm tired of my head hurting and getting confused and lost." She turned to Hunter. "But I'll miss you and Annie. And your burgers, Cokes, and pie."

Hunter and Annie both stood, and Hunter wrapped Clara in a big hug. "I'm so happy for you. I'll bet David will buy you hamburgers, Cokes, and pie anytime you ask."

She pulled away and eyed him. "Do you trust David? Do you think I should go with him?"

"Yes, I do. And so does the sheriff in the town where you lived. He gave me David's phone number and said he's been hunting for you every day since you disappeared. He told me that David is a good man, and he's been lonely, exactly like you. Also, your family attended a church there, and the entire church has been praying for you since you vanished. I think God has answered your prayers, Clara, and helped you find your way home."

Annie touched David's arm. "Please keep in touch with Hunter and let him know how Clara is doing. We don't want to lose touch with her after helping her find her way home."

"You've got it. I can't thank both of you enough. I'll owe you a debt of gratitude for the rest of my life." He held out his arm to his wife. "If you're sure you want to go home today, then I want you to come. Where do we find your belongings?"

"Yes, I'm sure." Then she shook her head. "I don't have anything worth going after. I think I left everything that mattered at home that day." Peering up at him, she narrowed her eyes. "Are you a good driver? You won't get in a wreck, will you? I think one is about all I can handle." She rubbed her head again. "Next time I might end up calling myself Gayle or Margo or something. At least I was close with Carla."

David threw back his head and laughed. "I'm an excellent driver. Come on, honey, let's go home."

Chapter Twenty-Six

SCOTT APPROACHED THE FRONT DESK OF the fanciest hotel he'd been able to find in Cave City, but it still didn't measure up to what he was used to in L.A. or the other big cities he frequented. Oh well, he wouldn't be here long. He tapped the bell on the counter, annoyed the woman with her back to him hadn't bothered to turn. Surely she'd heard him walking across the foyer. "Any messages for me?"

She pivoted, her pretty face breaking into a smile. "Oh, Scott. I mean, uh, Mr. Adson." Red swept into her cheeks. "I'm sorry, I'm a big fan of yours, and since you go by Scott on the show . . ." Her blush deepened.

He waved his hand. "Thanks." Another groupie. As much as he loved the spotlight, it might be nice to visit somewhere in this country without being recognized and the paparazzi showing up with their cameras. "Messages?"

"Oh, right." She reached into her pocket. "I didn't want to take a chance of losing it." She extended her hand, holding a folded note.

His fingers brushed hers as he took it, and she giggled. "Thanks." He looked at her nametag. "Uh, Lily. Have a good day."

She giggled again. "I hope everything works out with you and Ann."

He barely suppressed an eye roll and turned to go, opening the note as he did so. A quick glance was all it took to read the one line. He groaned and looked toward the restaurant door. Great. Just what he needed. He stepped into the open doorway and paused, looking around. The place only had a handful of people seated at the tables, as it was past the lunch hour. A few seconds later he spotted her.

"Scotty!" His mother stood and waved at him, her well-modulated voice carrying across the short distance.

Ann's PA sat next to Veronica. Gretchen something-or-other, if he remembered correctly.

"Mother?" He pushed down his annoyance and mustered a smile. "What are you doing here?" He covered the space in a few strides. Apparently, she was doing what she did best—trying to take over and manipulate his life. If he didn't need the success this show and her financial backing brought, he'd ditch both and walk. Convince Ann to run away with him and not look back. That thought had tempted him more than once lately.

Veronica tipped her head to the side and smirked. "She said no, didn't she?" She flipped her hand toward a chair. "Sit."

He slid into a chair, hating that he couldn't stand up to her, but not wanting to make a scene in front of the PA and the other diners in the room. Heads had already turned their way and whispers started as soon as Veronica Adson had stood to her feet. She was a presence to be reckoned with no matter where she went. "Yes. But I've got it handled. She'll come around if we give her time."

His mother sank into her seat but sat ramrod straight. "We don't have time to give her. I allowed you to do it your way, now we do it mine."

Scott held up his hand. "Wait. Hear me out."

"All right. Fine. You have five minutes to convince me." She tapped her manicured nails on the tabletop.

"Ann will stay here as long as her Amish friends and new boyfriend want her to. If they get tired of her and want her to leave, she'll have no choice but to go."

Gretchen's eyes widened.

Veronica relaxed against her chair. "And how do you propose to do that?"

Scott smiled. He finally had the upper hand. "I have a plan."

Hunter pushed away from his desk. It was stupid to stay and try to work any longer. He couldn't concentrate on designs or numbers. All he could see was Annie's face in front of him as she'd walked out that door yesterday. Her sadness. Her hurt and disbelief. He wanted to slam his fist on the desk in frustration. Why didn't she get it? Even more importantly, why hadn't she trusted him? He shook his hands to relax the tension, realizing he'd been gripping them into tight fists. This was as useless as trying to work. He'd been over this a hundred times in his mind and always came to the same conclusion. He cared more than she did. No matter what she claimed, her career and path to fame were more important than him.

He closed his laptop then stuffed it into a leather case. "Time to get out of here." Maybe coffee would clear his head—or a Coke. He smiled thinking of Clara and David. At least that was one part of his life where he'd been successful.

Guilt stung him as he strode toward his office door. That hadn't been only his doing. The idea had come from Annie. It was her compassion and curiosity—her insistence that had compelled him to help. Clara had been in town for months, and all he'd thought to do had been buy her an occasional meal. Annie showed up in town, and a week or so later, Clara was driving home with her husband to try to discover her way back to her old life.

He swung open the door leading onto the street and nearly knocked a man over. "Hey, sorry. I didn't see you."

"Mr. Lewis." The man he'd ran into stuck a microphone in his face and waved toward a cameraman who lifted his camera and moved a step closer. "We've been waiting to talk to you, sir. We know you were raised Amish, even if you aren't living among them now. Tell me, isn't it against your Amish religious beliefs to date a reality star from Hollywood?"

A camera flashed in his face, and Hunter held up a hand. "Who are you people?"

Another man stepped close, also holding a mic. "Are you going to appear on *Life with the Adsons* with Ann? Are you going to be the new love interest that tries to lure her away from Scott? Is that why he's here, to recruit you for the show?"

Hunter halted. "Hold it. I'm not saying a thing until I know who you are and why you're here."

The first man flashed a badge showing his face and words Hunter didn't have time to read before he tucked it into his pocket. "I'm with The Reel List." He gestured toward the other man. "And that's our competition. Trust me, you'd rather talk to me. We'll make sure to get the story right. Are you Ann's new love interest or not?"

"I'm not. How did you find me?"

The second reporter grinned. "An anonymous tip. We get them all the time, and this one led us to you. We heard she's staying at an Amish inn on the outskirts of town. Can you give us directions or tell us the name of the place?"

Hunter glared at the man, then pivoted and strode around his car parked nearby. No way was he telling these jerks anything. They'd make Annie's life miserable, not to mention the harm they could do to Sarah and her inn. He slammed his door and locked it as the first reporter knocked on his window. Somehow, he had to lose these guys, so they didn't follow him home or to Sarah's inn. He pulled onto the road and glanced in his mirror. Yep. They were racing for vans marked with the names of their publications. Great.

Sarah. He almost slammed on his brakes but hit the gas pedal instead. What if they showed up and the Bishop found out?

Chapter Twenty-Seven

ANNIE SAT ON THE PORCH SWING in the shadows, trying to think and pray. She'd been out here for close to an hour, sorting through her problems and options, but she still hadn't come to any conclusions. It seemed all she did lately was beg God to show her the way out and calm her soul. Peace was trickling in like a gentle, warm oil over her bruised heart, but she still didn't have any sense of what the Lord wanted her to do with her life. Hopefully, if she waited on Him long enough, that would come.

A movement caught her eye. An Amish buggy came down the road in front of the inn. She never tired of watching members of Sarah's community go about their lives. Their lives were simple, but the people were far from it. If Sarah was any indication, they had more wisdom and depth than almost anyone she'd met, other than her grandparents, and they had been rare.

Hmm. It appeared to be two men in the buggy, one bearded and one not, so the younger man without the beard must not be married. Might he be coming to call on Sarah? She sat a little straighter and tried to see their faces as the horse clopped steadily forward, growing closer with each step. She gasped and drew back into the shadows, lifting her feet from the floor and curling them beneath her, hoping to disappear and not be seen.

Bishop Swarey. Hunter's uncle. And that must be his son, Jeremiah. Yes. She could see now that it was. She'd like to slip into the house so they wouldn't see her, but hopefully they'd keep going and not stop. She held her breath, praying it would be so, as Sarah would say.

The buggy pulled to a stop at the end of the walk, and she held still, wondering what to do next.

Voices drifted to her, only twenty feet or so away. A gnarled hand waved from the front seat. "This is not our way."

"Sir?" Jeremiah's younger voice sounded curious. "I'm not sure what you mean?"

"These people."

Annie looked where the hand pointed. Two of Sarah's new guests wandered along the edge of her lawn, intent on their conversation. She prayed they wouldn't notice the buggy and rush over to try to take pictures. That would not go over well.

"Because they are *Englisch*?"

"*Ya.* Since we allowed Sarah to have a guest from outside our community, now she thinks she can open her doors to any *Englischers* who need a place to stay. This is not our way."

Annie sucked in a breath. Were they going to leave or come in?

A full minute elapsed in silence, then the Bishop clucked to his horse and drove it to the hitching rail a few yards past the path. Annie bolted. She didn't care if he saw her, she wasn't going to be on the porch when that man came up the steps.

She slipped through the door and closed it quietly behind her, then rushed to the kitchen where Sarah was lifting the steaming tea pot from a hot burner. "Sarah. Bishop Swarey and Jeremiah are here. He's tying up his horse now."

Sarah turned, and her brows rose. "I was not expecting him today. I wonder what he wants?" She pulled back a lace-edged curtain covering part of the kitchen window and gave a decisive nod. "Would you go to the door, Annie?"

"Me?" Annie squeaked the word. "I don't think he likes me. Maybe you should greet him. It might put him in a better mood if he doesn't see me. I'll slip into the living room and grab a book to read, if that's okay?"

"*Ya.*" Sarah nodded. "Maybe you are right, and that would be best. He's coming up the walk now. I will meet him."

Annie flew through the kitchen door and into the living room, settling into a comfortable, wing-backed chair right inside the door. Maybe she could keep out of the way and still hear what was going on, in case Sarah needed her support.

The front door opened in the nearby foyer, and Sarah's voice came clearly to Annie. "Please *kumm* in Bishop. I didn't know you and Jeremiah were coming to visit, or I would have prepared something to eat."

Footsteps followed her in, and the door closed. "We are not here to eat, Sarah. We have *kumm* to talk about your situation. The *Englischers* must leave your home."

A soft gasp was barely audible to Annie. She pushed to her feet and waited.

Sarah's voice remained calm. "Pardon me? I don't understand."

The Bishop's voice increased in intensity. "It is my duty to protect our community. You are bringing in outside influences that will disrupt our way of life. This Amish inn is being corrupted by people from outside our faith and our way of living. I can tolerate it no longer."

Annie couldn't tolerate it longer either, and she walked to the doorway of the living area opening onto the foyer. Jeremiah stood, hat in hand, clutching the brim to the point she was sure it would destroy the shape. His face was pale, but he didn't open his mouth to speak.

Sarah lifted her chin. "All of them? You want me to send my guests away when they have paid me to stay here?"

Annie rushed forward and stopped by Sarah's side. "Please, sir. This is my fault, not Sarah's. Don't blame her for the guests who are here now. I encouraged her to promote the inn."

He turned stormy eyes on her. "You have now proven my point, young woman. You are encouraging her in ways that are not ours. I must know what you mean by promote. In what way?"

She hunched a shoulder and forced a smile. "You know. The Internet."

His eyes widened, and his face flamed red.

Annie rushed on, hoping to deflect an explosion. "She did tell me this has always been an Amish inn, except for the few times she's taken someone in like me, who needed a place to stay for a short time. But she's been a blessing to me, and I wanted to help her business succeed. I showed her a way to reach beyond her current customer base. She needs the money, sir."

"*Nein.* This is not your concern. Sarah does not need the money. She can marry, and her husband will care for her." He gestured to Jeremiah who lowered his gaze to the floor. "We are done speaking of this. Sarah, you will return the money to your guests and tell them your inn is closing. That is all. Miss Stanway, you must leave as well. You have stayed long enough." He turned and stalked toward the door.

Jeremiah took a step forward, his jaw set. "Father. Maybe we could—"

"*Nein!*" The Bishop held up his hand. "I will not hear more."

"Wait!" Annie moved toward him and almost

grabbed his arm, but stopped herself in time. "Please."

He swung around. "It is not your place to speak on this. I have said what must be. Sarah knows this."

Annie nodded. "I understand, sir. And I apologize. But Wildwood Inn is important to Sarah. She needs it to succeed. Not just for herself, but to help preserve the memory of her husband and what he started here. Is that such a bad thing?"

His heavy brows drew together. "And when the inn fails, what then? She has no husband to support her. Will she go home to live with her parents and expect them to provide?" He wagged his head. "Will her memories feed her or keep her warm in the winter? She knows better than to depend on *Englischers* for her provision rather than *Gott* or her own people. Her pride and desire to do this on her own has blinded her and led her away from *Gott's* plan." He shook a finger at Annie. "And you have helped."

"Is it God's plan to force her to give up what she loves and live a life she may not want?" Annie crossed her arms. She would not let this man bully Sarah.

Sarah reached out and touched her arm. "Annie."

Annie took a deep breath and tried to relax. "I'm sorry, Bishop Swarey. I mean no disrespect, truly. But Sarah told me something recently that I didn't understand at the time. Now, however, I think I'm beginning to. She told me that God brought me here for a reason. That I have a purpose, even when I felt so lost. She gave me hope and reminded me where my peace came from. Not from the world or my life in it, but from my heavenly Father."

Sarah gave her a tentative smile.

Annie closed her eyes for a second, praying she could put into words what was burning in her heart. "Since Sarah welcomed me here, I've felt like I found a home for the first time in years. She made me remember what life is supposed to be and helped me discover who I am again. Maybe that's her purpose. Maybe God gave her this inn to reach out to struggling people in need like me, people who are trying to find their way. I was in the world, but I was also *of* the world. Sarah helped me to understand how I can be in it but not let it own me. What if that's her purpose and closing the inn would rob that from her?"

Annie knew in her heart she'd said enough. Possibly even too much. The words had poured out, but peace had come in their place.

Bishop Swarey eyed her with a speculative look. For a moment, she thought she noticed the hint of a smile as his eyes flicked to Sarah.

A movement through the window behind the Bishop caught her eye. What? She stared, trying to make out what was peeking through the bushes, aimed directly at the window. No. It couldn't be. *Oh no. Please God, no.*

She whirled toward Sarah and grabbed her hand. "You have to go upstairs. Close the door. Bishop, you and Jeremiah need to leave now. Go! You mustn't stay."

No one moved, even though she tugged at Sarah's hand. Suddenly, the front door burst open and Scott rushed in, wearing an agonized expression. "Ann. Thank God you're all right. I've been worried sick about you since you left L.A. without so much as a word." A camera crew followed him with Gretchen and a smiling Veronica in their wake.

Chapter Twenty-Eight

THE BISHOP THREW BACK HIS SHOULDERS and roared. "*Wat ist dieses*?" He turned and stepped close to Annie, shaking his finger in her face. "You say you want to help our Sarah, and this is how you repay her? You bring your world into her home? Into her place of business? *Mit der cameras*?"

Annie took a step away, her entire body shaking. What was happening here? She'd been so close to gaining the Bishop's approval and understanding. "I'm so sorry. I had no idea they were going to come here."

The front door slammed shut, leaving the cameramen outside. Hunter stalked into the room, his eyes stormy as he glared at Scott. "Annie." He stopped a few feet from her. "I came in through the kitchen door, and I've been standing there listening, trying to figure out what's going on in here." He motioned toward the front of the house. "I told those cameramen to get off the porch and away from the house. Why were reporters and cameramen waiting for me outside my office?" He gestured through the window. "Apparently, they followed me here, but I see it didn't matter, as some of their cohorts came ahead of them. What's going on?"

She shook her head. "I don't know. I—"

Hunter blew out a breath. "I thought you understood how important privacy is to the Amish community. The presence of your friends is going to cause a lot of upset and confusion. I appreciate what you told the Bishop, but this is too much. You need to tell these people to leave."

Annie opened her mouth to reply, but Veronica

Adson strolled into the room. She stopped in front of Annie and planted her hands on her hips as she looked Hunter over from head to toe. "So, you're the boyfriend Ann's gotten mixed up with here? I assume you're what's keeping her in this two-bit town." She waved at Scott and the cameras continuing to shoot through the window. "You don't like what you're seeing here, is that right?"

"That's exactly right. My uncle is the Bishop of the Amish community in Cave City, and as you can see, he's not pleased with what's going on."

Veronica turned a smile on the Bishop then over to Hunter, but it didn't reach her eyes. It had the predatory feel of a cat stalking a baby bird that had fallen from the nest. Only one more step and it would pounce.

Annie tried to keep her hands from shaking as she reached out and touched Veronica's arm. "Please. You can't do this. Sarah doesn't want this kind of publicity, and her people don't want their pictures taken. You need to respect that and leave her home."

Veronica arched one penciled brow. "Do I? Hmm." She swung toward Hunter. "We're going to keep the cameras here and in town until Ann changes her mind and decides to return with us to L.A. Where she belongs. And since you're Ann's new boyfriend, I'd say it's up to you to persuade her." The last words were said in a sharp staccato burst, all semblance of pleasantry tossed aside.

The Bishop cleared his throat. Annie's gaze swept to him. She'd almost forgotten the man, but his stiff stature and blazing eyes made it clear he had no intention of being forgotten. "Miss Stanway, I want you to leave this inn immediately. I think if you care for Sarah, you will go back to where you belong." He swiveled and pinned Sarah with his blue eyes. "Sarah, I am disappointed in you. We will talk later." He stalked to the door, his eyes straight ahead.

Hunter tossed one last sad look at Annie. "I'm sorry this happened, and I don't blame you. But if these people don't leave soon, I'll be back to see that they do. I'm going to talk to my uncle and see if I can smooth this out at all." He glared at Scott then at Veronica. He turned his attention to Sarah. "They have no right on your property. I won't interfere in Annie's business, but I won't stand by and see your rights trampled on. I'll call the police if they aren't gone soon. Call me if you need help. I won't be far away." He pivoted and followed the Bishop, shutting the door carefully behind him.

Annie wanted to run upstairs and throw herself on her bed and cry, but she had to think of Sarah. Somehow, she needed to save her friend from this mess. Scott. He hadn't said a word since his mother came in. He'd always hated how Veronica tried to manipulate his life. Maybe she could show him Veronica was doing it again. "Scott? You claim to still care about me, but you certainly aren't showing it right now by siding with your mother. Won't you help *me*?"

He bit his lip and glanced at his mother, then squared his shoulders. "I'm doing this for your own good, Ann. I want you to come home where you belong. With me."

She shook her head. "You have no idea what you're doing—the damage you're causing. *Please* turn off the cameras." She lifted her chin. "Hunter was right. I will call the police and force you to leave."

"I've come a long way, Ann, and I've made up my mind. I'm not leaving without you."

"Will you listen? This is not the way to win a girl's heart. You can't barge in here and destroy people's lives, then insist on your own way. If you ever cared about me, please do as I'm asking. Leave town and don't come back."

He smirked. "As for the police, we'll leave the house. We can even leave the yard. However, we have every right to be on the road in front of this inn and film anyone going in or out. We can also set up our cameras in town or on the country roads as other buggies pass by. That's not what you want, is it?" He held out his hand. "I'm not leaving without you, so you might as well get used to the idea."

Annie stared at his hand but didn't move. No way was she going to take it. Somehow, she had to make him understand. She looked deep into his eyes, trying to see a way to break him, but all she saw was determination. In fact, those eyes appeared more like his mother's than she'd ever thought possible.

As she swung her attention to Veronica, her stomach clenched, and a wave of nausea washed over her. The woman would have her way no matter how many lives she trampled to get it. "Fine. If I do what you say and go with you right now, will you turn off the cameras and send the press away? Leave these people alone and not come back? Will you promise?"

Veronica tipped her head to the side as she examined Annie's face. Then she smiled. "Let's cut." She waved her fingers in the air. "You'll return to L.A. with us and follow my directions. You'll be a part of the show again and finish this season and the next, to help get our ratings up. Then we'll decide where we go from there."

Annie gave a short bark of a laugh. "Right. That's what it's always been about, hasn't it? The ratings. Not love. Not family. It's all about ratings. How could I ever have missed that?"

Veronica smirked. "You're getting smarter, I see." She waved the photographers out, then turned to Gretchen. "Your PA will fill you in later on where we are in the shooting, as we decided to start shooting it early. Suffice it to say we've been playing up your little adventure already. You broke your contract by not returning or letting us know if you planned to continue, don't forget that. We had the right to a decision by now, and you ignored all of our calls. And don't forget what pressure we can bring through our attorney if you refuse to cooperate. All we need to do now is reshoot your reunion scene, since your Amish friends and your *boyfriend* messed that up for us. I'd love to use that footage, of course."

Sarah gasped, and Annie clenched her fists. "Don't you dare. Not if you want me to even consider returning to the show."

"Fine, fine. We'll do a new reunion scene between you and Scott in town. We can't do it in L.A., as our fans know you're here, so it must be believable. Lovesick hero travels clear across the country to rescue his sweetheart from herself and her poor choices. Our fans will eat it up and beg for more." She walked toward the door. "We're done here, people. Ann and Scott, come along."

Annie lifted her chin. "I need to pack."

"Fine. Gretchen can stay and drive you to the hotel. I'll ride with Scott." She stared at him. "Don't keep me waiting." Then she pivoted and walked out the door.

Scott's stiff stance relaxed as soon as she'd left, and he took a step toward Annie. "I'm sorry, Ann. This isn't how I wanted it to go, but you know Mother. And I really *have* been missing you. That part was true."

Annie didn't dare reply, as she knew she'd bite his head off. She swung around and headed up the stairs to her room, leaving him gaping after her.

Hunter sat at the counter in his favorite diner, wishing something would happen to distract him. He felt as though he was going to go crazy with the indecision and pain of losing Annie. He'd done it to himself, he realized that now. Sure, she hadn't been completely honest with him, but she'd tried to make it right, even if that had happened a bit late in the game. The thing that bothered him the most was he hadn't wanted to listen.

The ugly scene at Sarah's house made him want to strangle someone—preferably that arrogant jerk who pretended to be Annie's boyfriend. The way he'd charged into Sarah's inn and demanded Annie return to L.A. was nothing short of criminal. He should have thrown them all out of the house, but he could see how upset Sarah already was, and he didn't want to make the situation worse. But what it had shown him was Annie's heart—at least, what he hoped was the real Annie. He'd heard her impassioned speech to his uncle before he'd made his presence known—had that been real, or was that part of the act as well? He hated that he didn't know for sure—that he still had doubts. More than anything he wanted to believe what she'd said was true. He was still fighting hurt, anger, and confusion over the entire situation, but he somehow believed she'd been speaking the truth to the Bishop.

He set his glass of Coke on a napkin and stared at the food on his plate that he'd barely touched. Clara popped into his mind, and he smiled. Hopefully she was home and getting settled, and maybe even little snippets of memory would return. Funny that he missed her, but he did, even though he was happy they'd solved her mystery.

It still bugged him that Annie hadn't trusted him, and a part of him felt he'd been played for a fool. However, after he'd spent time praying before heading to the office this morning, he realized maybe he'd let his pride take over. The quiet voice of the Lord had reminded him that trust was a two-way street. He hadn't told Annie about his past, either. He hadn't shared his hurts and broken heart, or allowed her to see his vulnerability. And worse than that, he hadn't fought for her when Scott Adson showed up trying to drag her back home.

He bent his head and groaned. What a fool he'd been. And at the moment, he had no idea how to make it right. Or if he should even try. Maybe Annie deserved a second chance in Hollywood now that her fans were clamoring for her and her fame was increasing. Was it his place to try to take her away from that glamourous world when it might be what her heart really longed for? She'd said she didn't, and that she'd realized she wanted a different life, but had she thought that through? Wouldn't it be better if she returned to L.A., then if she returned to Cave City—to him—wouldn't it mean more?

It was all too much to figure out. More than likely Annie would find it hard to forgive him after the way he'd treated her. Maybe he should talk to Sarah tomorrow and get her perspective. That young woman had a lot of wisdom, and she'd gotten closer to Annie than anyone in the short time she'd lived here. In the meantime, he'd keep praying and see if the Lord opened a door.

Jimmy pulled up in his van. He'd heard gossip in town that a film crew had followed Hunter out of his office and more reporters had shown up at Sarah's. Had he missed out on all the action? This was his chance, and he couldn't blow it. He jumped out of the van and slammed the door behind him. Cameramen and crew got into their vans, and reporters stood around snapping pictures as two people came down the steps of the Wildwood Inn. Scott Adson, and that had to be his mother, Veronica. He hadn't watched the show much in the past, but he remembered his instant impression of dislike for the woman the couple of times he'd seen her.

He checked the collar of his dress shirt, making sure the top button was fastened. Dressing like this wasn't the norm for him, but he'd do whatever it took to make a good impression. After all, he'd made it this far and been smart enough to make that phone call to Scott Adson. The guy owed him now, big time. "Hey, Scott."

The man stopped and looked around, then his mouth pulled into a frown. "No autographs, sorry. But thanks for watching the show. You'll have to catch up with us later when we have more time." He headed toward the waiting car a few feet away.

"No." Jimmy shook his head and followed him. "I'm not here for an autograph. I'm Jim—uh, James. James Snyder. You remember—I'm the one who called you and told you where you could find Ann."

"Oh, right. I remember that now. Thanks, man. You sure came through for us. We appreciate the heads up." He lifted a hand. "I need to run. People waiting on me." He opened the car door.

"Stop!" Jimmy didn't know what was happening, but things were moving too fast and in the wrong direction. He had to grab control and make sure this guy understood who he was. Make him remember what he'd promised. "When do I go on the show? Are you going to fly me to Hollywood, or what?"

Scott's mouth twisted into something resembling a smile. "Yeah. That's right, I guess we kind of talked about that. We know how to reach you. Someone will be in touch in the future. See ya." He slipped into the car and slammed the door.

Jimmy stood staring as it pulled away and headed down the road toward town. Should he follow them? Find out where they were staying and demand they tell him when to fly out and what part he'd play? They'd promised. That was the only reason he'd done this. The only reason he'd betrayed Sarah and Annie. He shook his head. Where had that thought come from? He hadn't betrayed anyone. All he had done was try to help his own career—get out of this no-account town and make a name for himself. There wasn't anything wrong with that, was there?

A young woman walked down the path toward him. "You the guy who called the show and told Scott about Ann?"

He hesitated, not sure he liked what he saw in her face. Censure? Dislike? Maybe even a hint of disgust? And a flicker of something else. Pity? "Yeah. I'm Jimmy Snyder. What's with that guy, anyway? He made me a promise about being on the show, then he got in his car and drove off without telling me anything."

She gave a short laugh. "Don't feel bad, Jimmy. You aren't the first person they've duped, and I'm sure you won't be the last."

Annie threw the final pieces of clothing into her bag,

not caring that they weren't folded perfectly or that tears were dripping onto the bag as she zipped it closed. What was done was done. She couldn't change it, but for Sarah's sake, she would if she could.

Someone tapped on her door then it swung open before she could respond. Sarah stepped inside and gently shut the door behind her. "Annie? Are you all right?"

Guilt slammed into Annie like a fist to her gut. "I'm so sorry I dragged you into this. I didn't mean for this to happen, truly I didn't."

"Shh." Sarah sat beside her on the bed. "I know you did not. I don't blame you."

"But now you're going to lose your inn. That's not fair! I can't believe the Bishop would tell you to close this place and marry his son."

Sarah reached out and squeezed Annie's hand. "I am not worried about that now. It is you I am concerned for, not my inn. *Gott* will take care of me. He always has, and I know I can trust Him to keep doing so in the future. Besides, the Bishop will not force me to marry Jeremiah or anyone else. He wants me to, *ya*. But it is my decision, and only I can make it."

Annie swiped at the moisture on her cheeks with the back of her hand. "Are you sure about that?"

"*Ya*. I am sure. He is not a tyrant, our Bishop. He is a *gutt* man and cares what happens to me, just as Jeremiah does. I will continue to pray about my choice. But it is you I am worried about, not me."

She shrugged, not wanting to think about what her future might hold or what she'd be leaving behind. Right now, all that mattered was saving Sarah from the embarrassment of cameras crowding her home and invading her privacy, or keeping the Bishop from scolding her friend and making her miserable. "You don't need to worry about me. I'll be fine."

"But what will you lose if you return to this world where you do not belong? Surely that cannot be *Gott's* will for your life."

"I can't stay, Sarah. You heard what Veronica said before she pulled the camera crew out. Even if the Bishop allowed me to stay, which he won't, Veronica would keep the cameras pointed at your house and film every person who goes in or out the doors. We could keep them from coming in, even get the sheriff involved if they trespass, but that won't stop them from following you around town or harassing your people. I can't allow that."

Sarah gave a slow nod. "I understand. But what about Hunter? Have you thought of him?"

"Yes." Annie almost choked over the word. "Besides you, he's all I've thought about. But you saw his face and how disappointed and angry he was at me—at the entire situation. They came to his office and asked questions. I know these people. They won't leave him or you alone until they get what they want—me."

Sarah stood, her face sad. "So you will leave Hunter to return with this man who you do not love? Who you do not even respect? You will give up everything you could have here, to return to that life?"

Annie blinked away her returning tears. "Yes." She whispered the word. "To protect you, I have to. Besides, it's only a TV show. It's not like I'm going to marry Scott for real."

Sarah leaned over and gave Annie a hug, then walked toward the door. "I do not believe this will be goodbye. I am asking *Gott* to intervene." She tipped her head to the side. "You meant what you said to the Bishop?"

Annie rose and picked up a bag in each hand. "That

you've helped me more than I ever could have helped you? Yes. I meant every word. My life has been blessed and changed since coming here, and I'll be forever grateful." She hurried to the door and pushed it open, practically running down the porch stairs before she could change her mind.

Chapter Twenty-Nine

JIMMY COULDN'T BELIEVE WHAT GRETCHEN HAD said—the Adson family had duped a lot of people besides him? He didn't know if that should make him feel better or worse. He thought this would be his big break—that Scott Adson would keep his word and put him on the show, but if his indifference a few minutes ago was any indication, he seriously doubted that would happen.

He leaned over, placing his hands against his knees, his stomach rolling. What had he done to Annie, not to mention Sarah? Sarah had been his friend for years, and she had never been anything but kind. Her Amish community had helped him get a start a couple of years ago because she had recommended him as a good driver.

He'd sneaked in and stood near an open window when Scott's mother threatened to stay and keep filming Sarah and her people. He groaned. He'd had no idea the film crew would camp on the inn's doorstep and even invade her home. He assumed Annie would *want* to return to Hollywood at some point. Who wouldn't? He never would have left. He straightened as a new thought hit.

Hunter. He was the reason she wanted to stay in Cave City. Tendrils of jealousy snaked through his mind, but he shut them down before they could take root again. Annie wasn't his girl. Even though he'd hoped it might happen, she never would be—especially now that he'd ratted her out to Scott and his mother.

The woman who'd spoken to him—Gretchen—if he remembered correctly, leaned against her car, her face filled with curiosity. Well, let her look. Nothing mattered anymore. He was stuck in this two-bit town, and it served him right. He had no one to blame but himself for what happened to Sarah, as well as to Annie.

The front door swung open, and Annie slipped outside, juggling two suitcases. A minute later, Sarah walked out and hurried after her. Gretchen pushed upright from her post against the car, then dashed down the short walkway to the porch. "Hold on, Ann. Let me help."

Jimmy stood frozen. He probably should go help and not let them carry the bags alone, but somehow, he didn't think either of the women would care to have him do so. The thought stung. Sarah wouldn't let it show, as she was too kind, but no telling what Annie would say or do.

The two women were closing in on Gretchen's car when Annie's attention shifted to him, and she slowed, then came to a stop. "Hello, Jimmy."

Gretchen winced. "Sorry, Ann. I didn't think to warn you he was still here. Why are you still here, anyway? Didn't you get enough satisfaction by turning Ann in to the Adson family? You have to watch her leave so you can gloat?"

Ann touched Gretchen's arm. "It's okay. They would have found me eventually on their own, regardless. As soon as they found out what town I was staying in, they would have hunted me down. There was no good ending to this."

Guilt slammed Jimmy harder than he'd thought possible. He'd expected Annie to rail against him—tell him what a jerk he was and demand he never speak to her again. Instead, she said it was okay—that he wasn't to blame when he knew he was? He shook his head. None of this was okay. He was beginning to see that now. "I'm so sorry, Annie. I never should have followed you around or sent Scott that picture of you and Hunter. I didn't realize what a mess it would make. I thought I'd get to be on a reality show as a result of helping them, and now. . ." He spread his hands, clueless what more he could say or how he could set things right. "I guess I blew it, big time."

She raised her brows. "How much was the reward they paid you for turning me in?"

"I didn't accept the reward."

Gretchen smirked. "No, he had his own reward all figured out."

Jimmy's head started to pound, and he rubbed his forehead. "I only wanted to get a part on the show. I figured if I helped, they'd let me have a shot in Hollywood. And now?" He shrugged. "Pretty stupid, huh?" He scuffed his toe in the loose gravel at his feet, wanting nothing more than to crawl into a hole and disappear.

Annie gave a ghost of a smile. "Hey, it's as much my fault as anyone's. I should have been honest from the beginning with Sarah, Hunter, you—everyone. Don't beat yourself up over it, Jimmy. Maybe this will be the break you've been looking for. Enjoy your time in Hollywood."

Gretchen opened the trunk and swung one of Annie's bags in then reached for the other one. "They blew him off. I don't think he's going to get an invite to L.A. anytime soon."

Annie laughed. "Sorry. That laugh wasn't aimed at you, Jimmy. But I'm not a bit surprised. That's how the Adson family rolls. Even Scott's sister Carmen, who didn't come with them from L.A. is like that. It's all about them and rarely anyone else. Maybe this needed to happen so you can figure out what's important in your life, know what I mean? I've had to do a lot of deep soul searching since arriving here. Who knows? You might need to do the same."

Jimmy couldn't begin to think of a response. He was still reeling over Annie's lack of recrimination over his involvement in bringing the film crew here. The fact that she hadn't screamed at him made him feel even worse. He cleared his throat. "I meant it when I said I was sorry. If there's anything I can do to help make this right, say the word. Whatever it takes. I mean that."

She nodded. "Thanks. Now I'd better get out of here before I cause any more problems for Sarah." She patted his shoulder as she slipped past him on her way to her side of the car. A minute later, it moved slowly down the road headed for town.

Jimmy stared after it, his mind swimming, trying to sort out everything that had happened, when suddenly, it hit. Maybe he could be of use to Annie and undo at least part of the mess he'd created. He gave a short nod. Yes, sir, maybe he could, at that. If he hurried, he could follow a distance behind and see what hotel they stayed at. No telling what use his various skill sets could be put to before this was over.

Chapter Thirty

CONVERSATION BETWEEN VERONICA, SCOTT, AND AN occasional reply from Gretchen, flowed around Annie as they sat in the dining room at the hotel across town where they'd booked rooms for the entire crew. She barely registered what they were saying, because she didn't care. More than anything right now, she wanted to find a way out of this tangled, convoluted mess called her life. She'd meant what she'd said to Jimmy. Yeah, it was partly his fault that he'd gotten greedy and called Scott, but most of this was on her for not being honest from the beginning. All this time, she'd thought keeping quiet about who she really was, would protect her and provide some semblance of normalcy. Instead, it had badly hurt Sarah, the one person who had gone out of her way to make her feel at home and accepted.

And Hunter. She couldn't blame him for reacting the way he had and shutting her out of his life. At first, she'd been shocked that he'd think she'd lied to him, but thinking about it now, it made sense. She'd done everything in her power to keep any details about her life to herself—at least, any details that would lead to Hunter discovering the truth about who she was and where she came from. So she had lied, if only by omission, and she'd done so intentionally. She'd give anything to change the past.

"Ann." Veronica waved jeweled fingers in front of Annie's eyes. "Snap out of it and join us in the real world. You need to get your head together and listen. This is important. Got it?"

Annie lifted her chin. "The *real* world. Right. What do you need?"

Veronica settled into her chair and dismissed the waiter who hovered nearby with a flick of her wrist. "We're locked into the reunion episode when we get back. The producers love the idea. Due to all the social media the past couple of weeks, they're eating up the new storyline."

Annie almost laughed. Storyline. That shouldn't be a surprise. Her and Scott's grand reunion was only another piece of the impressive web the Adsons wove to keep their show moving forward.

Scott grinned. "Sounds great. Doesn't it, Ann?"

"Yeah. Wonderful." She couldn't muster an ounce of enthusiasm. They had her where they wanted her, sitting in this chair and heading to L.A. soon, and for now, that would have to be enough. Her insides felt drained with nothing left to give. But beneath it all simmered the peace she'd longed for. She'd done what was right. She'd put others ahead of herself, and she'd done it for the right reasons. *Thank you, Lord.*

Veronica looked from face to face, making sure she had their full attention. "I have another idea that will help make that episode even bigger. We can cause the ratings on that episode to go through the roof, if we play this right." She leaned forward. "Tomorrow, right here in this hotel, we're going to live stream the moment you two love-birds get back together."

Annie gaped at her. "Wait. What?"

"Not the whole thing, of course, only a couple of minutes. Enough to whet the appetites of our followers. A teaser, if you will. Our fans can watch in real time. If you two play it up right, they'll be sharing on every social media platform that exists. Our first episode showing the full reunion will be huge—very possibly, our biggest one yet."

Scott drummed his fingers on the table top. "And

the network is fine with this? They've given the go ahead?"

Veronica arched her penciled brows. "That's why Doyle is still in L.A. He's working behind the scenes, running interference for us, making sure they understand how big this will be. They're going to love what happens. Trust me, once they see the results, they won't be complaining."

Annie struggled to keep from rolling her eyes and snorting her disdain. What a hypocrite. "Aren't you the one who told me that no one wants to watch true love anymore? All they want is tragedy and conflict?"

Veronica turned icy eyes Annie's direction and stared. "That is not for you to worry about. All you need to remember is how to act like you're sorry you turned down Scott's proposal before you left and ran away and how happy you are that he's willing to take you back. You do understand, don't you, Ann?"

The muscles in Annie's neck tightened. "Perfectly." At one word from this power-hungry woman, the cameras would be camping on Sarah's and Hunter's doorsteps.

Veronica gave her a sugary smile. "As long as we understand one another, dear."

Thirty minutes later, Annie pushed away her almost untouched plate of chicken alfredo. "I'm going to get a little fresh air then call it a night and head to my room. I'll see you tomorrow morning."

Scott pushed to his feet. "Want me to go with you? I hate to see you walk around the streets at night unaccompanied. You never know what could happen."

She shook her head. "This is Cave City, not L.A. I'll be fine, and I prefer to be alone. I won't be long. I'm tired and plan to be in bed within a few minutes." She nodded to Gretchen. "'Night."

Annie slipped out of the hotel, making sure she stayed in the shadows. If she were lucky, the paparazzi would all stay inside swarming around their golden boy, Scott. She slipped down the street away from the hotel, allowing her feet to take her where they wanted, without thinking about where she could end up. How had her life gotten to this place? She slowed her pace and looked up at the starry sky. "Lord, please help me find a way of escape. I'm tired of doing everything on my own. Please show me what to do. I don't want to return to my old life and all that entails. I'd like to stay here and see where this path leads me, even if it's without Hunter."

She came to a stop and glanced around, needing to get her bearings before heading to the hotel. An office building with the lights blazing directly across the street drew her attention. Strange that someone would be working this late. Her heart rate increased. That was Hunter's office—she'd been there in the daylight, but never at night, or she'd have realized where she was standing. Her gaze traveled to the window at the far-right front corner, and she gasped. "Hunter." He sat at his desk, head bowed and unmoving.

She started across the street without thinking. When she reached the mid-way point, she stopped, thankful no cars were on the road. What was she going to do, beat on the front door or his office window and demand he talk to her? It wouldn't work—not after the way he'd walked out of Sarah's home today without looking back. She retraced her steps and slowly made her way to the hotel.

Her footsteps lagged as she got within a few yards of the front door. Bed didn't even sound good right now. More than likely, it would be impossible to sleep.

"I don't care what you tell the network, Doyle."

Veronica's voice seared the night, her words clipped and tight. "All you have to do is hold them off until we've had a chance to do the live stream tomorrow. It's imperative this works, or we could both be in trouble."

Annie pressed herself against the wall in the shadows, praying Veronica hadn't seen her. Something about this conversation wasn't right, and she intended to find out what was going on.

"I already told you! After we do the live stream for two or three minutes, the fans will clamor for more. The network won't have a choice. They'll stop this ridiculous idea of giving Scott his own show and cutting me out of the storyline. There is no *Life with the Adsons* if Scott's sister and I aren't in the show. It would be *Life with Scott Adson*, and that's not good enough. I built this show into what it is, and I will not be cut for anyone, not even my son."

Annie worked to keep her breathing shallow, hoping no one would walk by on their way to the hotel and see her huddled against the wall.

"I know I made the decision to cut Ann and bring Jessie in." Veronica's voice rose a notch, making it easier to hear each word. "How was I to know Jessie would throw fits and make demands and be impossible to work with? Besides, I had to get rid of Ann. She was getting way too popular, and the way it was going, she would have gotten a higher-paying contract than the rest of us." She gave a derisive laugh. "She's not even an Adson, and she never will be, if I have anything to say about it." Veronica stepped into the light from the door. "Make sure that doesn't happen. If you value your job, you'll make sure the suits are watching tomorrow and don't miss a word." She snapped her phone shut and pushed through the front door.

Chapter Thirty-One

THE NEXT MORNING, HUNTER STOOD BACK and studied his sanding job on the inside of Sarah's front door. It could stand a little more before he applied the stain and varnish, but it was almost there. If only she'd allow him to put a deadbolt on the inside for security, should that intrusive camera crew return—but no, Sarah would have none of it. All were welcome at her inn, as she'd reminded him only minutes before when he'd tried to suggest it.

"Hunter?" Sarah walked across the foyer toward him. "I brought coffee. Would you like to rest for a moment?"

He pulled a rag from his hip pocket and wiped off the dust from the door. "Sure. Sounds good. You make the best coffee lately."

She smiled. "That's Annie's doing. She taught me the right proportions for a perfect cup."

His answering smile faded. "Right. Annie." He motioned toward the door. "This will be lovely once it's stained and coated."

"*Ya.* I am sure the new owner will appreciate it, once it is sold."

"I'm sorry, Sarah. I hate that you're considering selling this place when you love it so much. And I'm sorry about Annie. I'd like to talk to you about that . . . about what Annie did and how you feel about it all. I have so many questions about why she would try to fool us all when she came, instead of being honest. And that doesn't count issues of my own I'm trying to work through and probably need to deal with. Issues that concern Annie."

She handed him the mug of coffee. "*Ach*, that is not true, Hunter. *Nein.* She did nothing of the sort. You do not understand. She is fooling *Scott*, not us."

He took a sip and frowned, wanting to believe what his heart had told him last night, wanting to be free of his pride that kept dragging him down every time he thought about Annie not telling him the truth. "I'm afraid I don't follow. I know Annie said Adson isn't her boyfriend, yet she left with him and his crew. You heard Adson's mother demand that Annie return to Hollywood and be a part of the show again, and she decided to go with them. I assumed that meant she wants another shot at her career."

"Annie and I talked before she left here. She does not wish to go back to their world. She has been trying to discover who she wants to be—who *Gott* wants her to be—ever since she arrived here. I think she finally figured it out, and she made her decision. She loves it here and said it's the first time she's felt as though she'd come home in years. You will see—she respects our ways and has no desire to harm me or our community. The Bishop will eventually see that and understand as well."

Hunter shook his head. "She tried to tell me that, and I didn't listen. I was so hurt, believing that she'd deliberately used me to help get her ratings up, that I refused to listen when she tried to explain. I heard what she said to Uncle and you. I wanted to believe it, then I started second-guessing myself again. But now—"

Sarah took the cup from his hand. "Whatever you need to say, you must say to her, not to me. Before it is too late."

His heart lurched as sudden realization set in. He might never see Annie again. He'd as good as sent her away when he'd let her think he didn't trust her or forgive her—would never forgive her. Some Christian he'd proved to be. He'd judged Annie for not trusting him, but he'd done virtually the same thing to her. Had he completely blown any chance he might have with Annie? "Thanks, Sarah."

He yanked open the front door and raced for his truck, praying God would give him another opportunity to find out if the woman he'd thought he'd known really existed, as Sarah had said, or if the old Ann Stanway was the real woman behind the mask Annie had been wearing. He jammed his key into the ignition and shot up another quick prayer for wisdom and discernment. He could really use help with this one.

Annie sat next to Gretchen in front of a make-shift mirror and make-up area in the dining room of the hotel where the crew had set up. They were ready to begin the shoot any moment, and since it was between breakfast and lunch, the hotel had allowed them to cordon off the entrance doors and only let in the extras and crew working on the upcoming live stream. *Lead me the rest of the way. Help me pull off what Jimmy suggested.* She'd been shocked when she'd received a note from Jimmy earlier, but she showed it to Gretchen, and they'd been in agreement. It might just work.

Gretchen leaned in close to Annie's ear, her voice pitched low. "Are you sure this is the right way to handle this?"

"Yes. I need to make things right if I can. Did you talk to Jimmy? Is he ready to go if you give him the signal?"

"He's waiting in the lobby."

"Good." Annie nodded then pasted on a fake smile as Scott strode over to the table.

He waved Gretchen out of the way and slipped into the chair she'd vacated. "You ready for this?" Excitement blazed from his eyes—the same eyes Annie thought she could get lost in only a couple of weeks ago, before her world started to unravel.

"As ready as I'll ever be."

He didn't seem to get the hidden message, but she didn't care. Hopefully, this would all be over soon, one way or the other. She prayed it wouldn't blow up in her face and make her life more miserable than it had become the past twenty-four hours.

Scott flipped open his laptop and put it on the table, then punched a couple of keys. "Take a look at this." He positioned the screen so they could both see it. "I put the word out last night that something big was going to take place today. The count shows we have over six million people tuned in to see what's happening. I expect that to increase as we get close to air time. Pretty amazing, huh?"

"Yeah. Great." She worked to infuse a measure of excitement into her voice, but Scott was so immersed in his own future glory, it probably wouldn't have mattered if she hadn't answered at all. "When do we go live?"

"Soon. The cameras are almost in place. We don't want to make it look like we're already together. They need to see us meet for the first time, know what I mean?"

"Right." She had all she could do not to laugh. Third or fourth time was more like it, but who was counting? It was all an illusion, anyway.

"They'll signal that the cameras are about to start rolling, and that will be the start of the live stream. I'll get up, leave the room, then come in and see you sitting at the table. Any final thoughts or do you have your part all down?"

"I think I've got it. But I do have one request. You remember that guy, Jimmy Snyder? The one who called you?"

"I guess. What about him?"

"He's bummed about not getting a part in the show like he'd hoped. What do you think about using him as an extra? We need a few people in the background to make it look natural, right?"

He laughed. "Toss the guy a bone to keep him happy. I hear you. Sure, we can do that."

"Thanks." She ran a brush through her long blonde hair one last time and set the brush on the table. "I think I saw him out in the lobby. Maybe you can send one of the crew out to get him?"

"Sure thing." He motioned to a man then gave him a description of Jimmy. "Bring him in and tell him where to mill around with the other extras and try to look natural. A couple of them should sit at nearby tables. You know the drill."

"No problem. I'll get him and be right back. We're about ready to roll."

A few minutes later, Annie, Veronica, and Scott sat together at a round table, with Annie and Scott side-by-side, a laptop open in front of Veronica, the webcam on top directed toward where Annie and Scott sat, close together. Annie let out a soft sigh. Jimmy was sitting at the table next to theirs, studiously working on his own computer, a cup of coffee near his left hand. Another extra sat across from him, with several more sprinkled around the room. Now if only this would work the way she, Jimmy, and Gretchen had planned.

Scott pointed to the corner. "Mother, you see this

area? As soon as the cameraman gives the signal, hit this button. The red light will come on to show we're live. The cameras are rolling now, to be sure we catch everything in case there are any hiccups, but the live stream will be picked up and relayed by the webcam. When I walk up toward the table, that's your signal to start the live stream on the computer. Our film footage will get edited to when the webcam is activated, so no worries about anything happening on TV now. Got it?"

Veronica huffed. "I wasn't born yesterday, Scott. Of course, I have it." She pointed at the readout to the right of the screen where the live feed would be displayed. "Is this right? We're at eight million people watching now? That's incredible!"

Annie caught movement out of the corner of her eye and glanced toward the door. Somehow Hunter had managed to gain entrance. More than likely he knew one of the local guards stationed there to keep out anyone not tagged as an extra. She caught his eye for a brief moment, then he walked to a corner within hearing distance of their table.

Scott puffed out his chest. "Yeah, it's very cool. You were right, Mom. Our first episode will be huge with us staging this little reunion scene today."

Annie nodded. "Yes. As you both always say: we have to do what's best for the show, right?"

Veronica gave her a tolerant smile. "I'm glad to see you've finally come around, Ann. It's about time you understood that what's good for the show is also good for you."

Annie glanced to the side and briefly met Jimmy's eyes. He gave a slight nod and a smile. She drew in a deep breath. "I'm curious about one thing you never explained. When you replaced me with Jessie on the show, it was because of my ratings. At least, that's what

I remember you saying at the time."

Veronica shrugged. "It happens to the best of us at times."

"I understand. I mean, you certainly didn't want me to get too popular and take over the show. That wouldn't look good for the family."

Scott's head rose with a quick jerk. "Wait—what?"

Veronica's smile was brittle. "I think you must be confused."

Annie's brows rose. "Like I'm confused that the network wasn't at all happy that you brought Jessie onto the show?"

"Sometimes things don't work out the way we hope."

Annie smiled into Veronica's hard eyes. "Right. Like you worrying your career might be going down the drain when you heard they planned to fire you from your own show?"

Veronica emitted a snarl.

Scott blinked, his face mirroring confusion and shock. "Mom?"

She waved away his concern. "That's ridiculous. Where did you hear this garbage, anyway?"

Annie worked to keep the butterflies at bay warring in her stomach. "Why, from you. Who else? I was taking a walk last night and overheard you talking to Doyle. You told him there was no way you were going to allow the network to drop you and give Scott his own show. That you'd do whatever it took to keep that from happening."

Scott rounded on his mother. "My own show? You didn't tell me? And if that had happened, I'd become Executive Producer, not you."

She reached out a hand toward him. "Scott—honey."

He pulled away. "I want to know what Ann's talking about. She obviously overheard you talking. What's going on that I don't know about? What have you been trying to hide from me?"

"She's upset and trying to get even. Ignore her. Remember, you, your sister, and I are family. Family is always the most important part of this show, right? We can't forget that."

Annie gave a low chuckle. "Yeah. Right. Carmen has always been a minor character in the show—not even in it enough to be a threat. Sure, family is always the most important, until the success of one of them threatens to upstage you."

Veronica glared at Annie, all pretense of civility gone. "That will be enough from you, young lady. Not another word. You are trying to sabotage this program. You should be grateful. We pulled you off that catering business and gave you the chance to be a star. And not a very good one at that. If it wasn't for Scott and me taking you under our wing, you'd be nothing now. You don't even know how to act."

"I never wanted to be a star." Annie's eyes skimmed over Scott and flew to Hunter's. "The only thing I ever wanted was to be loved and appreciated for who I was. Nothing more."

Veronica gave an unladylike snort. "But you didn't turn down the role either, did you? And now, thanks to the show that was my brainchild—the show that's been a success due to my guiding hand—the world has this misguided idea that you are even remotely interesting."

Scott frowned. "Hey, that's not fair. Enough."

"Stop being so naïve, Scott. Ann is nothing more than a boring young woman who we worked hard to make into someone remotely interesting. We've managed to trick our audience into thinking she's special." She gave an unladylike snort. "Don't you get it? That shows how easily fans can be manipulated, if you play them correctly. They think all of this is real, and it's all a big game."

"But . . ." Scott shook his head as though to clear it. "I have real feelings for Ann. You know that."

"Ha." His mother's face contorted in a grimace. "You'd fall in love with any woman the network and producers told you to. Face it, this is a reality show, and you're just part of the act that makes it work. We all are. And our audience is dumb enough to buy into it all."

Scott leaned heavily into his chair, his face masked in shock. He opened his mouth but no sound came out.

A phone rang in the distance, then another one closer by, all inside the perimeter of the dining room.

Veronica stood and glared. "Who left their phone on? Whoever it is, you're fired." She waved at the cameras. "Stop rolling. Destroy every bit of this footage. We're going to start over." She rounded on Annie. "*You* will do as you're told and say what you're told, or you're off this show forever. And believe me, you and your Amish friends will live to regret your actions if that happens. We'll make sure we film them all and make them look like idiots. How will you like that, young lady?"

Multiple phones began to ring. Annie's glance strayed to the top corner of the laptop. Scott followed her glance and froze. "Mom?"

She waved her arms in the air. "I said turn off those phones. Now! Or clear the room!"

Scott's hand shook as he pointed at the steady red light in the corner of the screen. "Mom. When did you push that button?"

Veronica's eyes narrowed. "What button?" She bent

over and peered at the screen. "I didn't push any button."

Scott's voice rose in pitch. "We've been live-streaming for over five minutes."

She fell into her chair, her anger turning to confusion. "What are you talking about?"

Annie smiled, pleasure bubbling inside that this had gone as she'd hoped. "He's talking about the ten million people who have been watching the show on the live stream the past few minutes—and all the lovely things you said about your fans that you can't take back."

"But. . ." She shook her head, dislodging a few perfectly placed curls. "That's impossible. I didn't touch that laptop. Scott?" She swung toward him. "You must have bumped it." She nearly spat the words at Annie. "I'd say you did it if you were sitting where you could reach the button without Scott or me noticing."

Annie motioned toward Jimmy. "You remember Jimmy Snyder? The guy who tried to help your show by giving me up—the guy who you blew off and ignored after making him a promise to let him have a part on your show?"

He lifted a hand and waved.

"Among other things, he's a computer genius."

Jimmy gave a slow smile. "You should read a few of these comments coming in from your fans."

"Shut it off!" Veronica said the words through gritted teeth while trying to smile. "Now!"

Scott reached out and slapped the laptop shut.

Veronica's phone vibrated, and she glanced at the screen. All the color ebbed from her face. "It's the president of the network."

"You just called ten million of his viewers dumb, but I'm sure you'll be fine." Part of Annie felt bad for what must be coming for Veronica, but mostly she hoped this wouldn't spill over on Scott. He'd been part of this fiasco in getting her back, but she'd sensed his heart hadn't been in it, and he'd been worried for her.

Veronica rose to her feet, staring down at Annie. "Get out." She pointed toward the door of the dining room. "You're fired. Your contract will not be renewed."

Annie slipped out of her seat and looked where Hunter had been standing. The spot was empty. Her gaze roamed over the rest of the room. Nothing. Disappointment hit her hard. Hadn't he seen or heard what she'd been trying to do? Did he still have so little faith in her that he'd leave? She lifted her chin and walked away from the table.

Veronica's voice came distinctly across the room. "Hello? Charles! Yes, this is Veronica Adson. How are you, sir?"

Annie smiled. Sometimes wishes did come true. At least, some of them.

Chapter Thirty-Two

HUNTER LOUNGED AGAINST THE OUTSIDE WALL of the hotel, praying Annie would come out before either of the Adsons or their crew started to exit. Maybe he should have waited to see what would happen, but as soon as all the phones in the room started ringing and the president of the network had called that obnoxious woman, he'd slipped outside. He needed time to figure out what he wanted to say to Annie—how he could apologize for not trusting her and assuming the worst.

He held his breath as the door swung open, waiting to see who it was. Annie emerged, pulling a pair of wheeled cases behind her. His breath whooshed out, and he stepped forward, extending his hand. "Need any help, lady? I take tips."

She bit her lip and eyed him. "I doubt I could afford to pay you what you deserve."

"We'll have to see about that. Do you need a ride to Sarah's?" He gave her a soft smile and slipped his hand over hers, squeezing it, then took the handle of her bag. "By the way, that was quite the show you put on in there. I've never seen anything like it."

"Hmm—that was my finale. I'm done with show business. And I'm not sure where I'm headed next, to be honest. But I'll take the offer of a ride, and maybe I'll figure it out before we get wherever we're headed." She smiled as he helped her into the truck then stashed her bags in the back. As he slipped into the other side, she turned toward him. Her eyes met his, and time hung suspended for several mesmerizing seconds.

He'd never realized the fathomless depths of her eyes before. Or how incredibly lovely they were. And those lips. He moistened his own. He had no right to kiss her after what had happened between them, but longing hit him so hard he wanted nothing more than to lean forward and draw her close. He shook himself. This wasn't the time—he had to make things right and discover where they stood—or if there ever could be a 'they.'

Suddenly, flashes went off outside the windows on both sides. Knuckles tapped on the glass. "Hey, Ann! What's going on? Are you staying on the show or starting one of your own?"

Another voice lifted above that one. "Come on, Ann. Give us a break out here. Veronica stormed off and wouldn't tell us a thing, and Scott started swearing at us. Give us a scoop, won't you?"

Hunter stuck his key in the ignition and turned it, but Annie held up her hand. "Wait. I owe them this, then I want you to get me as far away as you can." She rolled down her window an inch and tipped her chin so her lips were close to the opening. "It's over. I'm finished with *Life with the Adsons*. I have no idea what Veronica will be doing, but my guess is Scott will have his own show. Now get out of the way before you get run over."

They jumped back as Hunter put the truck in gear and punched the accelerator. The truck roared down the road and took a corner. Hunter peered in his rear-view mirror. "Looks like that did the trick. I'm guessing all the vultures have flown inside to see if they can pick up any more scraps from Scott or his mother." He took another corner at a slower speed. "I guess we shouldn't head for Sarah's just yet."

"Where are we going?"

"I'll take the road that leads to the caves. The reporters probably aren't familiar with it, so we should be safe there." He pulled to a stop in a few minutes, and Hunter released a long sigh. "About the show. I'm sorry for all the things I said to you. I was a class A jerk. I should have listened when you came to my office and tried to explain. I was wrong, and I'm so sorry. When I found out you were returning with Scott to be on *Life with the Adsons*, I thought . . ."

She touched his hand. "First, thank you for getting me out of there, oh knight in shining armor." She smiled. "You were saying . . . what did you think when you believed I was going back?"

He pushed the words out in a rush. "That you'd be going to L.A. forever, and I'd never see you again. Never get the chance to tell you what I'm feeling. That scared me worse than almost anything I've experienced before, and it made me sick at the same time."

"Exactly what are you feeling?" She edged a little closer across the bench seat, her gaze hopeful.

He reached out and wrapped his arm around her shoulders, pulling her close. "That my feelings for you are about as strong and real as they get—that I fell for the 'real' Annie, not the fake Ann Stanway. I care for the Annie I met in Cave City. The Annie Farley I kissed in the cavern. And I was terrified that you would leave and turn into Ann Stanway again."

"Never." Her hand slipped up his chest until she cupped his cheek. "I don't even know that girl—in fact, she never existed—she was only a fabrication."

He couldn't rein in his emotions any longer. He bent his head and captured her lips with his own, as warmth spread, mixing with pure joy. He smoothed her hair away from her face, then placed a gentle kiss on her forehead, on each cheek, then his lips met hers again.

She gave a contented sigh a minute later and

snuggled into his chest. "Do you think your uncle would mind if I stay in Cave City for a while?"

He drew back a few inches, so he could look into her eyes. "And how long is a while?"

"Hmm." She said the word with a dreamy note. "I was thinking I might want to sell my house in L.A. and buy a little cottage in a town where it's peaceful and nothing ever happens—other than to help rescue homeless women, fight off film crews and angry Bishops, and in the future maybe, just maybe, date the handsomest man in town—if he'll have me that is."

He tipped his head to the side and frowned. "Should I be jealous? Do I happen to know this handsome man?"

She laughed and pulled his head down. "I'm about to kiss him, so he'd better hurry up and figure it out."

AUTHOR NOTE

So much has gone into the journey from the concept of this book to the production of the movie, that it's hard to sort out all the pieces. But there's one thing that stands out, and that's how it all began. You would think that would be when I received the call from my (now) producer, Chevonne O'Shaughnessy in the late spring of 2015, but it started much earlier. In fact, what happened has the definite feel of the Hand of God in bringing it all to pass.

Rewind to early 2011. I had a finished manuscript, an old west romance set in ranch country outside of Sundance, Wyoming, titled *Outlaw Angel*, that my agent was shopping. I'd written and published three books with Summerside Press, all part of their Love Finds You series. In fact, my agent had presented the book set in Sundance as another *Love Finds You* book, but it was turned down as the location had already been assigned to another well-known author. I'd decided the manuscript would become the first in a series of three old west romances, but by that point it hadn't found a home.

My editor with Summerside contacted me in January or February of that year, saying they were in desperate need of a book with that setting for their *Love Finds You* line, and asked if I had sold mine yet. I said no—my agent was shopping it as a three-book series. Long story short, their author had some kind of setback, and she was unable to fulfill the contract. They offered me the contract, but at a lower rate than my agent or myself wanted to accept. Finally, I reluctantly decided to move forward and give up my dream of it becoming a series. After all, I'd first written it thinking it might be a good fit for the LFY line.

The book was published in the late summer of 2011, a very fast turnaround time. A couple of years later, I got word that a Hollywood production company had optioned several of the LFY titles, including mine set in Sundance. Three *Love Finds You* movies were made and aired on the UP Channel over the next two years, but nothing more was said about *Sundance*.

Then, in 2015, I received an email from Chevonne, followed by a phone call. Imagine my surprise when she asked if I'd be willing to write a book for them. They were no longer producing the *Love Finds You* books into movies and were working on a totally different project for UP TV, a possible three-movie series. She hoped I might be able to work with them. As anyone would be, I was curious why she'd chosen me. She explained that she'd optioned Sundance two or three years earlier, and loved it. Of the thirty-five or so titles she'd read of the line, that was her favorite. However, UP didn't want to make historical or old west movies, so she'd shelved it for now.

During that time period, I'd gotten my rights returned to all of my LFY books and had retitled them *Finding Love in Last Chance, California*, *Finding Love in Tombstone, Arizona*, and *Finding Love in Bridal Veil, Oregon.* Sundance became *Outlaw Angel*, and all four are still in print.

Here's the amazing part. I came very, very close to turning down that contract offer with Summerside for *Sundance*. I was disappointed in the advance and royalty rate, and shortly after they released it, they sold the line to Guideposts, and that company didn't continue the line much longer. Understandably, sales waned on their final releases, and I was disappointed with my sales from that final book as all three of my others had done quite well. For a long time, I wished I hadn't taken that contract and instead had held out for one with another company for a three-book series. However, had I done that, I doubt *Runaway Romance* would ever have been written. It was *Sundance* that grabbed Chevonne's attention and caused her to contact me. After reading it, she asked if I could write a brand-new contemporary romance, as she no longer had the right to produce any *Love Finds You* books and needed to start with something completely new. And the rest, as they say, is history.

The journey had its ups and downs, with three different projects pitched before UP TV decided on *Runaway Romance*. We're currently working on the second movie, and I'm excited to get that book written as well. Months later, I pitched the idea of taking my book *Finding Love in Bridal Veil, Oregon*, and changing it into a contemporary mystery/romance rather than a historical romance. The rights to it had been returned to me months before, and since we knew we couldn't use it the way it was, they optioned it, then I changed the title to *Secrets of the Veil, A Bridal Veil Mystery*. It will hopefully be filmed for an international audience soon, and possibly also be purchased for a US audience. *Outlaw Angel* has also been optioned, in the hope that one day an interest in western movies will return.

Also since that time, I've become the publisher at Mountain Brook Ink, a small Christian press. We have now released close to forty titles, including award-winning books, two of which have also been optioned by ACI, Chevonne and George's company.

I was blessed to meet George and Chevonne at a film festival in May of 2017, where we presented and promoted *Runaway Romance*, and I plan to be on set for the filming of the second movie in the next few months. I hope you've enjoyed this book, and that you'll watch for the second one coming next spring. It will mostly be Sarah's story, but you'll still see a lot of Hunter and Annie as they continue their journey in Cave City, Kentucky.

If you'd care to connect with me, you can do so at the following places: My website/blog and newsletter sign-up: www.miraleeferrell.com

Twitter: www.twitter.com/miraleeferrell

Facebook Author Group:
https://www.facebook.com/groups/82316202888/

Mountain Brook Ink website:
www.mountainbrookink.com

I prefer to interact on FB in my author group, rather than adding more friends, so please connect with me there rather than sending a friend request. Thank you all for taking the time to read my newest book, and if you have time, check out some of my other fiction, which you can find by doing a search on Amazon under Miralee Ferrell.

Please consider posting a review if you enjoyed this book, and share the book with friends and family. Doing both of those are a wonderful blessing to an author, and helps assure we'll have readers for our books in the future. Thank you all!

Book two will release in mid-to-late 2019.

A PEEK AT Another book by Miralee Ferrell

OUTLAW ANGEL—A Historical Romance

Chapter One

Texas Panhandle, 1887

ANGEL RAMIREZ WOKE WITH A START, her heart pounding a rolling beat in her chest. Someone was in her room.

Inching her fingers under the edge of her pillow, her hand brushed against the cold steel of her Colt revolver. She eased the gun out and waited, allowing her vision to adjust to the partial darkness of the muggy August night. Uncle Jose had taught her to wait, never to rush when confronting an intruder—the first shot might be her only one.

Rolling over onto her side, she pointed the gun at the door. "Who's there?"

A half moon sent tentative fingers of light through the small window near the foot of her bed, and a dark form stepped forward. "It's Jose. Put your gun down, *m'ija.*" Her uncle's accented drawl was absent—the words short and clipped. "Get dressed and meet me outside. Hurry now." He slipped out the door and closed it carefully behind him.

Angel drew on her trousers and long-sleeved shirt,

tugged on her boots, and shoved her sombrero onto her close-cropped curls. After a quick look around the room, she grabbed her rifle and headed outside. Jose raised his hand for silence and drew her into the nearby stand of trees, not far from their small, three-room cabin. “Keep your voice down. I don’t want any of the men in the *banda* to hear.”

The hair on the back of Angel’s arms stood on end. “What’s wrong?”

“Another cattle raid. I won’t leave you behind. It’s not safe for you here.”

“With the men?”

“Yes. Bart Hinson’s up to something.”

Angel sucked in a breath between her teeth. “Hinson. He’s the worst of this bunch. I don’t like the way he looks at me.”

Jose stifled what sounded like a curse and gripped her arm. “If anything happens to me tonight, promise you’ll ride out of here and never come back.”

Her heart rate accelerated, but she patted his hand. “Nothing’s going to happen to you.”

He swung her toward him and leaned close, dropping his voice. “I don’t trust Hinson. An outlaw banda is no place for a girl, even if you *were* raised here. You’re eighteen and can take care of yourself away from this place.” Her uncle pointed to the rifle near her knee. “That rifle will take you far—you shoot better than most men. Keep dressing like a boy and get work on ranches as a hunter or horse wrangler.”

She tried to laugh off his concern, but the effort nearly choked her. “This is my home. You’ve had these feelings before, and you’ve always come back safely.”

Jose placed his arm around her shoulders and squeezed. “I wish I’d made other choices years ago, m’ija. If your parents were alive, they wouldn’t have chosen this life for you. I should have sent you back to your mother's people in Italy." He dug into the pocket of his denim jacket and removed a small bag. "There's gold in there—enough to keep you a couple of years, if you're careful and work when you can."

She drew back, hating the thought of taking it. She'd never considered where Jose's money came from, but accepting a bag of gold procured from other people's loss didn't set right. Besides, her uncle's words implied he might not be along. "You're scaring me."

He closed her fingers over the handful of gold. "I plan on living for a long time, m'ija, but you must be ready." He swung away from her and called softly over his shoulder. "Saddle Bella, bring a bedroll, and put whatever you value most in your saddlebags—quick. And whatever you do, stay close to me on the trail."

Angel swung into the saddle and picked up Bella's reins, her black Spanish-Arabian mare. She shoved the Winchester lever-action rifle into the saddle scabbard and tugged her hat over her forehead.

The pale moon shone over the encampment, offering little in the way of light, but the deep reaches of the sky were lit by myriad stars sparkling against the dark backdrop. Dust rose as the outlaws' horses stamped their hooves and pawed at the churned-up ground. Sweat trickled down between Angel's shoulder blades. A horse bumped against Bella. Angel tightened her reins and turned sideways in her saddle.

Bart Hinson swiveled toward her and leered, his narrow lips tipping up the corners of his sun-baked, flat face. "Finally gonna become a true outlaw and help us rustle some cattle, hey, Angel?"

She raised her chin and backed her mare a couple of steps. "I rustle nothing. Jose asked me to come, but I'll not take part." Deliberately she touched her spur to the mare's flank and swung away from the man.

"Think you're too good for us, do you?" He laughed, and a shiver of apprehension ran across Angel's skin. "Once you ride with us, you'll share all that we stand for."

She'd lived among these men and their wives since she was eight years old, and had never been on a cattle raid before—for that matter, she'd never felt fear until recently—and then, only around a handful of the outlaws. Hinson's attentions had increased over the past couple of months, and she'd done her best to stay clear of the man. A sudden understanding of her uncle's concern coursed through her. Hinson wasn't a typical outlaw. He emanated something dark—a hint of evil deep at his core.

Jose moved up alongside her, inserting his sorrel gelding between Bella and Hinson's mount, effectively blocking the man's view of Angel. She was glad to have Bart's hawk-like scrutiny removed. She wanted to sink into a washtub and scrub the evil away.

Jose pressed his horse closer. "You all right, *pequeña*?"

Angel nodded. "*Si.*" She kept her gaze averted from Hinson as he spurred his horse the opposite direction.

Jose dropped his hand to the butt of his rifle. "Good. Let's pray this night will go well, and we'll be back in our beds by nightfall tomorrow."

"Pray, Uncle? You think God in heaven smiles on what we do tonight?"

"Maybe not, but we pray just the same, si?"

An hour later Bella snorted, sidestepped, and shook her head. Angel stroked the neck of her jigging black mare and stared out over the herd of restless cattle. Jose had insisted she stay back in the brush line, within sight of the men moving close to the herd but not near enough to be in danger.

Dust rose from the milling cattle. Calves bawled and their anxious mamas lowed as they searched for their young among the constantly moving melee. Angel struggled to see her uncle through the gloom as the approaching dawn withheld its gift of light. Ghostlike figures rode shadowy horses along the edge of the scrub brush, circling around and returning strays to the herd.

A shout rang out. A rider spurred his mount and charged after a bull racing away from the perimeter with three longhorn cows following close on his heels. The bay gelding stretched his neck and lengthened his stride, his one white stocking flashing against the dark background. His rider pushed the horse harder, leaning forward in his saddle. The pair leapt ahead of the bull, and the man swung his mount ever closer to the wicked horns, pushing the animals back in a wide arc toward the rest of the cattle.

Jose reined in beside Angel, pushed his sombrero back, and wiped his sleeve across his forehead. "It's warm, and the dust makes it worse."

Angel rested her hands on the pommel of her saddle, her reins draped loosely against Bella's neck. "What now?"

"We move the herd north into New Mexico." Jose dropped his voice. "You must leave tonight."

"Leave? I don't understand." She'd never known

anyone to leave the outlaw band. "What about you?"

"This is my life." He shrugged. "And I must stay here to make sure you can get away."

"It's gotten so bad?"

"Si."

"I won't go without you."

"You must promise me, little one."

She hesitated, but the determination bathing his face left her no room to argue. "I promise."

A shout went up from the fringe of the herd, and Jose swung his horse. "Stay out of sight, and don't return to the cabin." He peered back over his shoulder. "Angel?"

"Yes. I hear. Nothing will happen. Now go, before the men get angry at your absence."

He laid the big rowels of his California spurs to the flank of his gelding and cantered across the clearing, rejoining the ever-shifting herd.

Angel turned Bella and followed along parallel with the apex of the jostling cattle, watching the swift riders with grudging respect. These men were some of the best riders and ropers in Texas, and most of them were excellent shots. They had to be—their lives, not to mention their livelihood—depended on their horsemanship and speed with a gun.

The hours dragged as the men, horses, and cattle moved north and glimmering predawn colors appeared in the eastern sky, heralding a clear, hot day. Angel dropped back along the flank of the herd. She slipped her bandana over her nose to block the billows of dust rising from the dry streambed. She'd spoken to her uncle not long ago and knew the men were concerned about the lack of water.

The thirsty cattle bellowed, and restlessness crept through their numbers. A dozen cows and calves raced for freedom on the far side, seeming intent on returning the way they'd come. The animals had been traveling for over six hours now with no water, and the youngest started to lag. She wanted to urge Bella forward and help the men tighten the herd, but Jose wouldn't approve.

A glance over the heads of the jostling cattle showed her uncle riding not far from Hinson, with Junior Bailey just ahead.

Dust drifted on a light breeze, bringing with it the scent of sweat, manure, and fear. Angel drew Bella to a walk and moved off to the side. Tension knotted her stomach, and unease seemed to wrap itself over the atmosphere like a dark, looming thundercloud.

The other five men were spread from the point of the herd to the rear, hats drawn low and bandanas snugged up over their noses. All were alert, their posture in the saddle tense, and at least two had their rifles out of their scabbards.

She could see nothing moving in the rear. No. Wait. A dust trail rising in the east in the morning sun. Was that what had the men spooked?

Jose waved his arm and shouted. "Angel. Go. Hurry!" He reined his horse away from his position along the far edge of the cattle and broke into a hard trot. "Remember—"

An explosion of rifle fire severed his warning.

Five men rode into sight a hundred yards back on the cattle's flanks. They leaned low over their horses' necks, rifles extended in front of them, and Angel could see a flame erupt from the muzzle of the one in the lead.

Hinson let out a war whoop. "Rangers!" He aimed his six-shooter off to the side and let loose, firing a steady stream at the men approaching them at a ground-covering gallop. "Get the herd moving." Hinson turned his head and stared at Jose racing his gelding along the flank of the herd toward Angel. "Ramirez, get back to your post!"

Jose dug in his spurs and lashed his horse with the end of his reins, his attention fixed on Angel. "Get into the mesquite, *pequeña*. Hide!" He closed the gap to within ten yards of Angel and pointed toward a thick stand of brush. "Go, now!"

Angel hesitated, but her uncle's expression brooked no disobedience. Gripping Bella's reins, she leaned forward in the saddle and grazed the mare's side with her spur. Bella leapt forward, digging in her haunches and catapulting over the ground.

Another shot sounded and Angel turned her head, gazing back toward Hinson. He'd holstered his pistol and removed his rifle, aiming toward the Ranger and the posse. She ducked into the brush, reined Bella to a halt, and turned back toward the action unfolding before her.

Hinson sighted down the length of his rifle and squeezed the trigger. A loud report echoed across the hills, and Angel swung in the direction he'd aimed. She froze. Her uncle lurched in the saddle, blood soaking his arm. He gripped the saddle horn with the other; the reins lay useless on his horse's neck.

Another report erupted from Hinson's rifle and an explosion of sound followed, as Rangers, posse, and outlaws emptied their guns across the expanse. The rifle in Hinson's hands bucked, and the lead Texas Ranger tumbled from his horse's back, disappearing under the hooves of the stampeding cattle.

Angel sat frozen as her uncle's horse made his way toward her, seeming intent on reaching his pasture mate. Bella neighed, and Angel broke from her stupor.

She dismounted, tossed her reins over her horse's neck, and stepped to Jose's side as Rio drew to a stop.

"Uncle! How hard are you hit?" She caught Rio's reins.

"Not bad. Leave now, while they are busy with the posse." Blood oozed from between his fingers.

Angel yanked open her saddlebag. She withdrew a clean shirt and moved close to Rio. "Let me tie this around your arm. You're losing too much blood."

He grunted, held out his hand, and wrapped the shirt around the wound. "Knot it for me." He raised pain-filled eyes.

She tugged at the end of the fabric. "There. Promise me you'll be careful."

Jose gave her a tight smile. "I'm too tough to kill, m'ija. Your mother called you that. Do you remember? She always said that she named you Angel after taking one look at your sweet face on the day of your birth. And your papa, he called you pequeña—little one. Remember them, and remember me—your family."

"I won't leave you. I'll go back to the banda, and we'll stay away from Hinson."

"No! Hinson grows too powerful among the men. He fears me, but he's the kind of snake that will strike when your back is turned. If the posse wins this battle, you would go to jail along with the rest of us." Jose fixed a firm gaze on her. "Ride fast and go far. Stay on the path the cattle have made for now, then veer off when you hit rocky ground. I'll keep an eye on Hinson—make sure he doesn't follow." He laid his spurs into Rio's sides, and the big gelding bounded forward.

The renewed gunfire and the shouts of men brought her back to her immediate danger. She eased her horse deeper into the brush, knowing she should leave. *Uncle, be safe.*

Hinson had moved to the far side of the herd, engrossed in a gun battle with two men from the posse. Three of the outlaw band tried to head off stampeding cattle, two lay sprawled on the ground, and the sixth crouched behind a stand of mesquite, firing at another Ranger.

Angel's gaze returned to her uncle, trotting his horse across a small clearing, his rifle raised. She wanted to pull her own rifle from its sheath and turn it on Hinson, the good-for-nothing who'd turned her life upside down. But she'd made a promise, and she'd keep it.

"Come on, girl." She grazed Bella's flank with her spurs, then slumped in her saddle, numbness permeating her body. She laid her knotted reins on her mare's neck and rested her hands on the horn, trying to still the shaking.

Her uncle had been her only family for the last ten years. She had memories of her parents, but not many. Jose had raised her like his own daughter and showered her with love and attention. Spilling blood wasn't new to her, but the memory of her uncle's wound caused bile to rise in her throat. She pushed it down and picked up the reins—this wasn't the time to grieve.

Angel headed toward the rising sun, praying the intense rays of early morning light would blind anyone who looked her direction. Hopefully the men were too engaged in staying alive to notice her weaving through the brush several hundred feet from the action.

The men's shouts grew fainter, and she could no longer see anyone from the posse or the outlaw band. Only a small number of straggling cattle milled about when she bent forward over Bella's neck, urging her into a canter.

Angel glanced at the sun. At least an hour had passed and nothing appeared behind her on the horizon. Grief slammed into her like a herd of stampeding horses. Everything she'd known lay behind her, and an unknown future beckoned.

Alone.

She had the gold, her rifle, and Jose's instructions. Somehow she'd make it. But what should she do next? Angel straightened her shoulders and raised her chin. She'd not let Hinson find her.

Time to change direction. On the first leg of her journey, the goal had been escape. Now, she added another element.

Survival.

Over the past month, Hinson had dogged her steps in the banda. He wouldn't let her go without a fight. Every bit of the training she'd received from Jose would be bent on one thing—hiding her tracks as she moved toward country where she could disappear. If she didn't, her life wouldn't be worth living.

Bart Hinson holstered his gun and grunted with satisfaction. His men had killed the last of the posse as he tried to race away, hanging low on his horse's neck, undoubtedly to alert the rest of the Texas Rangers about their dead compadres. No way could they allow a man to return and sound the alarm, not after Bart had shot the Ranger heading the posse. They'd be hunted soon enough when the men didn't return, but no one knew who'd fired the shot that brought the Ranger down. No one but Angel Ramirez.

Bart scowled and spat to the side, then swung

around to the nearest man. "Where's the girl?"

Barnes tugged at a torn strip of cloth he'd knotted around a flesh wound in his arm. "Gone. Saw her ride off close to an hour ago."

Bart sprang at the man and backhanded him across the mouth. He leveled his pistol at Barnes's head. "You let her go? Give me a reason I shouldn't kill you now."

Barnes lay on his back, clutching his arm and groaning. "I'd just got winged. Weren't nothin' I could do to stop her."

"Why didn't you tell one of us?"

"Didn't think about it." The man's voice changed to a whine. "She ain't no account. Why you worried about her, anyway? We got most of the cattle."

Bart lowered his weapon, leaned over the man, and snarled a curse. "She saw me plug that Ranger, that's why." He jerked his head at the remaining four men. Two others had fallen in the battle, and Jose had been wounded and slipped away at some point. "Jose go with her?"

"Naw. He limped off a different direction not long ago. Bleedin' pretty bad. He probably won't make it."

"I want two of you to go after him. Hunt him down and kill him."

They'd take time to bury their dead. Their women wouldn't be happy that the bodies of the men weren't returned to the camp, but he refused to cart stinking bodies along the rest of the trip.

Once that was done, the men would start after Jose. Bart himself would find the girl. Jose must have schemed to fool Bart by going the opposite direction, so Angel would get away. Bart's lip curled in contempt. No woman could hide her tracks well enough that he couldn't find her. He smirked, thinking about Angel

Ramirez wearing men's trousers. He'd always fancied he'd have her one day.

He'd suspected Angel's uncle intended to take her away. When the bullets started flying, he knew—Jose planned to disappear, leaving the men to fight without him. It was one thing to be hunted as a cattle thief, but a Ranger's death would increase the intensity of a posse's hunt. No one walked away from this gang unless they were dead.

Angel would agree to be his woman, or die.

Made in the USA
Middletown, DE
23 March 2024

51974438R00152